JIMGRIM AND
ALLAH'S PEACE

JIMGRIM AND ALLAH'S PEACE

TALBOT MUNDY

WILDSIDE PRESS

To Jimgrim:
whose real name, rank, and military distinctions,
I promised never to make public.

JIMGRIM AND ALLAH'S PEACE

Published by Wildside Press, LLC
www.wildsidepress.com

CHAPTER ONE

"Look for a man named Grim."

There is a beautiful belief that journalists may do exactly as they please, and whenever they please. Pleasure with violet eyes was in Chicago. My passport describes me as a journalist. My employer said: "Go to Jerusalem." I went, that was in 1920.

I had been there a couple of times before the World War, when the Turks were in full control. So I knew about the bedbugs and the stench of the citadel moat; the pre-war price of camels; enough Arabic to misunderstand it when spoken fluently, and enough of the Old Testament and the Koran to guess at Arabian motives, which are important, whereas words are usually such stuff as lies are made of.

El Kudz, as Arabs call Jerusalem, is, from a certain distance, as they also call it, shellabi kabir. Extremely beautiful. Beautiful upon a mountain. El Kudz means The City, and in a certain sense it is that, to unnumbered millions of people. Ludicrous, uproarious, dignified, pious, sinful, naively confidential, secretive, altruistic, realistic. Hoary-ancient and ultra-modern. Very, very proud of its name Jerusalem, which means City of Peace. Full to the brim with the malice of certainly fifty religions, fifty races, and five hundred thousand curious political chicaneries disguised as plans to save our souls from hell and fill some fellow's purse. The jails are full.

"Look for a man named Grim," said my employer. "James Schuyler Grim, American, aged thirty-four or so. I've heard he knows the ropes."

The ropes, when I was in Jerusalem before the war, were principally used for hanging people at the Jaffa Gate, after they had been well beaten on the soles of their feet to compel them to tell where their money was hidden. The Turks entirely understood the arts of suppression and extortion, which they defined as government. The British, on the other hand, subject their normal human impulse to be greedy, and their educated craving to be gentlemanly white man's burden-bearers, to a process of compromise. Perhaps that isn't government. But it works. They even carry compromise to the point of not hanging even their critics if they can possibly avoid doing it. They had not yet, but they were about to receive a brand-new mandate from a brand-new League of Nations, awkwardly qualified by Mr. Balfour's post-Armistice promise to the Zionists to give the country to the Jews, and by a war-time promise, in which the French had joined, to create an Arab kingdom for the Arabs.

So there was lots of compromising being done, and hell to pay, with no one paying, except, of course, the guests in the hotels, at New York prices. The Zionist Jews were arriving in droves. The Arabs, who owned most of the land, were threatening to cut all the Jews' throats as soon as they could first get all their money. Feisal, a descendant of the Prophet, who had fought gloriously against the Turks, was romantically getting ready in Damascus to be crowned King of Syria. The French, who pride themselves on being realistic, were getting ready to go after Feisal with bayonets and poison-gas, as they eventually did.

In Jerusalem the Bolsheviks, astonishingly credulous of "secret" news from Moscow, and skeptical of every one's opinion but their own, were bolsheviking Marxian Utopia beneath a screen of such arrogant innocence that even the streetcorner police constables suspected them. And Mustapha Kemal, in Anatolia, was rumoured to be preparing a holy war. It was known as a Ghazi in those days. He had not yet scrapped religion. He was contemplating, so said rumour, a genuine old-fashioned moslem jihad, with modern trimmings.

A few enthusiasts astonishingly still laboured for an American mandate. At the Holy Sepulchre a British soldier stood on guard with bayonet and bullets to prevent the priests of rival creeds from murdering one another. The sun shone and so did the stars. General Bols reopened Pontius Pilate's water-works. The learned monks in convents argued about facts and theories denied by archaeologists. Old-fashioned Jews wailed at the Wailing Wall. Tommy Atkins blasphemously dug corpses of donkeys and dogs from the Citadel moat.

I arrived in the midst of all that, and spent a couple of months trying to make head or tail of it, and wondering, if that was peace, what war is? They say that wherever a man was ever slain in Palestine a flower grows. So one gets a fair idea of the country's mass-experience without much difficulty. For three months of the year, from end to end, the whole landscape is carpeted with flowers so close together that, except where beasts and men have trodden winding tracks, one can hardly walk without crushing an anemone or wild chrysanthemum. There are more battle-fields in that small land than all Europe can show. There are streams everywhere that historians assert repeatedly "ran blood for days."

Five thousand years of bloody terrorism, intermingling of races, piety, plunder, politics and pilgrims, have produced a self-consciousness as concentrated as liquid poison-gas. The laughter is sarcastic, the humour sardonic, and the credulity beyond analysis. For instance, when I got there, I heard the British being accused of "imperialistic savagery" because they had removed the leprous beggars from the streets into a clean place where they could receive medical treatment.

It was difficult to find one line of observation. Whatever anybody told you, was reversed entirely by the next man. The throat-distorting obligation to study Arabic called for rather intimate association with educated Arabs, whose main obsession was fear of the Zionist Jews. The things they said against the Jews turned me pro-Zionist. So I cautiously made the acquaintance of some gentlemen with gold-rimmed spectacles, and the things they said about the Arabs set me to sympathizing with the sons of Ishmael again.

In the midst of that predicament I met Jimgrim — Major James Schuyler Grim, to give him his full title, although hardly any one ever called him by it. After that, bewilderment began to cease as, under his amused, painstaking fingers, thread after thread of the involved gnarl of plots and politics betrayed its course.

However, first I must tell how I met him. There is an American Colony in Jerusalem — a community concern that runs a one-price store, and is even more savagely criticized than the British Administration, as is only natural. The story of what they did in the war is a three-year epic. You can't be "epic" and not make enemies.

A Chicago Jew assured me they were swine and horse-thieves. But I learned that the Yemen Jews prayed for them — first prayer — every Sabbath of the year, calling down blessings on their heads for charitable service rendered.

One hardly goes all the way to Palestine to meet Americans; but a journalist can't afford to be wilfully ignorant. A British official assured me they were "good blokes" and an Armenian told me they could skin fleas for their hides and tallow; but the Armenian was wearing a good suit, and eating good food, which he admitted had been given to him by the American Colony. He was bitter with them because they had refused to cash a draft on Mosul, drawn on a bank that had ceased to exist.

It seemed a good idea to call on the American Colony, at their store near the Jaffa Gate, and it turned out to be a very clean spot in a dirty city. I taxed their generosity, and sat for hours on a ten-thousand-dollar pile of Asian rugs behind the store; and, whatever I have missed and lost, or squandered, at least I know their story and can keep it until the proper time.

Of course, you have to allow for point of view, just as the mariner allows for variation and deviation; but when they inferred that most of the constructive good that has come to the Near East in the last fifty years has been American, they spoke with the authority of men who have lived on the spot and watched it happen.

"You see, the Americans who have come here haven't set up governments. They've opened schools and colleges. They've poured in education, and taken nothing. Then there are thousands of Arabs, living in hovels because there's nothing better, who have been to America and brought back memories with them. All that accounts for the desire for an American mandate — which would be a very bad thing, though, because the moment we set up a government we would lose our chance to be disinterested. The country is better off under any other mandate, provided it gives Americans the right to teach without ruling. America's mission is educational. There's an American, though, who might seem to prove the contrary. Do you see him?"

There were two Arabs in the room, talking in low tones over

by the window. I could imagine the smaller of the two as a peddler of lace and filigree-silver in the States, who had taken out papers for the sake of privilege and returned full of notions to exploit his motherland. But the tall one — never. He was a Bedouin, if ever a son of the desert breathed. If he had visited the States, then he had come back as unchanged as gold out of an acid bath; and as for being born there —

"That little beady-eyed, rat-faced fellow may be an American," I said. "In fact, of course he is, since you say so. But as for being up to any good —"

"You're mistaken. You're looking at the wrong man. Observe the other one."

I was more than ever sure I was not mistaken. Stately gesture, dignity, complexion, attitude — to say nothing of his Bedouin array and the steadiness with which he kept his dark eyes fixed on the smaller man he was talking to, had laid the stamp of the desert on the taller man from head to heel.

"That tall man is an American officer in the British army. Doesn't look the part, eh? They say he was the first American to be granted a commission without any pretense of his being a Canadian. They accepted him as an American. It was a case of that or nothing. Lived here for years, and knew the country so well that they felt they had to have him on his own terms."

You can believe anything in Jerusalem after you have been in the place a week or two, so, seeing who my informant was, I swallowed the fact. But it was a marvel. It seemed even greater when the man strolled out, pausing to salute my host with the solemn politeness that warfare with the desert breeds. You could not imagine that at Ellis Island, or on Broadway — even on the stage. It was too untheatrical to be acting; too individual to be imitation; to unself-conscious to have been acquired. I hazarded a guess.

"A red man, then. Carlisle for education. Swallowed again by the first desert he stayed in for more than a week."

"Wrong. His name is Grim. Sounds like Scandinavian ancestry, on one side. James Schuyler Grim — Dutch, then, on the other; and some English. Ten generations in the States at any rate. He can tell you all about this country. Why not call on him?"

It did not need much intelligence to agree to that suggestion; but the British military take their code with them to the uttermost ends of earth, behind which they wonder why so many folks with different codes, or none, dislike them.

"Write me an introduction," I said.

"You won't need one. Just call on him. He lives at a place they call the junior Staff Officers' Mess — up beyond the Russian Convent and below the Zionist Hospital."

So I went that evening, finding the way with difficulty because they talk at least eighteen languages in Jerusalem and, with the exception of official residences, no names were posted anywhere. That was not an official residence. It was a sort of communal boarding-house improvised by a dozen or so officers in preference to the bug-laden inconvenience of tents — in a German-owned (therefore enemy property) stone house at the end of an alley, in a garden full of blooming pomegranates.

I sent my card in by a flat-footed old Russian female, who ran down passages and round corners like a wet hen, trying to find a man-servant. The place seemed deserted, but presently she came on her quarry in the back yard, and a very small boy in a tarboosh and knickerbockers carried the card on a tray into a room on the left. Through the open door I could hear one quiet question and a high-pitched disclaimer of all knowledge; then an order, sounding like a grumble, and the small boy returned to the hall to invite me in, in reasonably good English, of which he seemed prouder than I of my Arabic.

So I went into the room on the left, with that Bedouin still in mind. There was only one man in there, who got out of a deep armchair as I entered, marking his place in a book with a Damascus dagger. He did not look much more than middle height, nor more than medium dark complexioned, and he wore a major's khaki uniform.

"Beg pardon," I said. "I've disturbed the wrong man. I came to call on an American named Major Grim."

"I'm Grim."

"Must be a mistake, though. The man I'm looking for is taller than you — very dark — looks, walks, speaks and acts like a Bedouin. I saw him this afternoon in Bedouin costume in the American Colony store."

"Yes, I noticed you. Sit down, won't you? Yes, I'm he — the Bedouin abayi[1] seems to add to a man's height. Soap and water account for the rest of it. These cigars are from the States."

It was hard to believe, even on the strength of his straight statement — he talking undisguised American, and smiling at me, no doubt vastly pleased with my incredulity.

"Are you a case of Jekyll and Hyde?" I asked.

"No. I'm more like both sides of a sandwich with some army mule-meat in the middle. But I won't be interviewed. I hate it. Besides, it's against the regulations."

His voice was not quite so harshly nasal as those of the Middle West, but he had not picked up the ultra-English drawl and clipped-off consonants that so many Americans affect abroad and overdo.

I don't think a wise crook would have chosen him as a subject for experiments. He had dark eyes with noticeably long lashes; heavy eyebrows; what the army examination-sheets describe as a medium chin; rather large hands with long, straight fingers; and feet such as an athlete stands on, fully big for his size, but well shaped. He was young for a major — somewhere between thirty and thirty-five.

Once he was satisfied that I would not write him up for the newspapers he showed no disinclination to talk, although it was difficult to keep him on the subject of himself, and easy to let him lose you in a maze of tribal history. He seemed to know the ins and outs of every blood-feud from Beersheba to Damascus, and warmed to his subject as you listened.

"You see," he said, by way of apology when I laughed at a string of names that to me conjured up only confusion, "my beat is all the way from Cairo to Aleppo — both sides of the Jordan. I'm not on the regular strength, but attached to the Intelligence — no, not permanent — don't know what the future has in store — that probably depends on whether or not the Zionists

---

1   Long-sleeved outer cloak.

get full control, and how soon. Meanwhile, I'm my own boss more or less — report direct to the Administrator, and he's one of those men who allows you lots of scope."

That was the sort of occasional glimpse he gave of himself, and then switched off into straight statements about the Zionist problem. All his statements were unqualified, and given with the air of knowing all about it right from the beginning.

"There's nothing here that really matters outside the Zionist-Arab problem. But that's a big one. People don't realize it — even on the spot — but it's a world movement with ramifications everywhere. All the other politics of the Near East hinge on it, even when it doesn't appear so on the surface. You see, the Jews have international affiliations through banks and commerce. They have blood-relations everywhere. A ripple here may mean there's a wave in Russia, or London, or New York. I've known at least one Arab blood-feud over here that began with a quarrel between a Jew and a Christian in Chicago."

"Are the Zionists as dangerous as the Arabs seem to think?" I asked.

"Yes and no. Depends what you call danger. They're like an incoming tide. All you can do is accept the fact and ride on top of it, move away in front of it, or go under. The Arabs want to push it back with sword-blades. Can't be done!"

"Speaking as a mere onlooker, I feel sorry for the Arabs," I said. "It has been their country for several hundred years. They didn't even drive the Jews out of it; the Romans attended to that, after the Assyrians and Babylonians had cleaned up nine-tenths of the population. And at that, the Jews were invaders them-selves."

"Sure," Grim answered. "But you can't argue with tides. The Arabs are sore, and nobody has any right to blame them. The English betrayed the Arabs — I don't mean the fellows out here, but the gang at the Foreign Office."

I glanced at his uniform. That was a strange statement coming from a man who wore it. He understood, and laughed.

"Oh, the men out here all admit it. They're as sore as the Arabs are themselves."

"Then you're on the wrong side, and you know it?" I suggested.

"The meat," he said, "is in the middle of the sandwich. In a small way you might say I'm a doctor, staying on after a riot to stitch up cuts. The quarrel was none of my making, although I was in it and did what I could to help against the Turks. Like everybody else who knows them, I admire the Turks and hate what they stand for — hate their cruelty. I was with Lawrence across the Jordan — went all the way to Damascus with him — saw the war through to a finish — in case you choose to call it finished."

Vainly I tried to pin him down to personal reminiscences. He was not interested in his own story.

"The British promised old King Hussein of Mecca that if he'd raise an Arab army to use against the Turks, there should be a united Arab kingdom afterward under a ruler of their own choosing. The kingdom was to include Syria, Arabia and Palestine. The French agreed. Well, the Arabs raised the army; Emir Feisul, King Hussein's third son, commanded it; Lawrence did so well that he became a legend. The result was, Allenby could concentrate his army on this side of the Jordan and clean up. He made a good job of it. The Arabs were naturally cock-a-hoop."

I suggested that the Arabs with that great army could have enforced the contract, but he laughed again.

"They were being paid in gold by the British, and had Lawrence to hold them together. The flow of gold stopped, and Lawrence was sent home. Somebody at the Foreign Office had changed his mind. You see, they were all taken by surprise at the speed of Allenby's campaign. The Zionists saw their chance, and claimed Palestine. No doubt they had money and influence. Perhaps it was Jewish gold that had paid the wages of the Arab army. Anyhow, the French laid claim to Syria. By the time the war was over the Zionists had a hard-and-fast guarantee, the French claim to Syria had been admitted, and there wasn't any country left except some Arabian desert to let the Arabs have. That's the situation. Feisul is in Damascus, going through the farce of being proclaimed king, with the French holding the seaports and getting ready to oust him. The Zionists are in Jerusalem, working like beavers, and the British are getting ready to pull out as much as possible and leave the Zionists to do their own worrying. Mesopotamia is in a state of more or less anarchy. Egypt is like a hot-box full of explosive — may go off any minute. The Arabs would like to challenge the world to mortal combat, and then fight one another while the rest of the world pays the bill —"

"And you?"

"The French, for instance. Their army is weak at the moment. They've neither men nor money — only a hunger to own Syria. They don't play what the English call 'on side.' They play a mean game. The French General Staff figure that if Feisul should attack them now he might beat them. So they've conceived the brilliant idea of spreading sedition and every kind of political discontent into Palestine and across the Jordan, so that if the Arabs make an effort they'll make it simultaneously in both countries. Then the British, being in the same mess with the French, would have to take the French side and make a joint campaign of it."

"But don't the British know this?"

"You bet they know it. What's the Intelligence for? The French are hiring all the Arab newspapers to preach against the British. A child could see it with his eyes shut."

"Then why in thunder don't the British have a showdown?"

"That's where the joker comes in. The French know there's a sort of diplomatic credo at the London Foreign Office to the general effect that England and France have got to stand together or Europe will go to pieces. The French are realists. They bank on that. They tread on British corns, out here, all they want to, while they toss bouquets, backed by airplanes, across the English Channel."

"Then the war didn't end the old diplomacy?"

"What a question! But I haven't more than scratched the Near East surface for you yet. There's Mustapha Kemal in Anatolia, leader of the Turkish Nationalists, no more dead or incapacitated than a possum. He's playing for his own hand — Kaiser Willy stuff — studying Trotzky and Lenin, and flirting with Feisul's party on the side. Then there's a Bolshevist element among the Zionists — got teeth, too. There's an effort being made from India to intrigue among the Sikh troops employed in Palestine. There's a very strong party yelling for an American mandate. The Armenians, poor devils, are pulling any string they can get hold of, in the hope that anything at all may happen. The orthodox Jews are against the Zionists; the Arabs are against them both, and furious with one another. There's a pan-Islam movement on foot, and a pan-Turanian — both different, and opposed. About 75 per cent of the British are as pro-Arab as they dare be, but the rest are strong for the Zionists. And the Administrator's neutral! — strong for law and order but taking no sides."

"And you?"

"I'm one of the men who is trying to keep the peace."

He invited me to stay to dinner. The other members of the mess were trooping in, all his juniors, all obviously fond of him and boisterously irreverent of his rank. Dinner under his chairmanship was a sort of school for repartee. It was utterly unlike the usual British mess dinner. If you shut your eyes for a minute you couldn't believe that any one present had ever worn a uniform. I learned afterward that there was quite a little competition to get into that mess.

After dinner most of them trooped out again, to dance with Zionist ladies at an institute affair. But he and I stayed, and talked until midnight. Before I left, the key of Palestine and Syria was in my hands.

"You seem interested," he said, coming with me to the door. "If you don't mind rough spots now and then, I'll try to show you a few things at first hand."

CHAPTER TWO

"No objection; only a stipulation."

The showmanship began much sooner than I hoped. The following day was Sunday, and I had an invitation to a sort of semi-public tea given by the American Colony after their afternoon religious service.

They received their guests in a huge, well-furnished room on the upper floor of a stone house built around a courtyard filled with flowers. I think they were a little proud of the number of fierce-looking Arabs, who had traveled long distances in order to be present. Ten Arab chieftains in full costume, with fifteen or twenty of their followers, all there at great expense of trouble, time and money, for friends sake, were, after all, something to feel a bit chesty about. Every member of the Colony seemed able to talk Arabic like a native and, as they used to say in the up-state papers, a good time was being had by all. The Near East adores ice-cream, and there was lots of it.

Two of the Arab chiefs were Christians; the rest were not. The peace and war record of the Colony was what had brought them all there. Hardly an Arab in the country was not the Colony's debtor for disinterested help, direct or indirect, at some time in some way. The American Colony was the one place in the country where a man of any creed could go and be sure that whatever he might say would not be used against him. So they were talking their heads off. Hot air and Arab politics have quite a lot in common. But there was a broad desert-breath about it all. It wasn't like the little gusty yaps you hear in the city coffee-shops. A lot of the talk was foolish, but it was all magnificent.

There was one sheikh named Mustapha ben Nasir dressed in a blue serge suit and patent-leather boots, with nothing to show his nationality except a striped silk head-dress with the camel-hair band around the forehead. He was a handsome fellow, with a black beard trimmed to a point, and perfect manners, polished no doubt in a dozen countries, but still Eastern in slow, deferential dignity. He could talk good French. I fell in conversation with him.

The frankness with which treason is mooted, admitted and discussed in the Near East is one of the first things that amaze you. They are so open about it that nobody takes them seriously. Apparently it is only when they don't talk treason openly that the ruling authorities get curious and make arrests. To me, a total stranger, with nothing to recommend me but that for an hour or two that afternoon I was a guest of the American Colony, Mustapha ben Nasir made no bones whatever about the fact that the was being paid by the French to stir up feeling over Jordan against the British.

"I receive a monthly salary," he boasted. "I am just from Damascus, where the French Liaison-officer paid me and gave me some instructions."

"Where is your home?" I asked him.

"At El-Kerak, in the mountains of Moab, across the Dead Sea. I start this evening. Will you come with me?"

"Je m'en bien garderai!"

He smiled. "Myself, I am in favor of the British. The French pay my expenses, that is all. What we all want is an independent Arab government — some say kingdom, some say republic. If it is not time for that yet, then we would choose an American mandate. But America has deserted us. Failing America, we prefer the English for the present. Anything except France! We do not want to become a new Algeria."

"What is the condition now at El-Kerak?"

"Condition? There is none. There is chaos. You see, the British say their authority ceases at the River Jordan and at a line drawn down the middle of the Dead Sea. That leaves us with a choice between two other governments — King Hussein's government of Mecca, and Feisul's in Syria. But Hussein's arm is not long enough to reach us from the South, and Feisul's is not nearly strong enough to interfere from the North. So there is no government, and each man is keeping the peace with his own sword."

"You mean; each man on his own account?"

"Yes. So there is peace. Five — fifteen — thirty throats are cut daily; and if you go down to the Jordan and listen, you will hear the shots being fired from ambush any day."

"And you invite me to make the trip with you?"

"Oh, that is nothing. In the first place, you are American. Nobody will interfere with an American. They are welcome. In the second place, there is a good reason for bringing you; we all want an American school at El-Kerak."

"But I am no teacher."

"But you will be returning to America? It is enough, then, that you look the situation over, and tell what you know on your return. We will provide a building, a proper salary, and guarantee the teacher's life. We would prefer a woman, but it would be wisest to send a man."

"How so? The woman might not shoot straight? I've some of our Western women do tricks with a gun that would —"

"There would be no need. She would have our word of honour. But every sheikh who has only three wives would want to make her his fourth. A man would be best. Will you come with me?"

"On your single undertaking to protect me? Are you king of all that countryside?"

"If you will come, you shall have an escort, every man of whom will die before he would let you be killed. And if they, and you, should all be killed, their sons and grandsons would avenge you to the third generation of your murderers."

"That's undoubtedly handsome, but —"

"Believe me, effendi," he urged, "many a soul has been consoled in hell-fire by the knowledge that his adversaries would be cut off in their prime by friends who are true to their given word."

Meaning to back out politely, I assured him I would think the offer over.

"Well and good," he answered. "You have my promise. Should you decide to come, leave word here with the American Colony. They will get word to me. Then I will send for you, and the escort shall meet you at the Dead Sea."

I talked it over with two or three members of the Colony, and they assured me the promise could be depended on. One of them added:

"Besides, you ought to see El-Kerak. It's an old crusader city, rather ruined, but more or less the way the crusaders left it. And that craving of theirs for a school is worth doing something about, if you ever have an opportunity. They say they have too much religion already, and no enlightenment at all. A teacher who knew Arabic would have a first-class time, and would be well paid and protected, if he could keep his hands off politics. Why not talk with Major Grim?"

It was a half hour's walk to Grim's place, but I had the good fortune to catch him in again. He was sitting in the same chair, studying the same book, and this time I saw the title of it — Walter Pater's *Marius the Epicurean* — a strange book for a soldier to be reading, and cutting its pages with an inlaid dagger, in a Jerusalem semi-military boarding-house. But he was a man of unexpectedly assorted moods.

He laughed when I told of ben Nasir. He looked serious when I mooted El-Kerak — serious, then interested, them speculative. From where I sat I could watch the changes in his eyes.

"What would the escort amount to?" I asked him.

"Absolute security."

"And what's this bunk about Americans being welcome anywhere?"

"Perfectly true. All the way from Aleppo down to Beersheba. Men like Dr. Bliss[2] have made such an impression that an occasional rotter might easily take advantage of it. Americans in this country — so far — stand for altruism without ulterior motive. If we'd accepted the mandate they might have found us out! Meanwhile, an American is safe."

"Then I think I'll go to El-Kerak."

Again his eyes grew speculative. I could not tell whether he was considering me or some problem of his own.

"Speaking unofficially," he said, "there are two possibilities. You might go without permission — easy enough, provided you

---

2   President of the American College at Beirut. Died 1920, probably more respected throughout the Near East than any ten men of any other nationality.

don't talk beforehand. In that case, you'd get there and back; after which, the Administration would label and index you. The remainder of your stay in Palestine would be about as exciting as pushing a perambulator in Prospect Park, Brooklyn. You'd be canned."

"I'd rather be killed. What's the alternative?"

"Get permission. I shall be at El-Kerak myself within the next few days. I think it can be arranged."

"D'you mean I can go with you?" I asked, as eager as a schoolboy for the circus.

"Not on your life! I don't go as an American."

Recalling the first time I had seen him, I sat still and tried to look like a person who was not thrilled in the least by seeing secrets from the inside.

"Well," I said, "I'm in your hands."

I think he rather liked that. As I came to know him more intimately later on he revealed an iron delight in being trusted. But he did not say another word for several minutes, as if there were maps in his mind that he was conning before reaching a decision. Then he spoke suddenly.

"Are you busy?" he asked. "Then come with me."

He phoned to some place or other for a staff automobile, and the man was there with it within three minutes. We piled in and drove at totally unholy speed down narrow streets between walls, around blind right-angle turns where Arab policemen stood waving unintelligible signals, and up the Mount of Olives, past the British military grave-yard, to the place they call OETA.[3] The Kaiser had it built to command every view of the country-side and be seen from everywhere, as a monument to his own greatness — the biggest, lordliest, most expensive hospice that his architects could fashion, with pictures in mosaic on the walls and ceilings of the Kaiser and his ancestors in league with the Almighty. But the British had adopted it as Administration Headquarters.

3   Headquarters: Occupied Enemy Territory Administration.

All the way up, behind and in front and on either hand, there were views that millions[4] would give years of their lives to see; and they would get good value for their bargain. Behind us, the sky-line was a panorama of the Holy City, domes, minarets and curved stone roofs rising irregularly above gray battlemented walls. Down on the right was the ghastly valley of Jehoshaphat, treeless, dry, and crowded with white tombs — "dry bones in the valley of death." To the left were everlasting limestone hills, one of them topped by the ruined reputed tomb of Samuel — all trenched, cross-trenched and war-scarred, but covered now in a Joseph's coat of flowers, blue, blood-red, yellow and white.

There were lines of camels sauntering majestically along three hill-tops, making time, and the speed of the car we rode in, seem utterly unreal. And as we topped the hill the Dead Sea lay below us, like a polished turquoise set in the yellow gold of the barren Moab Mountains. That view made you gasp. Even Grim, who was used to it, could not turn his eyes away.

We whirled past saluting Sikhs at the pompous Kaiserish entrance gate, and got out on to front steps that brought to mind one of those glittering hotels at German cure-resorts — bad art, bad taste, bad amusements and a big bill.

But inside, in the echoing stone corridors that opened through Gothic windows on a courtyard, in which statues of German super-people stared with blind eyes, there was nothing now but bald military neatness and economy. Hurrying up an uncarpeted stone stairway (Grim seemed to be a speed-demon once his mind was set) we followed a corridor around two sides of the square, past dozens of closed doors bearing department names, to the Administrator's quarters at the far end. There, on a bare bench in a barren ante-room, Grim left me to cool my heels. He knocked, and entered a door marked "private."

It was fully half an hour before the door opened again and I

---

4   This is no exaggeration. There are actually millions, and on more than one continent, whose dearest wish, could they have it, would be to see Jerusalem before they die.

was beckoned in. Grim was alone in the room with the Administrator, a rather small, lean, rigidly set up man, with merry fire in his eye, and an instantly obvious gift for being obeyed. He sat at an enormous desk, but would have looked more at ease in a tent, or on horseback. The three long rows of campaign ribbons looked incongruous beside the bunch of flowers that somebody had crammed into a Damascus vase on the desk, with the estimable military notion of making the utmost use of space.

Sir Louis was certainly in an excellent temper. He offered me a chair, and looked at me with a sort of practical good-humour that seemed to say, "Well, here he is; now how shall we handle him?" I was minded to ask outright for what I wanted, but something in his attitude revealed that he knew all that already and would prefer to come at the problem in his own way. It was clear, without a word being said, that he proposed to make some sort of use of me without being so indiscreet as to admit it. He reminded me rather of Julius Caesar, who was also a little man, considering the probable qualifications of some minor spoke in a prodigious wheel of plans.

"I understand you want to go to El-Kerak?" he said, smiling as if all life were an amusing game.

I admitted the impeachment. Grim was standing, some little way behind me and to one side; I did not turn my head to look at him, for that might have given a false impression that he and I were in league together, but I was somehow aware that with folded arms he was studying me minutely.

"Well," said Sir Louis, "there's no objection; only a stipulation: We wouldn't let an Englishman go, because of the risk — not to him, but to us. Any fool has a right to get killed, but not to obligate his government. All the missionaries were called in from those outlying districts long ago. We don't want to be held liable for damages for failure to protect. Such things have happened. You see, the idea is, we assume no responsibility for what takes place beyond the Jordan and the Dead Sea. Now, if you'd like to sign a letter waiving any claim against us for protection, that would remove any obstacle to your going. But, if you think that unreasonable, the alternative is safe. You can stay in Jerusalem. Quite simple."

That had the merit of frankness. It sounded fair enough. Nevertheless, he was certainly not being perfectly frank. The merriment in his eyes meant something more than mere amusement. It occurred to me that his frankness took the extreme form of not concealing that he had something important in reserve. I rather liked him for it. His attitude seemed to be that if I wanted to take a chance, I might on my own responsibility, but that if my doing so should happen to suit his plans, that was his affair. Grim was still watching me the way a cat watches a mouse.

"I'll sign such a letter," said I.

"Good. Here are pen and paper. Let's have it all in your handwriting. I'll call a clerk to witness the signature."

I wrote down the simple statement that I wished to go to El-Kerak for personal reasons, and that I waived all claim against the British Administration for personal protection, whether there or en route. A clerk, who looked as if he could not have been hired to know, or understand, or remember anything without permission, came in answer to the bell. I signed. He witnessed.

Sir Louis put the letter in a drawer, and the clerk went out again.

"How soon will you go?"

I told about the promised escort, and that a day or two would be needed to get word to ben Nasir. I forgot that ben Nasir would not start before moonrise. It appeared that Sir Louis knew more than he cared to admit.

"Can't we get word to ben Nasir for him, Grim?"

Grim nodded. So did Sir Louis:

"Good. There'll be no need, then, for you to take any one into confidence," he said, turning to me again. "As a rule it isn't well to talk about these things, because people get wrong ideas. There are others in Jerusalem who would like permission to go to El-Kerak."

"I'll tell nobody."

He nodded again. He was still considering things in the back of his mind, while those intelligent, bright eyes smiled so disarmingly.

"How do you propose to reach the Dead Sea?" he asked.

"Ben Nasir's escort will probably meet you on the shore on this side."

"Oh, hire some sort of conveyance, I suppose."

"Couldn't we lend him one of our cars, Grim?"

Grim nodded again.

"We'll do that. Grim, can you get word to ben Nasir so that when the escort is ready he may send a messenger straight to the hotel with the information? D'you get my meaning?"

"Sure," said Grim, "nobody else need know then."

"Very well," said Sir Louis. He rose from his chair to intimate that the precise moment had arrived when I might leave without indiscretion. It was not until I was outside the door that I realized that my permission was simply verbal, and that the only document that had changed hands had been signed by me. Grim followed me into the ante-room after a minute.

"Hadn't I better go back and ask for something in writing from him?" I suggested.

"You wouldn't get it. Anyhow, you're dealing with a gentleman. You needn't worry. I was afraid once or twice you might be going to ask him questions. He'd have canned you if you had. Why didn't you?"

I was not going to help Grim dissect my mental processes.

"There's a delightful air of mystery," I said, "I'd hate to spoil it!"

"Come up on the tower," he said. "There's just time before sunset. If you've good eyes, I'll show you El-Kerak."

It is an enormous tower. The wireless apparatus connected with it can talk with Paris and Calcutta. From the top you feel as if you were seeing "all the kingdoms of the world in a moment of time." There are no other buildings to cut off the view or tamper with perspective. The Dead Sea was growing dark. The Moab Hills beyond it looked lonely and savage in silhouette.

"Down there on your left is Jericho," said Grim. "That winding creek beyond it is the Jordan. As far eastward as that there's some peace. Beyond that, there is hardly a rock that isn't used for ambush regularly. Let your eye travel along the top of the hills — nearly as far as the end of the Dead Sea. Now — d'you see where a touch of sunlight glints on something? That's the top of the castle-wall of El-Kerak. Judge what strategists those old crusaders were. That site commands the ancient high road from Egypt. They could sit up there and take toll to their hearts' content. The Turks quartered troops in the castle and did the same thing. But the Turks overdid it, like everything else. They ruined the trade. No road there nowadays that amounts to anything."

"It looks about ten miles away."

"More than eighty."

The sun went down behind us while we watched, and here and there the little scattered lights came out among the silent hills in proof that there were humans who thought of them in terms of home.

Venus and Mars shone forth, yellow and red jewels; then the moon, rising like a stage effect, too big, too strongly lighted to seem real, peering inch by inch above the hills and ushering in silence. We could hear one muezzin in Jerusalem wailing that God is God.

"That over yonder is savage country," Grim remarked. "I think maybe you'll like it. Time to go now."

He said nothing more until we were scooting downhill in the car in the midst of a cloud of dust.

"You won't see me again," he said then, "until you get to El-Kerak. There are just one or two points to bear in mind. D'you care if I lecture?"

"I wish you would."

"When the messenger comes from ben Nasir, go to the Governorate, just outside the Damascus Gate, phone OETA, say who you are, and ask for the car. Travel light. The less you take with you, the less temptation there'll be to steal and that much less danger for your escort. I always take nothing, and get shaved by a murderer at the nearest village. If you wash too much, or change your shirt too often, they suspect you of putting on airs. Can't travel too light. Use the car as far as Jericho, or thereabouts, and send it back when the messenger says he's through with it. After that, do whatever the leader of the escort tells you, and you'll be all right."

"How do I cross the Dead Sea?"

"That's ben Nasir's business. There's another point I'll ask you to bear in mind. When you see me at El-Kerak, be sure not to make the slightest sign of recognition, unless and until you get word from me. Act as if you'd never seen me in your life before."

I felt like an arch-conspirator, and there is no other sensation half so thrilling. The flattery of being let in, as it were, through a secret door was like strong wine.

"Is your memory good?" Grim asked me. "If you make notes, be sure you let everybody see them; you'll find more than one of them can read English. If you should see or overhear anything that you'd particularly like to remember because it might prove useful to me, note it down by making faint dots under the letters of words you've already written; or — better yet — take along a pocket Bible; they're all religious and respect the Bible. Make faint pencil lines underneath words or letters, and they'll think you're more than extra devout. There's nothing special to watch out for; just keep your ears and eyes open. Well, here's your hotel. See you again soon. So long."

I got out of the car and went to get ready for a Christian dinner served by Moslems, feeling like a person out of the Arabian Nights, who had just met the owner of a magic carpet on which one only had to sit in order to be wafted by invisible forces into unimaginable realms of mystery.

CHAPTER THREE

"Do whatever the leader of the escort tells you."

I never learned exactly how Jim Grim got word to ben Nasir. My suspicion is that he took the simple course of getting the American Colony to send one of their men; but as they never referred to it afterwards, and might have their own reasons for keeping silence, I took care not to ask them. We have most of us seen harm done by noisy gratitude for kindness, better covered up.

I kept close to the hotel for three days, studying Arabic. By the fourth afternoon discouragement set in. I began to believe that the whole affair had petered out; perhaps on reflection the Administrator had decided I was not a proper person to be turned loose out of bounds, and nobody could have blamed him for that, for he knew next to nothing about me. Or Grim might have been called off for some other important business. The chances seemed all against my going after all.

But on the fourth evening, just at sunset, when the sandwiches I had ordered in advance were all thoroughly stale and I had almost decided to unpack the small hand-grip and try to forget the whole affair, I noticed an Arab standing in the door of the hotel scrutinizing every one who passed him. I watched him for five minutes. He paid no attention to officers in uniform. I left my chair in the lobby and walked past him twice.

He had one eye, like a gimlet on a universal joint; he turned it this and that way without any corresponding movement of his head. It penetrated. You felt he could have seen you with it in the dark.

I started to pass him a third time. He held his hand out and thrust a small, soiled piece of paper into mine. The writing on it was in Arabic, so I went back to the seat in the far corner, to puzzle it out, he standing meanwhile in the doorway and continuing to quiz people as if I had meant nothing in his life. The message was short enough:

Bearer will accompany you to a place where the escort will be in readiness. God give your honour a good journey.
Mustapha Ben Nasir.

I went to the Governorate and phoned for the car to come and pick me up outside the Jaffa Gate. The Arab followed me, and he and I were both searched at the gate for weapons, by a Sikh who knew nothing and cared less about Near East politics. His orders were to search thoroughly. He did it. The man whose turn was next ahead of mine was a Russian priest, whose long black cloak did not save him from painstaking suspicion. He was still indignantly refusing to take down his pants and prove that the hard lump on his thigh was really an amulet against sciatica, when the car came for me.

It was an ordinary Ford car, and the driver was not in uniform. He, too, had only one eye in full commission, for the other was bruised and rather swollen. I got in beside him and let the Arab have the rear seat to himself, reflecting that I would be able to smell all the Arab sweat I cared to in the days to come.

We are governed much more by our noses than we are often aware of, and I believe that many people — in the East especially — use scent because intuition warns them that their true smell would arouse unconscious antagonism. Dogs, as well as most wild animals, fight at the suggestion of a smell. Humans only differ from the animals, much, when they are being self-consciously human. Then they forget what they really know and tumble headlong into trouble.

The driver seemed to know which road to take, and to be in no particular hurry, perhaps on account of his injured eye. He was an ex-soldier, of course: one of those under-sized Cockneys with the Whitechapel pallor overlying a pugnacious instinct, who make such astonishing fighting-men in the intervals between sulking and a sort of half affectionate abuse of everything in sight. Being impatient to begin the adventure, I suggested more speed.

"Oh!" he answered. "So you're another o' these people in an 'urry to get to Jericho! It's strynge. The last one was a Harab. Tyke it from me, gov'nor, I've driven the very last Harab as gets more than twenty-five miles an hour out o' me, so 'elp me —"

He tooled the car out on to the road toward Bethany, and down the steep hill that passes under the Garden of Gethsemane, before vouchsafing another word. Then, as we started to climb the hill ahead, he jerked his chin in the direction of the sharp turn we had just passed in the bottom of the valley. "Took that corner las' time on one wheel!"

"For the Arab?"

"Aye. Taught me a lesson. Never agayn! I ain't no Arabian Night. Nor yet no self-immolatin' 'Indoo invitin' no juggernauts to make no pancykes out o' me. 'Enceforth, I drives reasonable. All Harabs may go to 'ell for all o' me."

He was itching to tell his story. He was likely to tell it quicker for not being questioned; your Cockney dislikes anything he can construe into inquisition. I remarked that the road didn't seem made for speed — too narrow and too rough — and let it go at that.

He said no more until we reached the village of Bethany, and drew abreast of Lazarus' reputed tomb, where a pack of scavenger-dogs awoke and yelped around the wheels. He did his best to run over one of them, but missed. Then he could not hold his story any longer.

"Two nights ago," he said, "they gives me orders to take a Harab to a point near Jericho. After dark, I starts off, 'im on the back seat; engine ain't warm yet, so we goes slow. He leans forward after a couple o' minutes, an says 'Yalla kawam'!"[5] So I thinks to myself I'll show the blighter a thing or two, me not bein' used to takin' orders from no Harabs. Soon as the engine's 'ot I lets rip, an' you know now what the road's like. When we gets to the top o' that 'ill above Gethsemane I lets extry special rip. Thinks I, if you can stand what I can, my son, you've guts.

"Well, we 'its all the 'igh places, and lands on a bit o' level road just often enough to pick up more speed — comes round that sharp bend on 'alf a wheel, syme as I told you — kills three

5   Hurry up.

pye-dogs for sure, an' maybe others, but I don't dare look round — misses a camel in the dark that close that the 'air on my arms an' legs fair crawled up an' down me — 'it's a lump o' rock that comes near tippin' us into the ditch — an' carries on faster 'an ever. By the time we gets 'ere to Bethany, thinks I, it's time to take a look an' see if my passenger's still in the bloomin' car. So I slows down.

"The minute I turns my 'ead to 'ave a peer at 'im, 'Kawam!' 'e says. 'Quick! Quick!'

"So it strikes me I weren't in no such 'urry after all. Why 'urry for a Harab? The car's been rattlin' worse 'n a tinker's basket. I gets down to 'ave a look — lights a gasper[6] — an' takes my bloomin' time about it. You seen them yellow curs there by Lazarus' tomb? Well, they come for me, yappin' an' snarlin' to beat 'ell. I'm pickin' up stones to break their 'eads with — good stones ain't such easy findin' in the dark, an' every time I stoops 'alf a dozen curs makes a rush for me — when what d'you suppose? That bloomin' Harab passenger o' mine vaults over into my seat, an' afore I could say "'ell's bells' 'e's off. I'd left the engine runnin'. By the luck o' the Lord I 'angs on, an' scrambles in — back seat.

"I thought at first I'd reach over an' get a half-nelson on 'im from behind. But, strike me blind! I didn't dare!

"Look where we are now. Can you see the 'air-pin turn at the bottom of this 'ill, with a ditch, beyond it? Well, we takes that turn in pitch-dark shadow with all four wheels in the air, an' you'd 'a thought we was a blinkin' airplane a doin' stunts. But 'e's a hexpert, 'e is, an' we 'olds the road. From there on we goes in one 'oly murderin' streak to a point about 'alf way up the 'ill where the Inn of the Good Samaritan stands on top. There we 'as two blow-outs simultaneous, an' thinks I, now, my son, I've got you! I gets out.

"'You can drive,' I says, 'like Jehu son o' Nimshi what made Israel to sin. Let's see you make bricks now without no bleedin' straw!' I knew there weren't no tools under the seat — there

6   Anglice — canteen cigarette.

never are in this 'ere country if you've left your car out o' your sight for five minutes. 'You take off them two back tires,' I says, 'while I sit 'ere an' meditate on the ways of Harabs! Maybe you're Moses,' I says, 'an' know 'ow to work a miracle.'

"But the only miracle about that bloke's 'is nerve. 'E gets out, an' begins to walk straight on up'ill without as much as a by-your-leave. I shouts to 'im to come back. But 'e walks on. So I picks up a stone off the pile I was sittin' on, an' I plugs 'im good — 'its 'im fair between the shoulder-blades. You'd think, if 'e was a Harab, that 'ud bring 'im to 'is senses, wouldn't you? But what d'you suppose the blighter did?

"Did you notice my left eye when you got in the car? 'E turns back, an' thinks I, 'e's goin' to knife me. But that sport could use 'is fists, an' believe me, 'e done it! I can use 'em a bit myself, an' I starts in to knock 'is block off, but 'e puts it all over me — weight, reach an' science. Mind you, science! First Arab ever I see what 'ad science; an' I don't more than 'alf believe it now!

"Got to 'and it to 'im. 'E was merciful. 'E let up on me the minute 'e see I'd 'ad enough. 'E starts off up'ill again. I sits where 'e'd knocked me on to a stone pile, wishin' like 'ell for a drink. It was full moonlight, an' you could see for miles. After about fifteen minutes, me still meditatin' murder an' considerin' my thirst I seen 'em fetch a camel out o' the khan at the Inn o' the Good Samaritan; an' next thing you know, 'e's out o' sight. Thinks I, that's the last of 'im, an' good riddance! But not a bit of it!

"The men what fetched the camel for 'im comes down to me an' says the sheikh 'as left word I'm to be fed an' looked after. They fixes me up at the inn with a cot an' blankets an' a supper o' sorts, an' I lies awake listenin' to 'em talkin' Arabic, understandin' maybe one word out of six or seven. From what I can make o' their conjecturin', they think 'e ain't no sheikh at all, but a bloomin' British officer in disguise!

"Soon as morning comes I jump a passing commissariat lorry. As soon as I gets to Jerusalem I reports that sheikh for arson, theft, felo de se, busting a gov'ment car, usin' 'is fists when by right 'e should ha' knifed me, an' every other crime I could think of. An' all I gets is laughed at! What d'you make of it? Think 'e was a Harab?"

I wondered whether he was Jimgrim, but did not say so. Grim had not appeared to me like a man who would use his fists at all readily; but he was such an unusual individual that it was useless trying to outline what he might or might not do. It was also quite likely that the chauffeur had omitted mention of, say, nine-tenths of the provocation he gave his passenger. What interested me most was the thought that, if that really was Jimgrim, he must have been in a prodigious hurry about something; and that most likely meant excitement, if not danger across the Dead Sea.

We caught sight of the Dead Sea presently, bowling past the Inn of the Good Samaritan and beginning to descend into the valley, twelve hundred feet below sea level, that separates Palestine from Moab. The moon shone full on the water, and it looked more wan and wild than an illustration out of Dante's Inferno. There was no doubt how the legends sprang up about birds falling dead as they flew across it. It was difficult to believe that anything could be there and not die. It was a vision of the land of death made beautiful.

But the one-eyed Arab on the rear seat began to sing. To him that view meant "home, sweet home." His song was all about his village and how he loved it — what a pearl it was — how sweeter than all cities.

"'Ark at 'im!" The driver stopped the car to fill his pipe. "You'd think 'e lived in 'eaven! I've fought over every hinch o' this perishin' country, an' tyke it from me, guv'nor, there ain't a village in it but what's composed of 'ovels wi' thatched roofs, an' 'eaps o' dung so you can't walk between 'em! Any one as wants my share o' Palestine can 'ave it!"

We bumped on again down a road so lonely that it would have felt good to see a wild beast, or an armed man lurking in wait for us. But the British had accomplished the impossible: They had so laid the fear of law along those roads that, though there might be murders to the right and left of them, the passer-by who kept to the road was safe, for the first time since the Romans now and then imposed a temporary peace.

At last, like two yellow streams glistening in moonlight, the road forked — one way toward Jericho. The other way appeared to run more or less parallel with the Dead Sea. At that point the one-eyed Arab left off singing at last and clutched the driver's shoulder.

"All right! All right!" he answered impatiently, and stopped. "Out you get, then!"

He did not expect the tip I gave him. He seemed to think it placed him under obligation to wait there and talk for a few minutes. But my one-eyed guide waved him away disgustedly with the hand that did not hold my bag, and we stood in the road watching until he vanished up-hill out of sight. Then the guide plucked my sleeve and I followed him along the righthand road. We walked half a mile as fast as he could set foot to the ground.

At last we reached a pretense of a village — a little cluster of half a dozen thatched stone huts enclosed within one fence of thorn and cactus. Everything showed up as clearly in the moonlight as if painted with phosphorus. The heavy shadows only made the high lights seem more luminous. A man and two donkeys were waiting for us outside the thorn hedge. The man made no remark. My guide and I mounted and rode on.

Presently we turned down a track toward the Dead Sea, riding among huge shadows cast by the hills on our right hand. The little jackals they call foxes crossed our path at intervals. Owls the size of a robin, only vastly fluffier, screamed from the rocks as we passed them. Otherwise, it was like a soul's last journey, eerie, lonely and awful, down toward River Styx.

Long before we caught sight of the water again, through a ragged gap between high limestone rocks, I could smell a village. The guide approached it cautiously, stopping every minute or so to listen. When we came on it at last it was down below us in abysmal darkness, one light shining through a window two feet square in proof we were not hesitating on the verge of the infinite pit.

The donkeys knew the way. They trod daintily, like little ladies, along a circling track that goats made and men had certainly done nothing to improve. We made an almost complete ellipse around and down, and rode at last over dry dung at the bottom, into which the donkeys' feet sank as into a three-pile carpet. You could see the stars overhead, but nothing, where we were, except that window and a shaft of yellow light with hundreds of moths dazzled in it.

We must have made some noise in spite of the donkeys' ve'vet foot-fall. As we crossed the shaft of light a door opened within six feet of the window. A man in Arab deshabille with a red tarboosh awry, thrust out his head and drew it in again quickly.

"Is that the American?" he asked. He held the door so that he could slam it in our faces if required.

The guide made no answer. I gave my name. The man opened the door wider.

"Lailtak sa'idi, effendi! Hishkur Allah! Come in, mister!" The guide led the donkeys away to some invisible place. I crossed the threshold, my host holding his tin lantern carefully to show the two steps leading down to a flag-stone floor. He bolted the door the moment I was inside. He seemed in a great state of excitement, and afraid to make any noise. Even when he shot the bolt he did it silently.

It was a square room, moderately clean, furnished only with a table and two chairs. There were other rooms leading off it, but the stone partitions did not reach as high as the thatch and I could hear rustling, and some one snoring. I sat on one of the chairs at his invitation, and rather hoped for supper, having had none. But supper was not in his mind; it seemed he had too much else to worry him. He looked like a man who worried easily, and likely enough with good reason, for his long nose and narrow eyes did not suggest honesty.

"There was to be an escort to meet me here," I said.

"Yes, yes. Thank God, mister, you have come at last. If you had only come at sunset! Ali has gone to bring them now."

"Who is Ali?"

"He with one eye. He who brought you. Your escort came at sunset. Because I am Christian they would not listen to me or wait for you in my house. There are twenty of them, led by Anazeh, who is a bad rascal. They have gone to raid the villages. There has been trouble. I have heard two shots fired. Now they will come back to my house, and if the Sikh patrol is after them they will be caught here, and I shall be accused of helping them.

May the fires of their lying Prophet's Eblis burn Anazeh and his men forever and ever, Amen! May God curse their religion!"

That was a nice state of affairs. I did not want to be caught there by a lot of truculent Sikhs under one of those jocularly incredulous young British subalterns that Sikhs adore. In the first place, I had nothing whatever in writing to prove my innocence. The least that was likely to happen would be an ignominious return to Jerusalem, after a night in a guard-house, should there be a guard-house; failing that, a night in the open within easy reach of Sikhs' bayonets. In Jerusalem, no doubt, Sir Louis would order me released immediately. But it began to look as if the whole mystery after all was nothing but a well-staged decoy, using me for bait. Not even tadpoles enjoy being used for live-bait without being consulted first. I began to spear about for remedies.

"If you're an honest man," I said, "you'd better simply deny all connection with the raid."

"Hah?"

He shrugged his shoulders. He did not look like an honest man. He wasn't one. He knew it. He retorted gloomily:

"Anazeh's scoundrels will have raided sheep, and perhaps cattle. If any one has resisted them, there will be wailing widows crying out for vengeance. They will put the sheep and cattle in their boats in which they came over the sea this afternoon. The boats will be found by the Sikhs, hauled up on the sand-pit just below my house, with my motor-boat beside them. I am ruined!"

Well, my own predicament was better than that. Nobody was likely to accuse me of having stolen sheep. But I could not feel sorry for my host, because he was so sorry for himself. He was one of those unfortunates who carry the conviction of their own guilt in their faces. I gave up all idea of relying on him in case the Sikhs should come.

My next idea was to ask for the loan of one of the donkeys, and to start back toward Jerusalem. But I had not more than thought of it when men's footsteps pattered on the yard dung, and an indubitable rifle-butt beat on the wooden door.

"For God's sake!" hissed the owner of the place. He ran to the door to open it as the thumping grew louder. As he drew the bolt somebody kicked the door open, sending him reeling backwards. For a second I thought the Sikhs had come.

But he was nothing like a Sikh who strode in, with a dozen ruffians at his tail and one-eyed Ali bringing up the rear. He was one of the finest-looking Arabs I had ever seen, although considerably past fifty and wrinkled so that his face was a network of fine lines, out of which his big, dark eyes shone with unaged intelligence. He was magnificently dressed, perhaps in order to do me honour. Except for the fact that he carried a modern military rifle on his elbow, in place of a shepherd's crook or a spear, he looked like one of those historic worthies who stalk through the pages of the Pentateuch. The dignity and charm with which he bowed to me were inimitable — unconveyable. But he turned on my Christian host like a prophet of old rebuking blasphemy.

Arabic when the right man uses it sounds like tooth-for-a-tooth law being laid down. Hebrew is all music and soft vowels; Arabic all guttural consonants. The Sheikh Anazeh (there was no doubt of his identity; they all kept calling him by name) fulminated. The other bleated at him. I learned his name at last. Ali of the one eye pressed forward, took him by the sleeve, and called him Ahmed. Ali seemed to be adding persuasion to Anazeh's threats. Whatever it was they were driving at, Ahmed began to look like yielding. So, as I could not untangle more than one brief sentence at a time from all those galloping arguments, I pulled Ahmed away into a corner.

"What do they all want?" I asked him. "Tell me in ten words." But he was not a brief man.

"They say the Sikhs are after them. They have put the stolen sheep into their boats, as I told you they would, mister. Now they order me to tow them with my motor-boat. But it cannot be done, mister, it cannot be done! I tell them there is government launch near Jericho that the Sikh patrol can use to overtake us. I have a swift boat, but if I take in tow two other loaded boats we shall be caught; and then who will save everything I have from confiscation?"

"How close are the Sikhs?" I asked.

"God knows, mister! They can come fast. Unless I consent to let them use my boat, Anazeh will order his men to kill me, and then they will take the boat in any case! There is only one thing: they must leave the sheep behind and all crowd into my boat, but I cannot persuade them!"

At that moment another of Anazeh's party burst in through the door. He evidently bore bad news. Catching sight of me, he lowered his voice to a whisper, and, whatever he said, Anazeh nodded gravely. Then the old sheikh gave an order, and four of his men came without further ado to seize Ahmed.

"Bear me witness!" the wretched man called back to me as they dragged him off. "I go under protest — most unwillingly!"

Somebody struck him with a butt-end. A woman's head appeared over the top of the partition, and began to jabber noisily. Several of Anazeh's men hurled jests: the highest compliment they paid her was to call her Um-Kulsum, the mother of sin. Anazeh beckoned to me. He did not seem to doubt for an instant that I would follow him.

I was in no mind to wait there and be arrested by the Sikh patrol. I wondered whether they were coming in open order, combing the countryside, or heading all together straight for a known objective; and whether in either case I could give them the slip and head back toward Jerusalem. In that minute I recalled Grim's advice:

"Do whatever the leader of the escort tells you and you'll be all right. You needn't be afraid to trust him."

That settled it. I did not suppose for a minute that Grim had contemplated any such contingency as this; but he had volunteered the advice, so the consequences would be his affair. I followed Anazeh into outer darkness, and one of his men pulled the door to after me.

There was something very like a panic down by the water-side, three hundred yards away from the house. It needed all Anazeh's authority to straighten matters out. There were divided counsels; and the raiders were working at a disadvantage in total darkness; the shadow of the hills fell just beyond the stern of the boats as they lay with their bows ashore.

They had already forced Ahmed into his own motor-boat, where he was struggling vainly to crank a cold engine. Some of the others were trying to push off a boat full of bleating sheep.

One man was carrying a fat sheep in his arms toward the motor-boat, splashing knee-deep in the water and shouting advice to everybody else, and in the end that was the only piece of plunder they got away with. Suddenly one man, who had been left behind to keep a look-out, came leaping like a ghost among the shadows, shouting the one word "askeri!" (Soldiers!) He jumped straight into the motor-boat. Anazeh bullied all the rest in after him. I climbed in over the bow. By that time you could not have crowded in one more passenger with the aid of a battering ram.

"Yalla!" barked Anazeh. But the engine would not start. Blood-curdling threats were hurled at the unhappy Ahmed. Some of the men got into the water and began to shove off, as if the engine could be encouraged by collaboration.

I was just as keen to escape as any one. I could not imagine a Sikh or subaltern stupid enough to believe me innocent. It was a military government. Soldiers have a drum-head method of leaving nothing to discuss except where the corpse is to be buried.

I forced my way aft — got some gasoline out of the tank into a tin cup — thrust aside Ahmed and two other men — and primed the engine liberally. The engine coughed next time they moved the wheel, and in thirty seconds more we had it going. Ahmed came in for a volley of mockery for having to be shown the way to start his engine; but from the sour way he looked at me I was nearly sure he had stalled deliberately.

We backed away from shore, and Anazeh steered the boat's nose eastward. Then somebody at the reversing lever threw it forward too suddenly, and the still chilled engine stopped. It took about another minute to restart it. We were just beginning to gain speed when some one shouted. All eyes turned toward the shore, the overloaded boat rocking dangerously as the crowd bent their bodies all in one direction together.

Down near the shore-line an electric torch flashed on the uniforms of half a dozen Sikhs, and we could hear an unmistakably British voice shouting an order.

We were out in the moonlight now, a perfect target. Bullets chanced at us could hardly fail to hit somebody. Two or three well-placed shots might sink us. But Anazeh had presence of mind. He changed helm, so as to present us end-on to the shore. Low in the water though the boat was, we were beginning to make good headway.

The Sikhs lost no time. Shots began to whizz overhead and to splash the water around us. But the boat was painted gray; as we increased the distance we must have looked like a moving patch of darker water with a puzzling wake behind us. The sea was still. The stars were reflected in it in unsteady dots and streaks. The moon cast a silver patch of light that shimmered, and confused the eye. Sikhs are not by any means all marksmen. At any rate, the shots all missed. Though some of our party, Anazeh included, returned the fire, none boasted of having hit any one. And an Arab boasts at the least excuse.

In a few minutes we were out of range and, since there was no pursuing launch in sight, could afford to jeer at the Sikhs in chorus. There were things said about their habits and their ancestry that it is to be hoped they did not hear, or at any rate understand, for the sake of any Arab prisoners they might take in future. It always struck me as a fool game to mock your enemy. If you fall in his power at any time he would be almost more than human if he did not remember it. It seemed to me unlikely that those Sikhs would forget to avenge the Arab compliments that must have sizzled in ears across that star-lit sea. After that the only immediate danger was from the wind that sometimes blows down in sudden gusts from between the mountain-tops. It would have needed only half a sea to swamp us. But the Dead Sea was living up to its reputation, quiet, inert, like a mercury mirror for the stars — a brooding place of silence.

The Arabs' spirits rose as we chugged toward their savage hills. They began to sing glorious songs about women and mares and camels. Presently Anazeh improvised an epic about the night's raid, abortive though it had been. He left out all the disappointing part. He sang first of the three shore-dwelling fools whose boats they had stolen. Then of the baffled rage of those same fools when they should learn their property was lost forever. Presently, as he warmed to the spirit of the thing, he sang about the wails of the frightened villagers from whom they had plundered sheep and goats; and of the skill and resourcefulness with which the party had escaped pursuit under his leadership, Allah favoring, "and blessed be His Prophet!"

Last, he sang about me, the honoured stranger, for whom they had dared everything and conquered, and whom they were taking to El-Kerak. He described me as a prince from a far country, the son of a hundred kings.

It was a good song. I got Ahmed to translate it to me afterwards. But I suspect that Ahmed toned it down in deference to what he may have thought might be my modesty and moralistic scruples.

CHAPTER FOUR

"I am willing to use all means — all methods."

Ahmed knew the Dead Sea. He knew its moods and a few of its tricks, so he was suitably scared. He was more afraid of the treacherous sea than of his captors. They weren't treacherous in the least. They were frankly disobedient of any law except their own; respectful of nothing but bullets, brains and their own interpretation of the Will of Allah. They showed sublime indifference to danger that always comes of ignorance. Ahmed was for running straight across to cut the voyage short, because of the wind that sometimes blows from the south at dawn. He said it might kick up a sea that would roll us over, for the weight of the Dead Sea waves in a blow is prodigious.

They overruled his protest with loud-lunged unanimity and lots of abuse. Anazeh continued to steer a diagonal course for a notch in the Moab Hills that look, until you get quite close to them, as if they rose sheer out of the sea. The old chief was pretty amateurish at the helm, whatever his other attainments. Our wake was like a drunkard's.

What with the danger in that overcrowded boat, and the manifestly compromising fact that I had now become one of a gang who boasted of the murder they had done that night, I did some speculation that seems ridiculous now, at this distance, after a lapse of time. It occurred to me that Grim might be disguised as a member of Anazeh's party. As far as possible in the dark I thoroughly scrutinized each individual. It is easy to laugh about it now, but I actually made my way to Anazeh's side and tried to discover whether the old Sheikh's wrinkles and gray-shot beard were not a very skillfully done make-up. At any rate, I got from that absurd investigation the sure knowledge that Grim was not in the boat with us.

I could not talk with Anazeh very well, because when he tried to understand my amateurish Arabic and to modify his flow of stately speech to meet my needs, he always put his head down, and the helm with it. It seemed wisest to let him do one unaccustomed thing at a time. I did not care to try to talk with any of his men, because that might possibly have been a breach of etiquette. Arab jealousy is about as quick as fulminate of mercury: as unreasonable, from a western viewpoint, as a love-sick woman's.

But there did not seem any objection to talking with Ahmed. He was at least in theory my co-religionist, and not a person any Moslem in that boat was likely to be jealous of. He jumped at the notion of making friends with me. He made no secret of the reason.

"You are safe, effendi. They will neither rob you, nor kill you, nor let you get killed. You are their guest. But as for me, they would cut my throat as readily as that sheep's, more especially since they have discovered that you know how to start the engine. My best chance was to make them believe that the engine is difficult to understand. Because of your knowledge they now feel independent of me. So I must yield to them in everything. And if they force me to swear on a Bible, and on my father's honour, and in the name of God, that I will not give evidence against them, I shall have to swear."

"An oath given under compulsion —" I began. But he laughed cynically.

"Ah! You do not know this land — these folk, effendi. If I were to break such an oath as that, they would burn my house, steal my cattle, ravish my wife, and hunt me to the death. If I ran away to America, Arabs in Chicago and New York would continue the hunt. This is a land where an oath is binding, unless you are the stronger. I am weak — an unimportant person."

"What is your business?" I asked.

"There is no business for a man like me. The regulations forbid commerce in the only goods for which there is a real demand among Bedouins."

"So you're a smuggler, eh?"

He laughed, between pride and caution, and changed the subject.

"I shall do what they order me, effendi. I think they will keep my boat over there to bring you back again. But when I get back the Sikhs will arrest me. So I ask you to bear me witness that I was compelled by threats and force to go with these people. In that way, with a little ingenuity — that is to say, the ingenious use of piastras — perhaps I can contrive to get out of the difficulty without being punished by both Arabs and British."

I promised to tell no more than I had seen and heard. On the strength of that we became as fast friends as suspicion permitted. We trusted each other, because we more or less had to, like a couple of thieves "on the lam." It suited me. He was a very good interpreter and slavishly anxious to please. But I lived to regret it later. When my evidence had cleared him of collusion in the raid, he chose on the strength of that to claim me as his friend for life. He turned up in the United States and tried to live on his wits. I had to pay a lawyer to defend him in Federal Court. He writes me piously pathetic letters from Leavenworth Penitentiary. And when he gets out I suppose I shall have to befriend him again. However, at the moment, he was useful.

It was just dawn when old Anazeh ran the launch into a cove between high rocks. Ahmed let out a shriek of anguish at the violence done the hull. They pitched the sheep overboard to wade ashore without remembering to untie its legs; it was almost drowned before it occurred to any one to rescue it. Perhaps it was dead. I don't know. Anyhow, one fellow prayed in a hurry while his companion cut the sheep's throat to make it lawful meat.

"God is good," old Anazeh remarked to me, "and blessed be His Prophet, who forbade us faithful, even though we hunger, to defile ourselves with the flesh of creatures whose blood did not flow from the knife of the slayer."

After that they all prayed, going first into the oily-feeling, asphaltic water for the ceremonial washing. They were quite particular about it. Then they spread prayer-mats, facing Mecca. Every single cut-throat had brought along his prayer-mat, and had treasured it as carefully as his rifle.

Ahmed and I sat on a rock and watched them. Ahmed pretended he wanted to pray, too. To impress me, he said he was a very devout Christian and that nothing should prevent the practice of his religion. But he was very quick to take my advice not to start anything that might bring on a breach of the peace. Old Anazeh's short preliminary sermon to his followers, about the need of always keeping God in mind, was not addressed to us.

Prayers finished, they proceeded to cut up and cook the sheep. Ahmed and I subdued the voice of conscience without noticeable effort and ate our share of the stolen goods. Ahmed said that, seeing how little was left for him when the rest had all been served, he sinned only in small degree, but that my share, as an honoured guest, was huge, and the sin proportionate. So I gave him some of my meat, and he ate it, and we were equally sinful — one more bond cementing an "eternal friendship!"

We had hardly finished eating when an Arab on a gray horse came riding furiously down a ravine that looked like a dry water-course. He was brought up all-standing fifty yards away. Every man in the party leveled a rifle at him. Anazeh beckoned me to come and get behind him for protection. He was very angry when I refused. He cursed the language and religion of whatever fool had taught me manners in a land where pigs are lawful food. However, after they had all had a good look at the horseman they let him draw near, and there followed a noisy conference, the man on the horse calling on Allah repeatedly with emphasis, and Anazeh and his followers all doing the same thing, but from an opposing viewpoint. I persuaded Ahmed to go up close and listen.

"The man is from El-Kerak," he said presently, while they all still fought with words, using tremendous oaths by way of artillery. "A council of the tribes has been summoned, to meet at El-Kerak, but each sheikh is only to take two men with him, because of the risk of fighting among themselves. Anazeh says there can be no proper council without his being present, and that he will attend the council; but as for taking only two men, he has pledged his word to escort you with twenty men to El-Kerak. He swears that he will carry out that pledge, even should he have to fight the whole way there and back again!"

Anazeh suddenly cut short the war of words. His gesture suggested that of Joshua who made the sun stand still. He tossed a curt order to one of his men, who went off at a run toward a village, whose morning smoke rose blue over a spur of the range a mile away. Then Anazeh sat down to await events, and took no more notice of the horseman's arguments. That did not worry the horseman much. He kept on arguing. Every few minutes one of Anazeh's men would go to him and repeat some tid-bit, as if the old sheikh had not heard it; but all he got for his pains was a gesture of contemptuous dismissal.

Ahmed kept growing more and more uncomfortable all the time. He had attended to his boat, making it properly fast and covering the engine, under the eyes of four men who were at pains to see that he did not crank up and desert. Now he was back beside me, trying to bolster up his own courage by making me afraid.

"They have determined to take me along with them to prevent me from escaping," he complained. "That man on the horse is saying that if more men go with Anazeh than you and two others, there will certainly be fighting. And Anazeh answers, he has pledged his word. Can you not say something to persuade Anazeh?"

I would rather have tried to persuade a tiger. Short of knocking the old raider on the head and standing off his twenty ruffians, I could not imagine a way of turning him from his set purpose. And at that, I had not a weapon of any kind. I was the goods, and the game old sportsman intended to deliver me, right side up, perhaps, but all in one piece and to the proper consignee.

"I don't see anything to worry about," said I.

"Wait till you hear the bullets!" Ahmed answered. Nevertheless, bullets or no bullets, I did not see what I could do about it. Again I remembered Grim's advice: "Do what the leader of the escort tells you." I had begun to feel sorry for Ahmed in spite of his self-pity, but his fear wasn't contagious and his advice wasn't worth listening to.

"Effendi, you are Anazeh's guest. He must do as you demand, if you ask in the Name of the Most High. Tell him, therefore, that you have an urgent business in El-Kudz. Demand that he send you back, with me, in my boat!"

"You are not his guest. He would simply shoot you and destroy the boat," I answered.

It was not more than half an hour before I saw horses coming in our direction from the village. At sight of them the man on the gray horse lost heart. With a final burst of eloquence, in which he spread his breast to heaven and shook both fists in witness that he was absolved and no blood-guilt could rest on his head, he rode away at top speed straight up the ravine down which he originally came.

The horses proved to be a very mixed lot — some good, some very bad, and some indifferent. But again they treated me as honoured guest and provided me a mare with four sound legs and nothing much the matter except vice. She came at me with open teeth when I tried to mount, but four men held her and I climbed aboard, somehow or other. As a horseman, I am a pretty good sack of potatoes.

That was the worst saddle I ever sat in — and Anazeh's second-best! The stirrups swung amidships, so to speak, and whenever you tried to rest your weight on them for a moment they described an arc toward the rear. Moreover, you could not sit well back on the saddle to balance matters, because of the high cantle. The result, whether you did with stirrups or without them, was torture, for anybody but an Arab, who has notions of comfort all his own.

They put Ahmed on a wall-eyed scrub that looked unfit to walk, but proved well able to gallop under his light weight. One of Anazeh's men took my bag, with a nod to reassure me, and without a word we were off full-pelt, Anazeh leading with four stalwarts who looked almost as hard-bitten as himself, six men crowding me closely, and the remainder bringing up the rear.

That is the Arab way of doing things — rush and riot to begin with. The steepness of the stony ravine we rode up soon reduced the horses to a walk, after which there was a good deal of attention to rifle-bolts, and a settling down to the more serious aspects of the adventure. The escort began to look sullenly ferocious, as only Arabs can.

There was a time, during the Turkish regime before the War, when Cook's Agency took tourists in parties to El-Kerak, and all the protection necessary was a handful of Turkish soldiers, whose chief employment on the trip was to gather fuel and pitch tents. Some one paid the Arabs to let tourists alone, and they normally did. But the War changed all that. A post-Armistice stranger in 1920, with leather boots, was fair quarry for whoever had rifle or knife.

We passed by a village or two, tucked into folds in the hills and polluting the blue sky with a smell of ageing dung, but nothing seemed disposed to happen. A few men stood behind stone walls and stared at us sullenly. The women looked up from their grindstones at the doors, covered their faces for convention's sake, and uncovered them again at once for curiosity. There was nothing you could call a road between the villages, only a rocky cattle-track that seemed to take the longest possible way between two points; and nobody seemed to own it, or to be there to challenge our right of way.

But suddenly, after we had passed the third village and were walking the horses up a shoulder of a steep hill-top, three shots cracked out from in front of us to left and right. Nobody fell, but if ever there was instantaneous response it happened then. Anazeh and his four galloped forward up-hill, firing as they rode for the cover of a breast-high ridge. One man on the off-side tipped me out of the saddle, so suddenly that I had no chance to prevent him; another caught me, and two others flung me into a hole behind a stone. I heard the rear-guard scatter and run. Two men pitched Ahmed down on top of me, for he was valuable, seeing he could run an engine; and thirty seconds later I peered out around the rock to get a glimpse of what was happening.

There was not a man in sight. I could see some of the horses standing under cover. The firing was so rapid that it sounded almost like machine-gun practice. A hairy arm reached out and pushed my head back, and after that, whenever I made the least movement, a man who was sniping from behind the sheltering rock swore furiously, and threatened to brain me with his butt-end. Beyond all doubt they regarded me as perishable freight; so I hardly saw any of the fighting.

Judging by the sound, I should say they fought their way up-hill in skirmish order, and when they got to the top the enemy — whoever they were — took to flight. But that is guesswork. There were two casualties on our side. One man shot through the arm, which did not matter much; he was well able to lie about what had happened and to boast of how many men he had slain before the bullet hit him. The other was wounded pretty seriously in the jaw. They came to me for first aid, taking it for granted that I knew something about surgery. I don't. I had a bad time bandaging both of them, using two of my handkerchiefs and strips from the protesting Ahmed's shirt. However, I enjoyed it more than they did.

When Anazeh shouted at last and we all rode to the hilltop there was a dead man lying there, stripped naked, with his throat cut across from ear to ear. One of our men was wiping a long knife by stabbing it into the dirt. There was also a led horse added to the escort. Anazeh looked very cool and dignified; he had an extra rifle now, slung by a strap across his shoulders. He was examining a bandolier that had blood on it.

We rode on at once, and for the next hour Ahmed was kept busy interpreting to me the lies invented by every member of the escort for my especial benefit. If they were true, each man had slain his dozen; but nobody would say who the opposing faction were. When I put that question they all dried up and nobody would speak again for several minutes.

It turned out afterward that there had been a sort of armistice proclaimed, and all the local chiefs had undertaken to observe it and cease from blood-feuds for three days, provided that each chief should prove peaceful intention by bringing with him only two men. Three men in a party, and not more than three, had right of way. The engagement may have been a simple protest against breach of the terms of the armistice, but I suspect there was more than that in it.

At any rate, we were not attacked again on the road, although there were men who showed themselves now and then on inaccessible-looking crags, who eyed us suspiciously and made no answer to the shouted challenge of Anazeh's men. When the track passed over a spur, or swung round the shoulder of a cliff, we could sometimes catch sight of other parties — always, though of three, before and behind us, proceeding in the same direction.

We sighted the stone walls of El-Kerak at about midafternoon, and rode up to the place through a savage gorge that must have been impregnable in the old days of bows and arrows. It would take a determined army today to force itself through the wadys and winding water-courses that guard that old citadel of Romans and crusaders.

We approached from the Northwest corner, where a tower stands that they call Burj-ez-Zahir. There were lions carved on it. It looked as if the battlements had been magnificent at one time; but whatever the Turks become possessed of always falls into decay, and the Arabs seem no better.

Beside the Burj-ez-Zahir is a tunnel, faced by an unquestionable Roman arch. Outside it there were more than a dozen armed men lounging, and a lot of others looked down at us through the ruined loop-holes of the wall above. Their leader challenged our numbers at once, and refused admission. Judging by Anazeh's magnificently insolent reply it looked at first as if he intended fighting his way in. But that turned out to be only his diplomatic manner — establishing himself, as it were, on an eminence from which he could make concessions without losing dignity.

The arrangement finally agreed to was Anazeh's suggestion, but showed diplomatic genius on both sides. The old man divided up his party into sets of three, and asserted that every set of three was independent. There were twenty-two of us all told, including Ahmed, but he described Ahmed as a prisoner, and offered to have him shot if that would simplify matters.

There was a great deal of windy discussion about Ahmed's fate, during which his face grew the color of raw liver and he joined in several times tearfully. Once he was actually seized and half a dozen of the castle guards aimed at him; but they compromised finally by letting him go in with hands tied. Nobody really wanted the responsibility of shooting a man who had smuggled stolen cartridges across the Dead Sea, and might do it again if allowed to live.

We rode for eighty or a hundred paces through an echoing tunnel into a city of shacks and ruined houses that swarmed with armed men, and it was evident that we were not the only ones who had ignored the rule about numbers. Anazeh explained in an aside to me that only those would obey that rule who did not dare break it.

"Whoever makes laws should be strong enough to enforce

them," he said sagely. "And whoever obeys such a law is at the mercy of those who break it," he added presently, by way of afterthought. To make sure that I understood him he repeated that remark three times.

Every house had its quota of visitors, who lounged in the doorways and eyed us with mixed insolence and curiosity. There were coffee-booths all over the place that seemed to have been erected for the occasion, where, under awnings made of stick and straw, men sat with rifles on their knees. Those who had provender to sell for horses were doing a roaring trade — short measure and high price; and the noise of grinding was incessant. The women in the back streets were toiling to produce enough to eat for all that host of notables.

To have had to hunt for quarters in that town just then would have been no joke. There was the mosque, of course, where any Moslem who finds himself stranded may theoretically go and sleep on a mat on the floor. But we rode past the mosque. It was full. I would not have liked a contract to crowd one more in there. Perhaps a New York Subway guard could have managed it. The babel coming through the open door was like the buzzing of flies on a garbage heap.

I was trying to sit upright in that abominable saddle and look dignified, as became the honoured guest with a twenty-man escort, when a courteous-looking cut-throat wearing an amber necklace worth a wheat-field, forced his way through a crowd and greeted Anazeh like a long lost brother. I examined him narrowly to make sure he was not Grim in disguise, but he had two fingers missing, and holes in his ears, which decided that question.

After he had welcomed me effusively he led us through a rat-run maze of streets to a good-sized house with snub-nosed lions carved on the stone doorposts and a lot of other marks of both Roman and crusader. No part of the walls was less than three feet thick, although the upper story had been rebuilt rather recently on a more economical and much less dignified scale. Nevertheless, there was a sort of semi-European air about the place, helped out by two casemented projections overhanging the narrow street.

There was no need to announce ourselves. The clatter of hoofs and shouts to ordinary folk on foot to get out of the way had done that already. Sheikh ben Nazir opened the door in person. His welcome to me was the sort that comes to mind when you read the Bible story of the prodigal son returning from a far-off country. I might have been his blood-relation. But perhaps I am wrong about that; bloodfeuds among blood-relations are notoriously savage. He was the host, and I the guest. Among genuine Arabs that is the most binding relation there is.

He was no longer in blue serge and patent-leather boots, but magnificent in Arab finery, and he was tricked out in a puzzling snowy-white head-dress that suggested politics without your knowing why. He had told me, when I met him at the American Colony, that he had made the pilgrimage to Mecca more than once; but that white linen thing had nothing to do with his being a haji, any more than the expensive rings on the fingers of both hands had anything to do with his Arab nationality.

After he had flattered and questioned me sufficiently about the journey to comply with etiquette I asked him whether Ahmed might not be untied, the thong cutting the man's wrists. Sheikh ben Nazir gave the necessary order and it was obeyed at once. The liquid-eyed rascal with the priceless amber necklace then led away the escort, Ahmed included, to some place where they could stall the horses, and — side-by-side, lest any question of precedence should be involved — Anazeh and I followed ben Nazir into the house.

We were not the only guests there. He ushered us into a square room, in which outrageous imported furniture, with gilt and tassels on it, stood out like loathsome sores against rugs and cushions fit for the great Haroun-al-Raschid's throne room. Any good museum in the world would have competed to possess the rugs, but the furniture was the sort that France sends eastward in the name of "culture" — stuff for "savages" to sit on and be civilized while the white man bears the burden and collects the money.

There were half a dozen Arabs reclining on two bastard Louis-something-or-other settees, who rose to their feet as we entered. There was another man, sitting on a cushion in a corner by himself, who did not get up. He wore a white head-dress exactly like our host's, and seemed to consider himself somebody very important indeed. After one swift searching glance at us he went into a brown study, as if a mere sheikh and a Christian alien were beneath his notice.

We were introduced first of all to the men who had stood up to greet us, and that ceremony took about five minutes. The Arab believes he ought to know all about how you feel physically, and expects you to reciprocate. When that was over ben Nazir took us to the corner and presented, first me, then Anazeh to the solitary man in the white head-dress, who seemed to think himself too important to trouble about manners.

Anazeh did not quite like my receiving attention first, and he liked still less the off-handed way in which the solitary man received us. We were told his name was Suliman ben Saoud. He acknowledged my greeting. He and old Anazeh glared at each other, barely moving their heads in what might have been an unspoken threat and retort or a nod of natural recognition. Anazeh turned on his heel and joined the other guests.

In some vague way I knew that Saoud was a name to conjure with, although memory refused to place it. The man's air of indifference and apparently unstudied insolence suggested he was some one well used to authority. Presuming on the one thing that I felt quite sure of by that time — my privileged position as a guest — I stayed, to try to draw him out. I tried to open up conversation with him with English, French, and finally lame Arabic. He took no apparent notice of the French and English, but he smiled sarcastically at my efforts with his own tongue. Except that he moved his lips he made no answer but went on clicking the beads of a splendid amber rosary.

Ben Nazir, seeming to think that Anazeh's ruffled feelings called for smoothing, crossed the room to engage him in conversation, so I was left practically alone with the strange individual. More or less in a spirit of defiance of his claim to such distinction, I sat down on a cushion beside him.

He was a peculiar-looking man. The lower part of his cheek — that side on which I sat — was sunk in, as if he had no teeth there. The effect was to give his whole face a twisted appearance. The greater part of his head, of course, was concealed by the flowing white kaffiyi, but his skin was considerably darker than that of the Palestine Arab. He had no eyebrows at all, having shaved them off — for a vow I supposed. Instead of making him look comical, as you might expect, it gave him a very sinister appearance, which was increased by his generally surly attitude.

Once again, as when I had entered the room, he turned his head to give me one swift, minutely searching glance, and then turned his eyes away as if he had no further interest. They were quite extraordinary eyes, brimful of alert intelligence; and whereas from his general appearance I should have set him down at somewhere between forty and fifty, his eyes suggested youth, or else that keen, unpeaceful spirit that never ages.

I tried him again in Arabic, but he answered without looking at me, in a dialect I had never heard before. So I offered him a gold-tipped cigarette, that being a universal language. He waved the offer aside with something between astonishment and disdain. He had lean, long-fingered hands, entirely unlike those of the desert fraternity, who live too hard and fight too frequently to have soft, uncalloused skin and unbroken finger-nails.

He did not exactly fascinate me. His self-containment was annoying. It seemed intended to convey an intellectual and moral importance that I was not disposed to concede without knowing more about him. I suppose an Arab feels the same sensation when a Westerner lords it over him on highly moral grounds. At any rate, something or other in the way of pique urged me to stir him out of his self-complacency, just as one feels urged to prod a bull-frog to watch him jump.

He seemed to understand my remarks, for he took no trouble to hide his amusement at my efforts with the language. But he only answered in monosyllables, and I could not understand those. So after about five minutes I gave it up, and crossed the room to ben Nazir, who seized the opportunity to show me my sleeping-quarters.

It proved to be a room like a monastery cell, up one flight of stone steps, with two other rooms of about the same size on either side of it. At the end of the passage was a very heavy wooden door, with an iron lock and an enormous keyhole, which I suppose shut off the harem from the rest of the house; but as I never trespassed beyond it I don't know. I only do know that a woman's eye was watching me through that key-hole, and ben Nazir frowned impatiently at the sound of female giggling.

"The Sheikh Anazeh will have the room on this side of you," he said, "and the Sheikh Suliman ben Saoud the room on the other. So you will be between friends."

"Suliman ben Saoud seems a difficult person to make friends with," I answered.

Ben Nazir smiled like a prince out of a picture-book — beautiful white teeth and exquisite benignance.

"Oh, you mustn't mind him. These celebrities from the centre of Arabia give themselves great airs. To do that is considered evidence of piety and wisdom."

I sat on the bed — quite a civilized affair, spotlessly clean. Ben Nazir took the chair, I suppose, like the considerate host he was, to give me the sensation of receiving in my own room.

"He wears the same sort of head-dress you do. What does it mean?" I asked.

"I wear mine out of compliment to him — not that I have not always the right to wear it. It is the Ichwan head-dress. It is highly significant."

"Of what?"

He hesitated for a moment, and then seemed to make up his mind that it did not much matter what he might divulge to an ignorant stranger soon to return to the United States.

"It is difficult to explain. You Americans know so little of our politics. It is significant, I might say, of the New Arabia — Arabia for the Arabs. The great ben Saoud, who is a relative of this man, is an Arabian chieftain who has welded most of Arabia into one, and now challenges King Hussein of Mecca for the caliphate. Hussein is only kept on his throne by British gold, paid to him from India. Ben Saoud also receives a subsidy from the British, who must continue to pay it, because otherwise ben Saoud will attack Hussein and overwhelm him. That, it is believed, would mean a rising of all the Moslem world against their rulers — in Africa — Asia — India — Java — everywhere. It began as a religious movement. It is now political — although it is held together by religious zeal. You might say that the Ichwans are the modern Protestants of Islam. They are fanatical. The world has never seen such fanaticism, and the movement spreads day by day."

"You don't look like a fanatic," I said, and he laughed again.

"I? God forbid! But I am a politician; and to succeed a politician must have friends among all parties. My one ambition is to see all Arabs united in an independent state reaching from this coast to the Persian Gulf. To that end I devote my energy. I use all means available — including money paid me by the French, who have no intention of permitting any such development if they can help it."

"And the British?"

"For the present we must make use of them also. But their yoke must go, eventually."

"Then if America had accepted the Near East mandate, you would have used us in the same way?"

"Certainly. That would have been the easiest way, because America understands little or nothing of our politics. America's money — America's schools and hospitals — America's war munitions — and then good-bye. I am willing to use all means — all methods to the one end — Arabia for the Arabs. After that I am willing to retire into oblivion."

Nevertheless, ben Nazir did not convince me that he was an altruist who had no private ends to serve. There was an avaricious gleam in ben Nazir's eyes.

CHAPTER FIVE

"D'you mind if I use you?"

For all his care to seem hospitable before any other consideration, ben Nazir looked ill at ease. He led me down again to a dining-room hung with spears, shields, scimitars and ancient pistols, but furnished otherwise like an instalment-plan apartment. He watched while a man set food before me. It seemed that Anazeh had gone away somewhere to eat with his men.

Ben Nazir's restlessness became so obvious that I asked at last whether I was not detaining him. He jumped at the opening. With profound apologies he asked me to excuse him for the remainder of the afternoon.

"You see," he explained, "I came from Damascus to Jerusalem, so I was rather out of touch with what was going on here. This conference of notables was rather a surprise to me. It will not really take place until tomorrow, but there are important details to attend to in advance. If you could amuse yourself —"

The man who could not do that in a crusader city, crammed with sons of Ishmael who looked as if they had stepped out of the pages of the Old Testament, would be difficult to please. I asked for Ahmed, to act as interpreter. Ben Nazir volunteered to provide me with two men in addition as a sort of bodyguard.

"Because Ahmed is a person who is not respected."

It did not take ten minutes to produce Ahmed and the two men. The latter were six-foot, solemn veterans armed with rifles and long knives. With them at my heels I set out to explore El-Kerak.

"There is nothing to see," said Ahmed, who did not want to come. But Ahmed was a liar. There was everything to see. The only definite purpose I had in mind was to find Grim. It was possible I might recognize him even through his disguise. Failing that, he could not help but notice me if I walked about enough; if so, he would find his own means of establishing communication.

But you might as well have hunted for one particular pebble on a beach as for a single individual in all that throng. Remembering Grim's disguise when I first saw him, I naturally had that picture of him in mind. But all the Bedouins looked about as much alike as peas in a pod. They stared at me as if I were a curio on exhibition, but they did not like being stared back at.

There was no hint of violence or interference, and no apparent resentment of an alien's presence in their midst. The loud-lunged bodyguard shouted out to all and sundry to make way for the "Amerikani," and way was made forthwith, although several times the bodyguard was stopped and questioned after I had passed, to make sure I was really American and not English. Ahmed assured me that if I had been English they would have "massacred" me. In view of what transpired he may have been right, though I doubt it. They might have held me as hostage.

Not that they were in any kind of over-tolerant mood. There was a man's dead body hanging by one foot from a great hook on a high wall, and the wall was splattered with blood and chipped by bullets. I asked Ahmed what kind of criminal he might be.

"He did not agree with them. They are for war. He was in favor of peace, and he made a speech two hours ago. So they accused him of being a traitor, and he was tried and condemned."

"Who tried him?"

"Everybody did."

"War with whom?" I asked.

"The British."

"Why?"

"Because they favor the Zionists."

"And that is what the conference is all about?"

"Yes. There is a man here from Damascus, who urges them to raid across the Jordan into Palestine. He says that the Palestinian Arabs will rise then, and cut the throats of all the Zionists. He says that Emir Feisul is going to attack the French in Syria, and that the British will have to go and help the French, so now is the time for a raid."

"Is my host, ben Nazir, the man who is talking that way? He has been to Damascus."

"No. Another, named Abdul Ali — a very rich sheikh, who

comes here often with caravans of merchandise, and gives rich presents to notables."

"Has ben Nazir anything to do with it?"

"Who knows? Mashallah! The world is full of mysteries. That Nazir is a knowing one. They say of him: whichever option is uppermost, that is always his opinion. He is a safe man to follow for that reason. Yet it is easier to follow water through a channel underground."

We made our way toward the castle at the south side of the town, but were prevented from entering by a guard of feudal retainers, who looked as if they had been well drilled. They were as solemn as the vultures that sat perched along the rampart overlooking a great artificial moat dividing the town from the high hill just beyond it.

Nobody interfered when I climbed on the broken town wall and looked over. The castle wall sloped down steeply into the moat, suggesting ample space within for dungeons and underground passages; but there was nothing else there of much interest to see, only dead donkeys, a dying camel with the vultures already beginning on him, some dead dogs, heaps of refuse, and a lot more vultures too gorged to fly — the usual Arab scheme of sanitation. I asked one of my bodyguard to shoot the camel and he obliged me, with the air of a keeper making concessions to a lunatic. Nobody took any notice of the rifle going off.

It was when we turned back into the town again that the first inkling of Grim's presence in the place turned up. A bulky-looking Arab in a sheepskin coat that stank of sweat so vilely that you could hardly bear the man near you, came up and stood in my way. Barring the smell, he was a winning-looking rascal — truculent, swaggering, but possessed of a good-natured smile that seemed to say: "Sure, I'm a rogue and a liar, but what else did you expect!"

He spoke perfectly good English. He said he wished to speak to me alone. That was easy enough; Ahmed and the bodyguard withdrew about ten paces, and he and I stepped into a doorway.

"I am Mahommed ben Hamza," he said, with his head on one side, as if that explanation ought to make everything clear to me at once. "From Hebron," he added, when I did not seem to see the light.

The wiser one looks, and the less one says, in Arab lands, the less trouble there's likely to be. I tried to look extremely wise, and said nothing.

"Where is Jimgrim?" he demanded.

"If you can tell me that I'll give you ten piastres," I answered.

"I will give you fifty if you tell me!"

"Why do you want to know?"

"He is my friend. He said I should see him here. But I have not seen him. He said also I should see you. You are the Amerikani? And you don't know where he is? Truly? Then, when you see him, will you say to him, 'Mahommed ben Hamza is here with nine men at the house of Abu Shamah?' Jimgrim will understand."

I nodded, and the man from Hebron walked away without another word.

"Did he steal your watch?" asked Ahmed. They are as jealous as children, those Arabs.

There was a second execution while I walked back through the city. A wide-eyed, panic-stricken poor devil with slobber on his jaws came tearing down-street with a mob at his heels. We stepped into an alley to let the race go by, but he doubled down the alley opposite. Before he had run twenty yards along it some one hit the back of his head with a piece of rock. A second later they had pounced on him, and in less than a minute after that he was kicking in the noose of a hide rope slung over a house-beam. I don't know what they hanged him for. No one apparently knew. But they used his carcase for a target and shot it almost to pieces.

I kept on looking for Grim, although the task seemed hopeless. Of course, I could not give a hint of my real purpose. But as Grim knew that the talk about a school-teacher was my passport to the place, it seemed possible that he might use that as an excuse for getting in touch with me. So I told Ahmed to show me the schools.

They weren't worth looking at — mere tumble-down sheds in which Moslem boys were taught to say the Koran by heart.

The places where Christian missionaries once had been were all turned into stores, and even into stables for the horses of the notables.

So I returned to ben Nazir's house, and found old Sheikh Anazeh sitting outside on the step, as motionless as a tobacco-store Indian but twice as picturesque. He still had his own rifle over his knees, and the plundered one slung over his shoulder by a strap; he never stirred abroad unarmed.

I asked him what the conference of notables was going to be about, and he told me to mind my own business. That struck me as an excellent idea, so, not having slept at all the previous night, I went upstairs and lay on the bed. There was no lock on the door, so I set the chair against it.

Ben Nazir was a man who had traveled a great deal, and picked up western notions of hospitality to add to the inborn eastern sense of sacredness in the relation between host and guest. It seems that an hour or two later he came to take me down to a Gargantuan meal, but, feeling the chair against the door, and hearing snores, he decided it was better manners to let me lie in peace.

So I did not wake up again until after midnight. The moon-light was streaming through a little high-perched window, and fell on the white-robed, ghostly-looking figure of a man, who sat with crossed legs on the end of the bed. I thought I was dead and in hell.

That is no picturesque exaggeration about a man's hair standing when he is terrified. It really does. I would have yelled aloud, if the breath would have come, but there is a trick of sudden fear that seems to grip your lungs and hold them impo-tent. The thing on the end of the bed had no eye-brows. It grinned as if it knew all about evil, and were hungry, and living men were its food.

I don't know how long I stared at the thing, but it seemed like a week. At last it spoke, and I burst into a sweat with the reaction.

"Good job you don't know how to fasten a door with a chair. I'll have to show you that trick, or you'll be dying before your time. Sh-h-h! Don't make a noise!"

I sat up and looked more closely at him. It was the Ichwan of the afternoon — Sheikh Suliman ben Saoud. And he was speaking unmistakable American. I began again to believe I was dreaming. He chuckled quietly and lit a cigarette.

"Aren't you wise to me yet?"

"Grim?"

"Who else?"

"But what's happened to your face? You're all one-sided."

"Oh, that's easy. I just take out my false teeth. The rest is done with a razor and some brown stain. I thought you were going to spot me when you first came. Did you? I didn't think so. Did you act as well as all that?"

"No. Looked all over town for you afterward."

"Uh-huh. I thought that was too natural to be acting. Pick up any news in town?"

"Saw a hanging, and met a man who calls himself Mahommed ben Hamza. He's waiting at the house of Abu Shamah."

"Any men with him?"

"Nine."

"Three more than he promised. Ben Hamza is the most honest thief and dependable liar in Palestine — a cheerful murderer who sticks closer than a brother. I saved him once from being hung, because he smiles so nicely. Any more news?"

"I expect none that you don't know. There's a sheikh named Abdul Ali from Damascus, preaching a raid into Palestine."

Grim nodded.

"I'm here to bag that bird."

"Where do I come in?" I asked.

"You are the plausible excuse, that's all. Thanks to you old Anazeh got into El-Kerak with twenty men. Two might not have been enough, even with ben Hamza and his nine."

"Then our host ben Nazir is in on your game?"

"Not he! Up at headquarters in Jerusalem we knew all about this coming conference. These folk are ready to explode. The only way to stop it is to pull the plug — The plug is Abdul Ali. We knew we could count on old Anazeh. But the puzzle was how to get him and his men into El-Kerak. When you told me ben Nazir had invited you, I saw the way to do it. There wasn't anybody else except Anazeh that ben Nazir could have sent to fetch you, and the old boy is a dependable friend of ours."

"That did not stop him from raiding two villages on the British side of the Dead Sea," I answered.

"Did he?"

"Sure. I had part of a raided sheep for breakfast."

"Um-m-m! Well of all the — damn his impudence! The shrewd old devil must have figured that we can't get after him for it, seeing how he's playing our game. Bloody old horse-thief! Well, he gets away with it, this time. You'll have to be mighty careful not to seem to recognize me. One slip and we're done for. You're safe enough. If they once get wise to me they'll pull me in pieces between four horses."

"What's your plan?"

"It's vague yet. Got to be an opportunist. I'm supposed to be a member of the ben Saoud family, recruiting members for the new sect — biggest thing in Arabia. I'm invited to the conference on the strength of my supposed connection with the big Ichwan movement."

"D'you propose to murder this Abdul Ali person, then, or have him murdered?" I asked.

"Uh-uh! Murder's out of my line. Besides, that'ud do no good. Worse than useless. They'd all cut loose. Abdul Ali has got them together. What with bribes and a lot of promises he has them keen on this raid. If he were killed they'd say one of our spies did it. They'd add vengeance to their other motives, which at present are mainly a desire for loot. No, no. Abdul Ali has got to disappear. Then they'll believe he has betrayed them. Then, instead of raiding Palestine they'll confiscate his property and curse his ancestors. D'you see the point?"

"More or less. But what good can I do?"

"Do you mind if I use you?"

I laughed. "That's a hell of a silly question. Any use my minding? You've already used me. You will do it again without consulting me. I like it, as it happens. But a fat lot you care whether I like it or not. Isn't it a bit late in the day to ask permission?"

"Oh, well. You know the hangmen always used to beg the

victim's pardon. Will you obey orders?"

"Yes. But it might be easier if I know what I'm doing."

"As soon as I know I'll explain," he answered. "Where you can fit into the puzzle at the moment is by rooting for the school idea. The worst robber chieftain from the farthest cluster of huts he calls his home town would like to see an American school here in El-Kerak. If there were one he'd send his sons to it."

"Okay. I'll root like a dog for a buried bone."

"Go to it. That gives you the right to ask questions. That will oblige ben Nazir to introduce you to any one you want to interview. That will explain without any further argument whatever weakness you seem to have for talking to men in the street like Mahommed ben Hamza. It would even explain away any politeness that I might show you in my capacity of Ichwan. For safety's sake, and to create an impression, I take the line of being rude to every one; but I might reasonably toss a few crumbs of condescension to an altruist from foreign parts. At any rate, I'll have to take that chance. D'you get me?"

"You mean, you'll use me as intermediary? Messages to and from ben Hamza and that sort of thing?"

"That's the idea, but there's more to it. Did you bring that Bible along? Are you superstitious? Any notions like Long John Silver's about its being bad luck to spoil a Bible? All right. Keep it in your pocket to make notes in. If you can't get the whole book to me, tear a page out and send that, or give it to me, with the message spelled in dots under the words. Make the dots faint, I've good eyes."

"What sort of notes do you want from me?"

"You mustn't mistake me for the prophet Ezekiel," he answered, grinning. "'Thus saith the Lord' is all right when you know what you're talking about. All I know for certain is that I've got to bag Abdul Ali. If you get information that looks important to you, get it to me in the way I've told you, that's all. Don't be caught talking to me. Don't look friendly. Don't seem interested."

"What else?"

"If you can, keep old Anazeh sober."

"Oh!"

Grim nodded meaningly: "I've known easier jobs!"

"The old sport thinks no more of me than of an express package he'd been hired to deliver," I answered. "Drunk or sober, he'd brush me aside like a fly."

"Well — wits were given us to use. I guess you'll have to use yours. Have you any?"

"How the hell should I know?" I retorted. "If you find I haven't any, don't blame me."

"I won't," he answered, and I believed him.

"What else besides being dry-nurse to the king of the Amale-kites?" I asked.

"Don't trust Ahmed."

"He's a good interpreter."

"Yeh — and a poor peg. You'll have to use him — some. But don't trust him."

"Does old Anazeh know you in that disguise?" I asked.

"No, and he mustn't. I'll tell you why. All these people are religious fanatics. A horrible death is the only fate they would consider for a man caught masquerading as a holy personage the way I'm doing. But their fanaticism has a way of petering out when the gang's not there to see. In his own village I think Anazeh would laugh if I talked this ruse over with him — after-wards. But if he knew about it here, with all these other fanatics alert and fanning, he wouldn't dare not to expose me. It's a good job you asked that. If I send any message to Anazeh through you, be sure you don't give me away."

"How shall I make him believe the message is from you, then?"

"Begin with 'Jimgrim says.' He'll recognize the formula. But if he questions that, say 'A lion knows a lion in the dark.' That'll serve a double purpose — convince him and jog his memory. He ignored a request of mine — once, and I was able to get back at him. Tell you the story some day. Nowadays he's more or less dependable, unless he gets a skin-full of redeye. Well, make the most of your chance to sleep; you may have to go short later. I'm going to saw off a cord or two myself."

He left the room as silently as a ghost. I don't doubt that he slept peacefully. Subsequent acquaintance with him convinced me that he can go to sleep almost anywhere in any circumstances. And that is a very great gift, for it enables its owner to wear down any dozen who must sleep for stated hours at fixed intervals. Grim snatches his whenever the chance comes, and goes without with apparent indifference. He told me once that he dreams nearly all the time he is asleep. But the dreams don't seem to trouble him. I believe he dreams out the key to whatever problem puzzles him at the moment.

My own sleep was done for that night, his advice notwithstanding. I lay listening to Anazeh's thunderous snores and naturally enough imagining every possible contingency and dozens that were totally impossible. Nothing turned out in the least like any of my forecasts; but that was not for want of trying to foresee it all. I don't seem to possess any of that quiet gift of waiting to deal with each development on its merits, as and when it comes. I have to speculate, and speculation is the enemy of peace.

Looking back, I don't think I felt a bit afraid of the immediate future; but that was due to ignorance of nearly all that the present held. I think that was part of Grim's reason for helping me to reach El-Kerak in the first place; he counted on my ignorance of danger to keep me cool-headed. It is true, it did dawn on me that if my host were to suspect me of intriguing under cover of his protection, the protection might cease with disconcerting abruptness. I realized to some extent what a predicament that would be. But on the whole, I think the only real worry was the definite task Grim had given me — the thankless, and very likely desperate, inglorious one of trying to keep old Anazeh sober.

Of course, the Koran forbids wine. But whiskey is not wine. And if you mix whiskey and wine together they cease to be either; they become a commodity of which the Prophet knew nothing and which he therefore did not forbid. But if you introduce such a mixture into the stomach, and thence into the brain of an already fiery Bedouin; and then introduce the Bedouin to trouble; and if, in addition to the trouble, you provide impertinent, alien, and what he calls infidel restraint, it is fair to presume that the mixture might explode.

It seemed to me I had been given too much to do. In order to get introductions to the notables I must first get ben Nazir into a proper frame of mind. Then, stammering in an alien tongue, I must make friends with chieftains who had never even heard of me; and that, when their minds were busy with another matter. I must keep in touch with ben Hamza, and convey his messages to Grim without being seen or arousing suspicion. In addition to all that I must keep sober by some means an old savage armed with two rifles and a knife, who had twenty cut-throats at his beck and call!

While I pondered the problem in all its impossible bearings, loud snores to right and left of me, tenor and bass by turns, announced that Jimgrim and Anazeh were as blissfully oblivious to my worries as the bedbugs were that had come out of hiding and discovered me. I began to feel homesick.

CHAPTER SIX

"That man will repay study."

I got my first shot at Anazeh at dawn, when the muezzin began wailing over the city; and I missed badly with both barrels. The old sheikh looked into my room, presumably to see if I was still alive, since he had guaranteed to see me safely back again across the Jordan, before rounding up his rascals for morning prayer. They prayed together whenever possible, Anazeh keeping count of their genuflections.

You could tell he had been drinking the night before the minute he thrust his head into the room. He smelt like the lees of a rum barrel, and the rims of his eyes were red.

Seeing I was awake he gave me the courteous, full-sounding "Allah ysabbhak bilkhair," and I asked him where he had dined the night before. He mumbled something into his beard that I could not catch, but he could not have told me much more plainly to go to hell, even in plain English. However, I had to get a foothold somewhere, so I said that I had heard that the liquor in El-Kerak was poisonous.

As far as I understood his answer, he implied that it likely would be poisonous in the sort of place where I would buy it, but that he, Anazeh, need not be told how to suck eggs by any such a greenhorn as me.

I tried him again. I said that liquor taken in quantity would kill a man.

"So will one bullet!" he answered. "But, whereas a bullet in the belly causes pain before death, moiyit ilfadda (aqua fortis) causes pleasure; and a man dies either way."

He turned to go, rattling two rifle-butts against the door, but I had one last try to get on terms and said I hoped to see him at breakfast, or shortly afterward.

"God is the giver both of eyesight and the things to see," he answered. "I go to pray. God will guide my footsteps afterward."

I did not feel I had really made much headway, but I fared rather better with my host downstairs, who either did not pray with such enthusiasm or else had forestalled the muezzin. At any rate, he was waiting for me near a table spread with sweet cakes and good French coffee. After the usual string of pleasantries he became suddenly confidential, over-acting the part a little, as a man does who has something rather disagreeable up his sleeve that he means to spring on you presently.

"I have been busy since an hour before dawn. I have been consulting with my friend Suliman ben Saoud. The situation here is very serious. As long as you are my guest you are perfectly safe; but if I were to send you away, the assembled notables might suspect you of being a spy, and might accuse me of harbouring a spy. Do you see? They would suppose you were returning to Jerusalem with information for the British. That would have most unpleasant consequences — for both of us!"

Clearly, Grim in the guise of ben Saoud had been busy, and it was up to me to seize my cue alertly. I was at pains to look alarmed. Ben Nazir grew solicitous.

"Rest assured, you are safe as my guest. But Suliman ben Saoud was annoyed to think a stranger should be here at such a time as this. He took me to task about you. He is also my guest, as I reminded him, but he is a truculent fellow. He insisted that the assembled notables have the right to satisfaction regarding your bona fides. It was no use my saying, as I did repeatedly, that I personally guarantee you. He asked me how much I know about you. I had to confess that what I actually know amounts to very little."

"Well?" I said. "What does the old grouch want?"

"He thinks that you should be presented to the assembled notables at noon today. In fact, he demands that they should catechize you regarding your ideas about a school."

"I have no objection."

"But, I am sorry to have to add this: it is probable the notables will insist on your remaining in El-Kerak until after that shall have taken place which they have been summoned to decide on. They will not risk your returning before the —"

"Before what?"

"The — ah — they contemplate a raid!"

"So I'm a prisoner?"

"No, no! Mon dieu, what do you think of me! Even the fanatical Suliman ben Saoud saw the force of the argument when I spoke of the sanctity of any guest here on my invitation. But he thinks — and I agree with him, that as a precaution you should first call on Sheikh Abdul Ali. You will find him a very agreeable man, who will receive you with proper courtesy. He is here from Damascus, and exercises a great influence. Once his mind is at ease about you, he will satisfy all the others. Are you agreeable?"

"Why not?"

So we smoked a cigarette together after the coffee, and then set forth on foot, for the distance was not great, preceded and surrounded by armed retainers. I imagine the armed men were more for the sake of appearance than protection. Ben Nazir seemed popular. But the escort drove other pedestrians out of the way as roughly as they did the unspeakable dogs that infested every offal-heap. The street that we followed was, of course, the open sewer for the houses on either hand, and its condition was a credit to the mangy curs that so resented our intrusion.

Abdul Ali's house, if his it was, was a fairly big square building near the middle of the town. It did not look unlike one of the old-time New York precinct stations, with its big windows protected by iron grilles, and a flight of stone steps leading up to a door exactly in the middle of the front wall.

There were thirty or forty capable-looking men hanging about the place. Abdul Ali owned more than one camel caravan, and every man connected with the business looked on himself as a member of one big feudal family. They were all armed. Most of them had modern rifles.

We were admitted into a room that faced on the street, furnished entirely in the eastern style, except for two gilt chairs against the wall. The walls were hung with carpets and the floor was covered with Bokhara rugs three deep.

No doubt in order to emphasize his own importance, Abdul Ali kept us waiting in that room for ten minutes before he condescended to enter. But when he did come at last he was at pains to seem agreeable, which was not quite his natural attitude.

I had never seen a more offensive personality, although at the first glance he did not arouse actual dislike. Distaste for him dawned, and grew. He was certainly not physically attractive, although the Syrian Arab costume made him picturesque. The first thing I noticed was the fatness of his hands — those of a giver of dishonest gifts. When he shook hands you felt in some subtle way that he was sure your conscience was for sale, that he would purchase it for any reasonable figure, and that he believed he had plenty of money with which to buy you and all your relatives.

He was a little puffy under the eyes, had a firm mouth, rather thick lips, and his small black moustache was turned up like the Kaiser's, which gave him a cockily self-assured appearance. For the rest, he was a rather military-looking person, although his flowing robe partly concealed that; stockily rather than heavily built; and of rather more than middle height. He wore one ring — a sapphire of extraordinary brilliance, of which he was immensely proud. When I noticed it he said at once that it had been given him by the late Sultan Abdul Hamid.

He spoke German from choice, so we conversed in German, which annoyed ben Nazir, who could not understand a word of it. And from first to last throughout that interview, and subsequently to the point where Jimgrim out-maneuvered and out-played him, he relied on the German philosophy of self-assertion that teaches how to get and keep the upper hand by making yourself believe in your own super-intelligence and then speaking, acting, making plans in logical accord with that belief. It works finely until somebody spoils the whole thing by pricking the super-intelligence bladder and letting out all the wind.

Although he spoke German, he was not by any means pro-German in his motives. He was at pains to make that clear. Evidently he had been pro-German once, until he saw the writing on the wall. He was conscious of the need to offset past prejudices before suggesting his enormous ability along advanced lines.

"You come at an interesting time," he said. "You find us in transition. Before the War, and almost until the end of it, most Arabs believed in the German destiny. English gold commanded the allegiance of an Arab army, but every last man in that army was ready to follow the German standard at the proper time. That only shows how ignorant these people are. As soon as it became evident that the Arab destiny lies in the hands of Arabs themselves most of them immediately began to clamour for an American mandate, because that would give them temporary masters who could protect them, yet at the same time who would be too ignorant of real conditions to prevent secret preparations for a pan-Arabian revolt. All very absurd, of course."

He had no idea how absurd he himself appeared. He launched into a tirade designed to make him seem a super-statesman in the eyes of a stranger who did not care what he was. The more he talked himself into a delirium of self-esteem the less his character impressed me. I even ran into the danger of under-estimating him because he liked himself so much.

"I'm here to look into the prospects for a school," I said.

"Yes, yes. Very estimable. You shall have my support." He paused for me to fawn on him, and my neglect to do it spurred him to further self-revelation.

"You must look to me for support if you hope for success. There is no cohesion here without me. I am the only man in El-Kerak to whom they all listen, and even I have difficulty in uniting them at times. But a school is a good idea, and under my auspices you will succeed."

For the moment I thought he suspected me of wanting to teach school myself. I hastened to correct the impression:

"All I promise to do is to tell people in the States who might be interested."

"Exactly." He had been coming at this point all along in his own way. "So there is no hurry. It makes no difference that you must stay in El-Kerak a little longer than you intended. You shall be presented to the council of notables under my auspices. In my judgment it is important that you remain here for some little time."

I suppose the men who can analyze their thoughts, and separate the wise impulses from the rash ones, are the people whom the world calls men of destiny and whom history later assigns to its halls of fame. The rest of us simply act from pique, prejudice, passion or whatever other emotion is in charge. I know I did. It was resentment. It was so immensely disagreeable to be patronized by this puffy-eyed sensualist that I could not resist the impulse to argue with him.

"I don't see the force of that," said I. "My plans are made to return to Jerusalem tomorrow."

I could not have done better as it happened. I suppose there is some theory that has been written down in books to explain how these things work, at any rate to the satisfaction of the fellow who wrote the book. But Grim, referring to it afterward, called it naked luck. I would rather agree with Grim than argue with any inky theorist on earth, having seen too many theories upset. Luck looks to me like a sweeter lady, and more worshipful than any of the goddesses they rename nowadays and then dissect in clinics. At any rate, by naked luck I prodded Abdul Ali where he kept his supply of mistakes. Instead of calling my bluff, as he doubtless should have done, he set out to win me over to his point of view. Whichever way you analyze it in the light of subsequent events, the only possible conclusion is that it was my turn to be lucky and Abdul Ali's to make a fool of himself. Nobody could have made a fool of him better than he did.

"I must dissuade you," he said, trying to hide wilfulness under an unpleasant smile. "I will offer inducements."

"They'll have to be heavy," I said, "to weigh against what I have in mind."

He had kept ben Nazir and me standing all this time. Now he offered me one of the chairs, took the other himself, and motioned ben Nazir to a cushion near the window. A servant brought in the inevitable coffee and cigarettes. Then he laid a hand on my knee for special emphasis — a fat, pale, unprincipled hand, with that great sapphire gleaming on the middle finger.

"It happens that this idea of a school comes just at the right moment. I have been searching my mind for just some such idea to lay before the notables. As we are talking a language that none else here understands, I can safely take you into confidence. A raid is being planned into British territory."

He paused to let that sink in, and tapped my knee with his

disgusting fingers until I could have struck him from irritation.

"There is, however, an element of disagreement. There is uncertainty as to the outcome, in the minds of some of the chiefs who live nearest to the border. The feeling among them is that perhaps I am urging them on in order to serve my own ambition at their expense. They appreciate the opportunity to loot; but they say that the British will hit back afterwards, and they, being nearest to the border, will suffer most; whereas I stand to gain all and to lose nothing. Very absurd, of course, but that is their argument."

"Surely," I said, "you don't expect me to take my coat off and preach a jihad against the British?"

"Um Gottes willen! No, no, no! This is my meaning: if I can go before them with the offer of a school for El-Kerak, which the very worst scoundrel among them desires with all his ignorant heart; and if I can produce a distinguished gentleman from America, present among them on my invitation for the sole purpose of making the arrangements for such a school, that will convince them that I have their interests really at heart. Do you see?"

Again the irritating fingers drumming on my knee. I did not answer for fear of betraying ill-temper.

"I am a statesman, sir. I understand the arguments with which whole nations may deceive themselves. I have made it my profession to detect the trends of thought and the tides of unrest. Psychological moments are for me a fascinating study. I can recognize them."

He laid the fat hand on my shoulder for a change, and tried to look into my eyes; but I was watching the edge of a curtain at the far end of the room.

"Now, to you, an American, our local dispute means nothing. This raid is no affair of yours. You wash your hands of it. You, an altruist, are interested only in a school. I offer you opportunity, building, subsidy, guarantees. You reciprocate by giving me a talking point. I shall make use of the opportunity. That is settled. And, let me see, I promised you inducements, didn't I?"

He looked, at me and I looked at him. He waited for a hint of some sort, but I made no move to help him out.

"What shall we say?"

I was as interested in the result of his appraisal as he was in making it. Whether complimentary or not, another's calculated judgment of your character is a fascinating thing to wait for.

"I think you will be getting full value. I shall introduce you to all the notables," he said at last. "To a man of your temperament it will be a privilege to attend the council, and to know in advance all that is going to happen. There will be no objection to that, because it is already decided you will remain in El-Kerak until after the — er — raid. The notables will understand from me that your mouth is sealed until after the event. You shall be let into our secrets. There — is that not equitable?"

It was shrewd. I did not believe for a minute that he would let me into all their secrets, but he could not have imagined a greater temptation for me. Since I would not have taken his word that black was not white, I did not hesitate to pretend to agree to his terms.

"I must have an interpreter," I said. "Otherwise I shall understand very little."

"I will supply you an interpreter — a good one."

"No, thank you. Any man of yours might only tell me what he thought correct for me to hear. If I'm to get a price for my services, I want the full price. I want to hear everything. I must be allowed to bring my own interpreter."

"Who would he be?"

"I don't know yet."

"That man Ahmed, for instance? I have been told he is one of your party. Ahmed would do very well."

"No, not Ahmed."

"Who then?"

"I will find a man."

He hesitated. If ever a man was reviewing all the possible contingencies, murder of me included, behind a mask of superficial courtesy, that man was he.

"He should be a man acceptable to the notables," he said at

last. "I ought to know his name in advance."

"I must have unfettered choice, or I won't attend the mejlis."[7]

"Oh, very well. Only the interpreter, too, will have to remain afterward in El-Kerak."

I looked at that curtain again, for it was moving in a way that no draft from the open window could account for. But at last the movement was explained. Before Abdul Ali could speak again a man stepped out from behind it, crossed the room, and went out through the door, closing it silently behind him. He was a man I knew, and the last man I had expected to see in that place. I suppose Abdul Ali noticed my look of surprise.

"You know him?" he asked.

"By sight. He was at Sheikh ben Nazir's house yesterday."

"That is Suliman ben Saoud, a stranger from Arabia, but a man of great influence because of his connection with the Ichwan movement. If you are interested in our types that man will repay study."

"Good. I'll try to study him," said I.

It was all I could do to keep a straight face. So Jimgrim was the source of Abdul Ali's inspirations! I wondered what subtle argument he could have used to make the sheikh so keen on baiting his hook with the school proposal. His nerve, in waiting behind that curtain until he knew his scheme had succeeded, and then walking out bold as brass to let me know that he had overheard everything, was what amused me. But I managed not to smile.

"What time is the mejlis?" I asked.

"At noon."

"Then I'll go and hunt up my interpreter."

Ben Nazir came out with me, in a blazing bad temper. He was as jealous as a pet dog, and inclined to visit the result on me.

"Very polite, I am sure! Most refined! Most courteous! In your country, sir, does a guest reward his host for hospitality by talking in a language that his host can't understand? Perhaps you

7   Council

would rather transfer your presence to Abdul Ali's house? Pray do not consider yourself beholden to me, in case you would prefer his hospitality!"

I tried in vain to pacify him. I explained that the choice of language had been Abdul Ali's, and offered to tell him now in French every word that had passed. But he would not listen.

"It would not be difficult for a man of your intelligence to make up a story," he said rudely. "Abdul Ali can talk French. If it had been intended that I should know the truth that conversation would have been in French. Shall I send your bag to Abdul Ali's house?"

"No," I said. "Give it to Anazeh. He is answerable for my safety until I reach Palestine again. Thank you for a night's lodging."

He walked away in a great huff, and I set out for the house of Abu Shamah, using my scant store of Arabic to ask the way. Mahommed ben Hamza was lolling on the stone veranda, gossiping with half a dozen men. He came the minute I beckoned him.

"I've seen Jimgrim," I said. "You're to come with me at noon to the mejlis as my interpreter."

He grinned delightedly.

"And see here, you smelly devil: Here's money. Buy yourself a clean shirt, a new coat, and some soap. Wash yourself from head to foot, and put the new clothes on, before you meet me at the castle gate ten minutes before noon. Those are Jimgrim's orders, do you understand?"

"Taht il-amr! (Yours to command)" he answered laughing.

I went and bought myself an awful meal at the house of a man who rolled Kabobs between his filthy fingers.

CHAPTER SEVEN

"Who gives orders to me?"

The wonderful thing about Moab is that everything happens in a story-book setting, with illustrations by Maxfield Parrish and Wyeth and Joe Coll, and all the rest of them, whichever way you look.

Imagine a blue sky — so clear-blue and pure that you can see against it the very feathers in the tails of wheeling kites, and know that they are brown, not black. Imagine all the houses, and the shacks between them, and the poles on which the burlap awnings hang, painted on flat canvas and stood up against that infinite blue. Stick some vultures in a row along a roof-top — purplish — bronze they'll look between the tiles and sky. Add yellow camels, gray horses, striped robes, long rifles, and a searching sun-dried smell. And there you have El-Kerak, from the inside.

From any point along the broken walls or the castle roof you can see for fifty miles over scenery invented by the Master-Artist, with the Jordan like a blue worm in the midst of yellow-and-green hills twiggling into a turquoise sea.

The villains stalk on-stage and off again sublimely aware of their setting. The horses prance, the camels saunter, the very street-dogs compose themselves for a nap in the golden sun, all in perfect harmony with the piece. A woman walking with a stone jar on her head (or, just as likely, a kerosene can) looks as if she had just stepped out of eternity for the sake of the picture. And not all the kings and kaisers, cardinals and courtezans rolled into one great swaggering splurge of majesty could hold a candle to a ragged Bedouin chief on a flea-bitten pony, on the way to a small-town mejlis.

So it was worth a little inconvenience, and quite a little risk to see those chiefs arrive at the castle gate, toss their reins to a brother cut-throat, and swagger in, the poorest and least important timing their arrival, when they could, just in advance of an important man so as to take precedence of him and delay his entrance.

Mindful of my charge to keep Anazeh sober, and more deadly afraid of it than of all the other risks, I hung about waiting for him, hoping he would arrive before Abdul Ali or ben Nazir. I wanted to go inside and be seated before either of those gentry came. But not a bit of it. I saw Anazeh ride up at the head of his twenty men, halt at a corner, and ask a question. His men were in military order, and looked not only ready but anxious to charge the crowd and establish their old chief's importance.

Mahommed ben Hamza, not quite so smelly in his new clothes, was standing at my elbow.

"Sheikh Anazeh beckons you," he said.

So the two of us worked our way leisurely through the crowd toward the side-street down which Anazeh had led his party. We found them looking very spruce and savage, four abreast, drawn up in the throat of an alley, old Anazeh sitting his horse at their head like a symbol of the ancient order waiting to assault the new. My horse was close beside him, held by Ahmed, acting servitor on foot.

The old man let loose the vials of his wrath on me the minute I drew near, and Mahommed ben Hamza took delicious pleasure in translating word for word.

"Is that the way an effendi in my care should be seen at such a time — on foot? Am I a maskin[8] that you do not ride? Is the horse not good enough?"

I made ben Hamza explain that I was to attend the mejlis as Sheikh Abdul Ali's guest. But that only increased his wrath.

"So said ben Nazir! Shall a lousy Damascene trick me out of keeping my oath? You are in my safekeeping until you tread on British soil again, and my honour is concerned in it! No doubt that effeminate schemer of schemes would like to display you at the mejlis as his booty, but you are mine! Did you think you are not under obligation to me?"

I answered pretty tactfully. I said that Allah had undoubt-

8   Poor devil.

edly created him to be a protector of helpless wayfarers and the very guardian of honour. Mahommed ben Hamza added to the compliments while rendering mine into Arabic. But though Anazeh's wrath was somewhat mollified, he was not satisfied by any means.

"Am I a dog," he demanded, "that I should be slighted for the sake of that Damascene?"

It looked to me like the proper moment to try out Grim's magic formula.

"You are the father of lions. And a lion knows a lion in the dark!" said I.

The effect was instantaneous. He puffed his cheeks out in astonishment, and sucked them in again. The overbearing anger vanished as he leaned forward in the saddle to scrutinize my face. It was clear that he thought my use of that phrase might just possibly have been an accident.

"Jimgrim says —"

"Ah! What says Jimgrim? Who are you that know where he is?"

"A lion knows a lion in the dark!" I said again, that there might be no mistake about my having used the words deliberately.

He nodded.

"Praised be Allah! Blessings upon His Prophet! What says Jimgrim?"

"Jimgrim says I am to keep by Anazeh and watch him, lest he drink strong drink and lose his honour by becoming like a beast without decency or understanding!"

"Mount your horse, effendi. Sit beside me."

I complied. Ben Hamza took the place of Ahmed, who went to the rear looking rather pleased to get out of the limelight.

"What else says Jimgrim?" asked Anazeh.

"There will be a message presently, providing Sheikh Anazeh keeps sober!"

To say that I was enjoying the game by this time is like trying to paint heaven with a tar-brush. You've got to be on the inside of an intrigue before you can appreciate the thrill of it. Nobody who has not had the chance to mystify a leader of cheerful murderers in a city packed with conspirators, with the shadow of a vulture on the road in front, and fanged death waiting to be let loose, need talk to me of excitement.

"Well and good," said Anazeh. "When Jimgrim speaks, I listen!"

Can you beat that? Have you ever dreamed you were possessed of some magic formula like "Open Sesame," and free to work with it any miracle you choose? Was the dream good? I was awake — on a horse — in a real eastern alley — with twenty thieves as picturesque as Ali Baba's, itching for action behind me!

"Abdul Ali of Damascus thinks he will enter the mejlis last and create a great sensation," said Anazeh. "That son of infamies deceives himself. I shall enter last. I shall bring you. There will be no doubt who is important!"

Just as he spoke there clattered down the street at right angles to us a regular cavalcade of horsemen led by no less than Abdul Ali with a sycophant on either hand. Cardinal Wolsey, or some other wisehead, once remarked that a king is known by the splendour of his servants. Abdul Ali's parasites were dressed for their part in rose-coloured silk and mounted on beautiful white Arab horses so severely bitted that they could not help but prance.

Abdul Ali, on the other hand, played more a king-maker's role, dark and sinister in contrast to their finery, on a dark brown horse that trotted in a business-like, hurry-up-and-get-it-done-with manner. He rode in the German military style, and if you can imagine the Kaiser in Arab military head-dress, with high black riding boots showing under a brown cloak, you have his description fairly closely. The upturned moustaches and the scowl increased the suggestion, and I think that was deliberate.

"A dog — offspring of dogs! Curse his religion and his bed!" growled Anazeh in my ear.

The old sheikh allowed his enemy plenty of time. To judge by the way the men behind us gathered up their reins and closed in knee-to-knee, they would have liked to spoil Abdul Ali's afternoon by riding through his procession and breaking its formation. But Anazeh had his mind set, and they seemed to know better than to try to change it for him. We waited until noises in the street died down, and then Ahmed was sent to report on developments.

"Abdul Ali has gone into the mejlis and the doors are closed," he announced five minutes later. That seemed to suit Anazeh perfectly, for his eyes lit up with satisfaction. Evidently being excluded from the council was his meat and drink. He gave no order, but rode forward and his men followed as a snake's tail follows its head, four abreast, each man holding his rifle as best suited him; that gave them a much more warlike appearance than if they had imitated the western model of exact conformity.

We rode down-street toward the castle at a walk, between very interested spectators who knew enough to make way without being told. And at the castle gate we were challenged by a man on foot, who commanded about twice our number of armed guards.

"The hour is passed," he announced. "The order is to admit no late-comers."

"Who gives orders to me?" Anazeh retorted.

"It was agreed by all the notables."

"I did not agree. Wallah! Thou dog of a devil's dung-heap, say you I am not a notable?"

"Nevertheless —"

"Open that gate!"

They opened it. Two of the men began to do it even before their chief gave the reluctant order. Anazeh started to ride through with his men crowding behind. But that, it seemed, was altogether too much liberty to take with the arrangements. Shouting all together, the gate-guards surged in to take hold of bridles and force Anazeh's dependents back. Teeth and eyes flashed. It looked like the makings of a red-hot fight.

"No retainers allowed within the gate! Principals only!" roared the captain of the guard, in Arabic that sounded like explosions of boiling oil.

Anazeh, Mahommed ben Hamza and I were already within the courtyard. Four of Anazeh's followers made their way through after us before any one could prevent them. At that moment there came a tremendous clattering of hoofs and the crowd outside the gate scattered this and that way in front of

about a hundred of the other chiefs' dependents, who had duti-
fully stayed outside and had sought shade some little distance
off.

Whether the sudden disturbance rattled him, or whether he
supposed that all the other truculent ruffians were going to try to
follow our example, at any rate the man on duty lost his head
and shouted to his men to shut the gate again. Before they could
do it every one of Anazeh's gang had forced his way through.
There we all were on forbidden ground, with a great iron-
studded gate slammed and bolted behind us. To judge by the
row outside the keepers of the gate had got their hands full.

In front of us was a short flight of stone steps, and another
great wooden door set in stone posts under a Roman arch. There
were only two armed men leaning against it. They eyed Anazeh
and our numbers nervously.

"Open!"

Anazeh could use his voice like a whip-crack. They fumbled
with the great bolt and obeyed, swinging the door wide. I
thought for a minute that my arrogant old protector meant to
ride up the steps and through the door into the mejlis hall with
all his men; but he was not quite so high-handed as that.

After a good long look through the door, I suppose to make
sure there was no ambush inside waiting for him, he dis-
mounted, and ordered his men to occupy a stable-building
across the courtyard, from which it would have been impossible
to dislodge them without a siege. Then, when he had seen the
last man disappear into it, he led me and Mahommed ben
Hamza up the steps.

Ben Hamza was grinning like a schoolboy, beside himself
with delight at the prospect of elbowing among notables, as well
as inordinately proud of his new clothes and the smell of
imported soap that hung about him like an aura. But Anazeh
looked like an ancient king entering into his own. Surely there
was never another man who could stride so majestically and
seem so conscious of his own ability to override all law.

We passed under the shadowy arch and down a cool stone
passage to yet another heavy door that barred our way. Anazeh
thundered on it with his rifle-butt, for there were no attendants

there to do his bidding. There was no answer. Only a murmur of voices within. So he thundered again, and this time the door opened about six inches. A face peered through the opening cautiously, and asked what was wanted.

"What is this?" asked Anazeh. "Is a mejlis held without my presence? Since when?"

"You are too late!"

The face disappeared. Some one tried to close the door. Anazeh's foot prevented.

"Open!" he demanded. The butt of his rifle thundered again on the wood.

There was a babel of voices inside, followed by sudden silence. Anazeh made a sign to Mahommed ben Hamza and me. We all three laid our shoulders against the door and shoved hard. Evidently that was not expected; it swung back so suddenly that we were hard put to it to keep our feet. The man who had opened the door lay prone on the floor in front of us with his legs in the air, and Anazeh laughed at him — the bitterest sign of disrespect one Arab can pay to another.

"Since when does the word of a Damascene exclude an honourable sheikh from a mejlis in El-Kerak?" asked Anazeh, standing in the doorway.

He was in no hurry to enter. The dramatic old ruffian understood too well the value of the impression he made standing there. The room was crowded with about eighty men, seated on mats and cushions, with a piece of carpeted floor left unoccupied all down the centre — a high-walled room with beautifully vaulted ceiling, and a mullioned window from which most of the glass was gone. The walls were partly covered with Persian and other mats, but there was almost no furniture other than waterpipes and little inlaid tables on which to rest coffee-cups and matches. The air was thick with smoke already, and the draft from the broken windows wafted it about in streaky clouds.

Every face in the room was turned toward Anazeh. I kept as much as possible behind him, for you can't look dignified in that setting if all you have on is a stained golf suit, that you have slept in. It seemed all right to me to let the old sheikh have all the limelight.

But he knew better. Perhaps my erstwhile host ben Nazir had understood a little German after all. More likely he had divined Abdul Ali's purpose to make use of me. Certainly he had poured the proper poison in Anazeh's ear, and the old man understood my value to a nicety.

He took me by the arm and led me in, Mahommed ben Hamza following like a dog that was too busy wagging its tail to walk straight. You would have thought Anazeh and I were father and son by the way he leaned toward me and found a way for me among the crowded cushions.

He had no meek notions about choosing a low place. Expecting to be taken at his own valuation, he chose a high place to begin with. There were several unoccupied cushions near the door, and there were half a dozen servants busy in a corner with coffee-pots and cakes. He prodded one of the servants and ordered him to take two cushions to a place he pointed out, up near the window close to Abdul Ali. There was no room there. That was the seat of the mighty. You could not have dropped a handkerchief between the men who wanted to be nearest the throne of influence. But Anazeh solved that riddle. He strode, stately and magnificent, up the middle of the carpet amid a mutter of imprecations. And when one more than ordinarily indignant sheikh demanded to know what he meant by it, he paused in front of him and laid his right hand on my shoulder. (There was a loaded rifle in his left.)

"Who offers indignity to a distinguished guest?" he demanded.

The question was addressed to everybody in the room. He took care they were all aware of it. His stern eyes traveled from face to face.

"My men, who escorted him here, are outside the door. They can enter and escort him away, if there are none here who understand how to treat the stranger in our midst!"

There was goose-flesh all over me, and I did not even try to look unembarrassed. A man's wits, if he has any, work swiftly when he looks like being torn to pieces at a moment's notice. It seemed to me that the less insolent I appeared, the less likely they were to vent their wrath on me. I tried to look as if I didn't understand I was intruding — as if I expected a welcome.

"Good!" Anazeh whispered in my ear. "You do well."

There was a murmur of remonstrance. The sheikh who had dared to rebuke Anazeh found the resentment turned against himself. Somebody told him sharply to mend his manners. Anazeh, shrewd old opportunist, promptly directed the servant to place cushions on the edge of the carpet, in front of the first row of those who wished to appear important. That obliged the front rank to force the men behind them backward, closer to the wall, so that room could be made for us without our trespassing on the forbidden gangway.

So I sat down in the front row, five cushions from Abdul Ali. Anazeh squatted beside me with his rifle across his knees. Then Mahommed ben Hamza forced himself down between me and the man on my left, using his left elbow pretty generously and making the best of the edges of two cushions. As far as I could see there were not more than half a dozen other men in the room who had rifles with them, although all had daggers, and some wore curved scimitars with gold-inlaid hilts.

As soon as I could summon sufficient nerve to look about me and meet the brown, conjecturing eyes that did not seem to know whether to resent my presence or be simply curious, I caught the eye of Suliman ben Saoud in the front row opposite, ten or twelve cushions nearer the door than where I sat. He did not seem to notice me. The absence of eyebrows made his face expressionless. He didn't even vaguely resemble the Major James Grim whom I knew him to be. When his eyes met mine there was no symptom of recognition. If he felt as nervous as I did he certainly did not show it behind his mask of insolent indifference.

There was still a good deal of muttered abuse being directed at Anazeh. The atmosphere was electric. It felt as if violence might break out any minute. Abdul Ali seemed more nervous than any one else; he rocked himself gently on his cushion, as if churning the milk of desire into the butter of wise words. Suddenly he turned to the sheikh on his left, a handsome man of middle age, who wore a scimitar tucked into a gold-embroidered sash, and whispered to him.

Ben Hamza whispered to me: "That sheikh to whom Abdul Ali speaks is Ali Shah al Khassib, the most powerful sheikh in these parts. A great prince. A man with many followers."

Ali Shah al Khassib called for prayer to bring the mejlis to order. He was immensely dignified. The few words he pronounced about asking God to bless the assembled notables with wisdom, in order that they might reach a right decision, would have been perfectly in place in the Capitol at Washington, or anywhere else where men foregather to decide on peace or war.

At once a muballir[9] on his left opened a copy of the Koran on a cushion on his lap and began to read from it in a nasal sing-song. There were various degrees of devoutness, and even of inattention, shown by those who listened. Some knelt and prostrated themselves. Others, including Anazeh, sat bolt upright, closing their eyes dreamily at intervals. Over the way, Jim Suliman ben Saoud Grim was especially formally devout. His very life undoubtedly depended on being recognized as a fanatic of fanatics.

But there were three Christian sheikhs in the room. One of them opposite me pulled out a Bible and laid it on the carpet as a sort of challenge to the Koran. It was probably a dangerous thing to do, although most Moslems respect the Bible as a very sacred book. The manner in which it was done suggested deliberate effort to provoke a quarrel.

Mahommed ben Hamza, dividing his time like a schoolboy in chapel between staring about him and attending by fits and starts, nudged me in the ribs and whispered:

"See that Christian! He would not dare do that, only on this occasion they like to think that Moslems and Christians are agreeing together."

The man who was reading to himself from the Bible looked up and caught my eye. He tapped the book with his finger and nodded, as much as to ask why I did not join him. At once I pulled my own from my pocket. He smiled acknowledgment as I

9   A Moslem priest who recites prayers.

opened it at random. Certainly he thought I did it to support his tactlessly ill-timed assertion of his own religion. Very likely my action, since I was a guest and therefore not to be insulted, saved him from violence. Incipient snarls of fanatical indignation died away.

But as a matter of fact my eye was on Jim Suliman ben Saoud Grim. As the reading from the Koran came to an end amid a murmur of responses from all the sheikhs, the crooked-faced Ichwan sat upright. In his sullen, indifferent way, he stared leisurely along the line until his eyes rested on me.

As his eyes met mine I marked the place where the Bible was open with a pencil, and closed the book, suspecting that he might be glad to know where a pencil could be found in a contingency.

He did not smile. The expression of his face barely changed. Just for a second I thought I saw a flicker of amused approval pass over the corners of his eyes and mouth.

So I left the book lying where it was with the pencil folded in it.

CHAPTER EIGHT

*"He will say next that it was he who set
the stars in the sky over El-Kerak,
and makes the moon rise!"*

Ali Shah al Khassib was the first to speak. He was heard to
the end respectfully, none interrupting. But it seemed obvious
from their faces that not a few sheikhs were disposed to question
both his leadership and most of what he said. Mahommed ben
Hamza kept up a running whisper of interpretation, breathing
into my ear until it was wet with condensed breath. I had to use a
handkerchief repeatedly.

Ali Shah al Khassib made no definite proposal. He said that a
man whom they all knew well had brought news to the effect
that Emir Feisul was ready to make war on the French in order to
drive them out of Syria. That in a case like that, of Moslems
against kafirs,[10] there could be no question on which side their
hearts or their interests lay. That several dependable men had
brought word of great unrest in Palestine. That in all likelihood
the British would send their army to help the French, in which
case the Arabs of Palestine were likely to rise in rebellion in the
British army's rear. That was the situation. They were invited to
consider it, and to decide what action, if any, seemed called for.

He sat down without having risked his leadership by any
statement of his own attitude. He had simply reported facts that
he believed to be true — facts that many of the notables plainly
did not yet believe, or believed only in part. There followed a
perfect babel of argument, during which the servants passed the
coffee and cakes around. After that, during every interval between speeches there was more coffee and more cakes — wonderful cakes made with honey and almonds, immensely filling;
but the more full an Arab gets of stodgy food the more his tongue

10   Unbelievers.

wags, until at last he talks himself to sleep.

For ten minutes men were shouting their opinions to one another to and fro across the room. From what I could make of it there was not a man who did not advocate putting the whole of Palestine to the sword forthwith. But it was noticeable that when their turns came to stand up and address the mejlis their advocacy was considerably toned down. Everybody seemed to want somebody else to father the proposal for a raid, although every man pretended to be anxious to take part in one.

Old Anazeh on my right sat in grim silence, quizzing each talker in turn with puckered eyes. The only comment he made was a sort of internal rumbling, suggestive of the preliminary notice of an earthquake.

At the end of ten minutes Sheikh Ali Shah al Khassib brought proceedings a step forward by calling for confirmation of the news of unrest in Palestine. Man after man got up, and, since he was speaking of others, not of himself, painted the discontent of the Palestinians in lurid terms. Each man tried to outvie the other. The first man said they were anxious regarding the Zionists and keen for a solution of the problem. The second said they hated the Zionists, and could see no way out of their predicament but by rebellion. The third said that no Arab in Palestine could eat for thinking of the Zionist outrage, and that the heart of every man in El-Kerak should bleed for his distressed brethren.

To judge by what the fourth and fifth and sixth said, Palestine was in a state of scarcely suppressed rebellion, and every living Arab in the country was sharpening his sword in secret for the butchering of Zionists at the first opportunity. The seventh man said that the Palestine Arabs had never under Turkish rule suffered and groaned as they did under the British, and that their cry was going up to heaven for relief from the ignominious tyranny of Zionist pretensions.

Ali Shah al Khassib chose that ringing appeal as the cue for his next move in the game. He called on Sheikh Abdul Ali, "as well known in Damascus as in this place," to address the mejlis.

There was instant silence. Even the coffee cups ceased rattling. Abdul Ali got to his feet with the manner of a man long used to swaying assemblies. He had just the right air of authority; exactly the right suggestion of deference; the quiet smile of the man with secrets up his sleeve; and he paused just long enough before speaking to whet curiosity and fix attention.

He did not speak floridly or fast, and he indulged in none of those flights of oratory that most Arabs love. There was ample time between his sentences for Mahommed ben Hamza to translate into my wet and itching ear. But every sentence of his speech had measured weight in it, and every word he used was chosen for its poison or its sting.

He began by reminding them of the war and of Emir Feisul's share in it. Of how they, and their fathers, and their sons had fought behind Feisul and helped to establish him in Damascus. Then he spoke of the British promise that the Arabs should have a kingdom of their own, with Damascus for its capital and borders to include all the peoples of Arab blood in the Near East. He paused for a full minute after that. Then:

"But the French are in Syria. The French, who also promised us an Arab kingdom. They have assembled at the coast an army that already threatens Emir Feisul. The British are in Palestine, where they are admitting a horde of Zionist Jews to displace us Arabs, rightful owners of the soil. The British are also in Mesopotamia, which they have seized for themselves for the sake of the oil which Allah, in His wisdom, created beneath the fertile earth. Feisul makes ready to defend Syria against the French. But the British will march to the aid of the French. Can anybody tell me how much of that promise to us Arabs has been kept, by either nation, French or British?"

So far he was on thoroughly safe ground. A man who preached against the French could hardly be suspected of being hired by the French to do it. There was nobody there but he who could say what Feisul's intentions actually were. You can say what you like against the British anywhere, at any time, and find some one to believe what you say. And it needed no wizardry to prove that the Allies had broken every promise they ever made to the Arabs.

"Are you going to sit idle, and let Emir Feisul and the Syrians fight the French alone?" he asked, and paused again.

There was a great deal of murmuring — not quite all of it, I thought, entirely in his favour.

"What is the alternative to sitting still like camels waiting to be doubly burdened? If you raid Palestine, the local Arabs will all rise to your assistance. The throat of every Zionist from the Lebanon to Beersheba will be cut. There will be plunder beyond reckoning. And you will help Feisul by holding back the British army from marching to the assistance of the French. The question is, are you men? — are you Arabs? — are you true Moslems? — or do you like to look down from these heights of El-Kerak over the home of your ancestors in the hands of so-called Zionists who are nothing but Jews, under a new name?"

He sat down before any one could answer him, and whispered to Ali Shah al Khassib, who called on another man to speak at once. It was a pretty obvious piece of concerted strategy, but he got by with it for the moment. The general feeling seemed to be in favour of a raid if only some one would start it. Nobody seemed to mind much how the decision was arrived at, so long as the responsibility was passed to some one else.

The man now called on was a smooth-tongued, tall, lean individual with shifty eyes, and a flow of talk of the coffeeshop variety. At the end of his first sentence any fool would have known that he had been put up to quiz Abdul Ali, in order that Abdul Ali might have an excuse to justify himself. He attacked him very mildly, with much careful hedging and apologetic gesture, on the ground that possibly the Damascene was ignoring their interests while urging them to take action that would suit his own.

Even with that mild criticism he set loose quite a murmur of minority agreement. For the first time since the speech-making began Anazeh barked approval. I thought for a moment the old man was going to get to his feet. But Abdul Ali was up again first, and launched on the seas of self-esteem.

If I had not listened to equally childish political maneuvers in the States, and seen them succeed for the reason that people who want something want also to be fooled into getting it by special arguments, it would have seemed incredible that a man, who had recently boasted of statesmanship, should dare to make such a public ass of himself. Yet, for fifteen minutes he carried the whole meeting with him, and the warmth of his self-satisfied emotion made him ooze resplendent sweat.

"Now he speaks of you, effendi," Mahommed ben Hamza whispered; and in confirmation of it Anazeh clutched my arm, as if to keep the tide of eloquence from washing me away.

Had the British done anything for the country this side of Jordan? Anything for the people's education, for instance? No! Instead, they had taken away the missionaries. Better than nothing were those missionaries. They had their faults. They undermined religion. But they taught. And the British had called them in, giving some ridiculous excuse about danger. It had remained then for him — Abdul Ali of Damascus and of El-Kerak — the same individual who was now urging them to strike for their own advantage — to take the first step for the establishment in El-Kerak of a school that should be independent of the British. He, Abdul Ali, greatly daring because he had the interest of El-Kerak at heart, had introduced that day into the mejlis a distinguished guest from the United States, whose sole desire — whose only object in life — whose altruistic and divine ambition was to establish an American secular school in El-Kerak!

He sat down, glowing with super-virtue. And then the fur flew. Anazeh was first on his feet.

"Princes!" he shouted. "That Damascene is a father of lies! It was I, Anazeh, who brought this man hither! That corrupter of honesty, who doles out other people's gold for hidden purposes, seeks to appear as your benefactor!" (It was fairly obvious that Anazeh had not received any of the gold.) "He will say next that it was he who set the stars in the sky over El-Kerak, and makes the moon rise! He is a foreigner, a father of snakes, and a born liar!"

Anazeh refused to sit down again, but stood with rifle on his arm, daring any one to challenge his statements. Abdul Ali flushed angrily, but laughed aloud. The next man on his feet was ben Nazir, my erstwhile host, who had repudiated me. And he repudiated me all over again, accusing me of abusing his hospitality by going over to Abdul Ali, who had never even heard of me before I came to El-Kerak.

There was no making head or tail of the storm of abuse and counter-abuse that followed, except that it did not look healthy for me. There seemed to be four or five different factions, all of whom regarded me as the bone of contention. Rather than betray anxiety I opened the Bible and began to make dots under letters, spelling out a message to Grim to the effect that I had no notion where to find lodgings for the night, and that if Anazeh elected to carry me off I should have to go with him.

I did not know how to get the message to him without arousing suspicion and making matters worse than they were, and it seemed best not to call attention to the fact that I was writing. So I made a few dots at a time, and looked about me. I saw Abdul Ali, laughing cynically, make a gesture with his arm as if he consigned me to the dogs. Then I caught Grim's eye — Suliman ben Saoud's. He, too, was making capital of my predicament.

He had got the attention of the men around him, and was pointing at the Bible while he reeled off a string of an angry rhetoric that sounded like a cat-fight. He shouted at me, and made angry gestures; but I knew that if he wanted me to understand his signals he would never make them openly, so I ignored them.

"The sheikh from Arabia demands to see the book," said Mahommed ben Hamza in my ear.

I passed it over the carpet with the pencil folded in it at the page I had begun to mark; and the men opposite handed it along, with remarks they considered appropriate. Jim Suliman ben Saoud Grim seized the book angrily, glared at it, denounced it, and wrote something on the fly-leaf. He showed it to the men beside him, and they laughed, nodding approval. He wrote again. They approved again. He turned and talked to them. Then, as if he had an afterthought, he wrote a third time. When they wanted to look at that he ran the pencil through it and wrote something else on the other side of the fly-leaf, at which they all laughed uproariously. Presently he tossed the book back to me with all the outward signs of contempt that a fanatic can show for another religion.

I have kept that Bible as a souvenir, with the verses from the Koran written on the flyleaf in Arabic in Grim's fine hand.

Underneath them, in Greek characters with a pencil line scrawled through them, is the only sentence that interested me at the moment:

"This looks good. Keep Anazeh quiet and sober."

Anazeh was beginning to hold forth again, shaking his fist at Abdul Ali and making the roof echo to his mighty bellowing. I tugged at the skirt of his cloak, and after a minute he sat down to discover what I wanted. He seemed to think I needed reassurance. He began to flood me with promises of protection. It was about a minute before I could get a word in edgeways. Then:

"Jimgrim says," said I.

"Jimgrim! Is he here?"

"He surely is."

"How do you know?"

"We have a sign. Jimgrim says, 'Be quiet, and drink no strong drink.'"

He leaned across to Mahommed ben Hamza, doubting his ears and my Arabic. I repeated the message, and ben Hamza translated.

"I don't believe Jimgrim is here!" said Anazeh. "I would know him among a million."

"It is true," said ben Hamza, grinning from ear to ear, "for I myself know where he sits!"

"Where then?" Anazeh demanded excitedly.

"Don't you dare!" said I, and ben Hamza grinned again.

"He is my friend. I say nothing," he answered.

Anazeh put in the next five minutes minutely examining every face within range, while the din of argument rose louder and more violent than ever, and suspicion of me seemed to be gaining.

But suddenly Suliman ben Saoud got to his feet and there was silence. They were all willing to listen to a member of the Ichwan sect, for the news of its power and political designs had spread wherever men talk Arabic. He spoke gutturally in a dialect that ben Hamza did not find it any too easy to follow, so I only got the general gist of Grim's remarks.

He said that he had much experience of raids and of making preparations for them. A raid aimed at the Zionists — at this moment — might be good — perhaps. They were better judges of that than he. But it was all-important to know who was in favour of the raid, and exactly why. The words men spoke were not nearly so impressive as the deeds they did. Therefore, when the illustrious Sheikh Abdul Ali of Damascus urged a raid on the one hand, and boasted of provision for a school in El-Kerak on the other, it would be well to examine this foreign effendi, whom Abdul Ali claimed to have introduced. The claim was disputed, but the claim was not made for nothing. In his judgment, based on vast experience of politics in Arabia, motives were seldom on the surface. All depended on the motives of the illustrious Abdul Ali. This stranger from America — he glared balefully at me — should be investigated thoroughly. As a man of vast experience with the interests of El-Islam at heart, he offered respectfully to examine this stranger thoroughly with the aid of an interpreter. He confessed to certain suspicions; should they prove unfounded, then it might be reasonable to credit the rest of Abdul Ali's statements; if not, no. He was willing, if the honourable mejlis saw fit, to take the stranger aside and put many questions to him.

When he had finished you could actually physically feel the suspicion directed at me. It was like a cold wind. Anazeh was just as conscious of it, and muttered something about its being time to go. Abdul Ali got up and asked indignantly why the Ichwan from so far away should have such an important voice; he himself stood there ready to answer all questions. Suliman ben Saoud retorted sourly that he proposed to question the Damascene in public after privately interrogating me.

"They shall not interfere with you! You are in my charge," Anazeh growled in my ear. "I will summon my men at the first excuse."

"Jimgrim says, 'Be quiet!'" I answered.

There was another uproar. Ali Shah al Khassib openly took the part of Abdul Ali. A dozen men demanded to know how much he had been paid to do it. Finally, Suliman ben Saoud beckoned me. I got up, and with Mahommed ben Hamza at my heels I followed him to a narrow door in a side wall that opened on a stone stairway leading to the ramparts. Anazeh came too, growling like a hungry bear, and after a couple of blood-curdling threats hurled at Suliman ben Saoud's back he took up position in the open door, facing the crowd, and dared any one to try to follow. He seemed to have confidence in Mahommed ben Hamza's ability to protect me, if necessary, on the roof.

The roof and ramparts appeared deserted. They were in the ruinous state to which the Turks reduce everything by sheer neglect, and in which Arabs, blaming the Turks, seemed quite disposed to leave things. The Ichwan led the way to the south-west corner, peering about him to make sure no guards were in hiding, or asleep behind projecting buttresses. Overhead the kites were wheeling against a pure blue sky. The Dead Sea lay and smiled below us, with the gorgeous, treeless Judean Hills beyond. Through the broken window of the hall came the clamour of arguing men.

"O, Jimgrim!" grinned Mahommed ben Hamza when we reached the corner.

Grim turned and faced us with folded arms, leaning his back against the parapet.

Ben Hamza continued: "You are a very prince of dare-devils! One word from me — one little word, and they would fling you down into the moat for the vultures to feed on!"

"I remember a time," Grim answered, "when a word from me saved you from hanging."

"True, father of good fortune! But a man must laugh. I will hold my tongue in El-Kerak like a tomb that has not been plundered!"

"You'd better! You've work to do. Where are your men?"

"All where I can find them."

"Good. You'll get turned out of the mejlis presently. Look down into the moat now."

We all peered over. The lower ramp of the wall sloped steeply, but all the way up the sharp southwest corner the stones were broken out, and a goat, or a very active man, could find foothold.

"Could you climb that?"

"Surely. Remember, Jimgrim, when I climbed the wall of El-Kudz (Jerusalem) to escape from the police!"

"Bring your men into the moat between dark and moonrise. Have a long rope with you — a good one. You and two men climb up here and hide. The remainder wait below. Oh, yes; and bring a wheat sack — a new, strong one. You may have to wait for several hours. When you see me, take your cue from me; but whatever happens, no murder! You understand? Nobody's to be killed."

Ben Hamza grinned and nodded. He seemed to be one of those good-natured rogues who ask nothing better than the sheer sport of lawless hero-worship. He would have made a perfect chief of staff for any brigand, provided the brigand took lots of chances.

"You'll be killed, if anybody finds you up here after dark! You realize that?"

"Trust me."

Grim nodded. He was good at trusting people, when he had to, and when the selection was his own.

"Affairs seem to be drifting nicely," he said, turning to me. "It's best not to let Anazeh know who I am just yet, if that can be helped. But if you must, when the time comes, you'll have to tell him. Do keep him sober. After the evening prayer there'll be a banquet; if he gets drunk we're done for. I'm going to make you out an awful leper, if you don't mind. They may yell for your hide and feathers before I've finished, but Anazeh will protect you. If he leaves the hall in a huff, don't make any bones about going with him. Let him ride out of town and wait for me about two miles down the track, at the point where that tomb stands above a narrow pass between two big rocks. Do you remember it?"

"What if he won't wait?"

"He must! Tell him I'll have a prisoner with me; then he'll be curious. But you can bet on old Anazeh when he's sober. But things may turn out so that it's simpler for you to stay and see this through with me. In that case you must persuade him to go without you, after explaining to him just where he's to wait."

"How shall I do that?" I said. "I haven't enough Arabic."

"I'll write it," he answered. "Give me that pencil."

"Say something, too, then about his keeping sober."

Grim nodded, and wrote quite a long letter in Arabic on a page of my notebook.

"The next move," he said, as I pocketed the letter, "is for me to get Abdul Ali's goat: I think — and I hope — he'll try to bribe me. If he does, he's my meat! The whole question of raid or no raid hangs on their confidence in him. If I throw suspicion on him, and he disappears directly afterwards, they'll abandon the plan, confiscate his goods and chattels, and quarrel among themselves instead of raiding Palestine. Get me?"

"Um-n-yes. I've sat on a horse I was warned against — felt safer — and gone to hospital at that."

He laughed.

"No hospitals up here! It'll be soon over if they get wise to us. But I think we're all right; and you're almost certainly safe. But don't be tempted to talk. Well — we've been up here long enough for me to have put you through the third degree. Better look a bit uncomfortable as you go down, as if I'd got under your skin with some awkward questions. You, too, ben Hamza; don't grin; look afraid."

"I am not at all afraid, Jimgrim. But I will try."

Grim studied for a moment.

"Don't forget," he added, "at the first suggestion that you're not wanted, make yourself scarce, and go and round up your men. If you're thrown out pretty roughly, keep your temper and run."

"Taht il-amr!" (Yours to command.)

"Come on, then. Let's go."

The sun was fairly low over the Judean Hills as we turned down the narrow stairs and found Anazeh waiting at the bottom.

CHAPTER NINE

"Feet downwards, too afraid to yell!" —

Abdul Ali of Damascus was holding the floor again when we returned. He had abandoned the cold air of mysterious authority and secrets in reserve. His claim to backstairs influence having been challenged, he had resorted to the emotional appeal that is the simplest means of controlling any crowd of men anywhere. The demagog who can find a million men all responsive to the same emotion can swing them as easily as a hundred if he knows his business. Loot was the tune he harped, with the old Ishmael blood-lust by way of obbligato.

He had them by the heart-strings, and there were long-necked bottles of liquor that smelt of aniseed being passed from hand to hand. We returned to our places almost unnoticed, and within the minute some one handed a full bottle to Anazeh; the accompanying cup was big enough to hold any ordinary drunk-ard's breakfast, and the old sheikh's eyes admired the size of it.

I laid my hand on the wrist that held the bottle. He shook it off angrily, and began to pour. Grim, over the way, looked anxious. It was up to me to play this hand, so I led my ace of trumps.

Suddenly, and very clumsily, I rocked sideways to reach my hip-pocket, contriving to jog his elbow and spill what was already in the cup. He turned his head to curse savagely, and I showed him the folded sheet from my notebook. His name was on it in Arabic:

"Sheikh Anazeh ben Mahmoud, from Jimgrim."

He seized it, setting the bottle down between his feet, where it was instantly reached for by some one else and handed down the line. Reading was evidently not Anazeh's favorite amuse-ment, but he knitted his brows over the letter and wrestled with it word by word, while Abdul Ali's fiery declamation made the vaulted roof resound. I could only make out snatches of the appeal to savagery — a word and a sentence here and there.

"Who are you, princes? Men with swords, or slaves who must obey? — Raid over the Jordan twenty thousand strong! —

What are Jews? Shall Jews take the home of your ancestors? Who says so? — Let the Jews be buried in the land they come to steal! — You say the Jews are cleverer than you. Cut their heads off, then they cannot think!"

"When did Jimgrim give you this?" Anazeh demanded, folding the letter and stowing it in his bosom.

"That is the message that I told you would come later if you waited."

"Do you know what is in the message?"

"No." That was perfectly true. I had talked with Grim, but had not read what he had written.

"He wishes me to go and wait for him in a certain place."

"Why not do it?"

"Rubbama." (Perhaps.)

"True-believers! Followers of the Prophet! Sons of warrior kings!" thundered Abdul Ali. "Will you do nothing to help Feisul, a lineal descendant of the Prophet? You have helped him to a throne. Now strike to hold him there!"

"Jimgrim says, I may go away and leave you here," growled Anazeh. "What say you?"

"Ala khatrak. (Please yourself.) Jimgrim is wise."

"He is the father of wisdom. Mashallah! I will consider it. There will be a banquet presently!"

"And loot! You can help yourselves!" shouted Abdul Ali of Damascus. Then he sat down amid a storm of applause. Suliman ben Saoud — Jimgrim — was on his feet before the tumult died away, and again they grew perfectly still to listen to him. If an Arab loves anything under heaven more than his own style of fighting, it is the action and reaction of debate. I could not understand a word of the mid-Arabian dialect, but Abdul Ali's retorts were plain enough; and from the way that Grim pointed at me and Mahommed ben Hamza it was fairly easy to follow what was happening.

He denounced me as possibly dangerous, and wondered why they permitted me to have an interpreter, who could whisper to me everything that was being said.

"Put out the interpreter!" sneered Abdul Ali, and there was a chorus of approval. Mahommed ben Hamza got up and hurried for the door while the hurrying was good and painless to himself, though it was hardly that to other people; forcing his way between the close-packed notables he kicked more than one of them pretty badly and grinned when they cursed him. I saw Abdul Ali of Damascus whisper to one of his rose-coloured parasites, who got up at once and made his way toward the door, too.

"The fellow is from Hebron," Abdul Ali sneered in a voice loud enough for all to hear. "It is best that he should not go back to Hebron to tell tales! I have attended to it."

My blood ran cold. I tried to catch Grim's eye, but he would not look in my direction. I wondered whether he had heard Abdul Ali's threat. It seemed to me that if Mahommed ben Hamza were either murdered or imprisoned Grim's whole chance of success was gone. The danger would be multiplied tenfold. Anazeh seemed the only remaining hope. The old-rose individual who followed ben Hamza had not reached the door yet.

"How about your men?" I asked.

"They are all right." Anazeh's eyes pursued the liquor bottle.

"Why not go and see?" I suggested.

"Ilhamdul'illah, they are good men. I know them. If there is trouble they will come and tell me."

The door opened softly. The gorgeous old-rose parasite slipped through. I had a mental vision of Mahommed ben Hamza lying face-downward with his new coat stained with blood. There was nothing for it, it seemed, but the magic formula to move Anazeh.

"Jimgrim says, 'See that ben Hamza gets safely away!'"

"Dog of a Hebron tanner's son — let him die! What is that to me?"

"It is Jimgrim's command."

"Wallahi haida fasl! (By God, this is a strange affair!) Wait here!"

Old Anazeh, with the name of the Prophet of God on his lips, cast an envious glare at the bottle of liquor and seized action by the forelock. There was nothing to excite comment in his getting up to leave the room. A dozen men had done that and come in again. He strode out, straight down the middle of the carpet.

Suliman ben Saoud — Jimgrim — went on talking, and to judge by Abdul Ali of Damascus' increasingly restless retorts he was getting that gentleman's goat as promised. Finally Abdul Ali got to his feet and said that if the Ichwan would see him alone he would show him certain documents that would satisfy him, but that it would not be policy to produce them in public. He offered to send for the documents, and to show them during or after the banquet.

So Jimgrim sat down, and there was a good deal of quiet nudging and nodding. Every one seemed to understand that the Ichwan was going to be bribed; they seemed to admire his ability to get for himself a share of the funds that most of them had tapped.

A man nearly opposite me leaned over and said in fairly good French, with the manner of a doctor assuring his patient that the worst is yet to come:

"It has been decided that you are to be detained here in the castle until there is no danger of your carrying away important news."

While I was turning that over in my mind Anazeh came back, grinning. Something outside had tickled him immensely, but he would not say anything. He sat down beside me and chuckled into his beard; and when his neighbour on the right asked what had amused him he turned the question into a bawdy joke.

"Did ben Hamza get away?" I whispered.

He only nodded. He continued chuckling until the man on duty by the door announced to the "assembled lords and princes" that the muezzin summoned them to prayer. All except three Christian sheikhs trooped up the narrow stairway in Ali Shah al Khassib's wake, Anazeh going last with a half serious joke about not caring to be stabbed in the back.

I expected the three non-Moslems would take advantage of the opportunity to ask me a string of questions. But they took exactly the opposite view of the situation. They avoided me, withdrawing into a corner by themselves. I suppose they thought that to be seen talking to me was more risky than the amusement merited.

So I went up to the ramparts, too, to watch the folk at prayer, minded to keep out of sight, for they don't like being regarded as a curious spectacle; and on the way up I did something that may have had a lot to do with our getting away alive, although I did not give much thought to it and could hardly have explained my motive at the time.

The door at the foot of the stairs opened inward. It was almost exactly the same width as the stairway, so that when it stood wide open you could not have put your hand between its edge and the stairway wall. Lying on the floor of the hall within a few feet of the nearest corner was a length of good sound olive-wood, about three inches in thickness, roughly squared and not particularly squared. Having stepped on it accidentally, I picked it up, and discovered more by accident than intention that it was longer than the width of the stairway. Then I noticed a notch in the stairway wall. Behind the opened door there was a deeper notch in the opposite wall. There was no lock on the door, no bolt. That length of wood had been cut to fit horizontally from notch to notch across the passage. Once that beam was fitted in its place, whoever wished to reach the roof would have to burn or batter down the door. I moved the door and placed the length of olive-wood on end behind it.

I found the view from the ramparts much more interesting than the soul-saving formalities of eighty or so potential cut-throats. While they prayed I stood watching the shadows deepen in the Jordan Valley, as no doubt Joshua once watched them from somewhere near that same spot before he marshalled his invading host. You could understand why people who had wandered forty years in a stark and howling wilderness should yearn for those coloured, fertile acres between the Jordan and the sea: why they should be willing to fight for them, die for them, do anything rather than turn back.

By the time we had filed down — Anazeh last again — the servants had nearly finished spreading a banquet. What looked like bed-sheets had been laid along the strip of carpet, and the whole length of them was piled with all imaginable things to eat, from cakes and fruit to whole sheep roasted and seethed in camel's milk and honey. There were no less than six sheep placed at intervals along the "table," with mountains of rice, scow-loads of apricots cooked in various ways, and a good sized flock of chickens spitted and smeared with peppery sauce. At a guess, I should say there were several pounds of meat, about two chickens, and a peck of rice per man, with apricots and raisins added; but they faced the prospect like heroes.

Perhaps what helped them face it was the sight of sundry bottles bearing labels more familiar in the West. Abdul Ali of Damascus, licking his lips like a cat that smells canary, took his place on a cushion up near the window again on the right of Ali Shah al Khassib, who was only the nominal host. Abdul Ali left no doubt in anybody's mind as to who was paying for the feast. It was he who gave orders to the servants in a bullying tone of voice; he who begged every one be seated.

Anazeh looked at the bottles of brandy — looked at me — and prayed under his breath; or, at any rate, it looked and sounded like a prayer. He may have been swearing. He and I were not very far from the door; the seats near the head of the table had all been taken. I sat down at once, so as not to be conspicuous, but Anazeh remained standing so long that at last Abdul Ali called to him to sit down and eat his fill, using the offensively magnanimous tone of voice that some men can achieve without an effort. I think Anazeh had been waiting for just that opening.

"I have twenty men outside," he announced. "Shall I eat, and not they?"

"This is a feast for notables," said Abdul Ali.

"A little bread with my own men is better than meat and drink at a traitor's table," Anazeh answered. "Wallahi! (By God!) I go to eat with honest men!" He laid a hand on my head. "Ye have said this effendi must stay in the castle. Well and good. Whoever harms him or offers him indignity shall answer to me and my men for it!" He bowed to me like a king taking leave of his court. "Lailtak sa'idi. Allah yifazak, effendi!" (Good night. God keep you, effendi!) With that he stalked out, and the door slammed shut behind him. Everybody, including Abdul Ali, laughed.

The banquet was a boresome business — an interminable competition to see who could eat and drink the most. With my interpreter gone, and everybody else too busy guzzling to trouble to speak distinctly for my benefit, I had to depend on my eyes for information and naturally used them to the utmost. I noticed that Abdul Ali of Damascus, Jimgrim Suliman ben Saoud and myself were the only men in the room, servants included, who ate and drank within the bounds of decency and reason. One of the servants, walking up and down the table-cloth with brandy and relays of vegetables, was drunk very early in the game and had to be thrown out.

Abdul Ali kept conversation going on the subject of the raid. The more the brandy bottles circulated the easier he found it to keep enthusiasm burning. He talked about me, too, several times, and every time that subject cropped up all eyes turned in my direction. I think he was making the most of the school idea, mixing up the raid with education and serving the mixture hot, as it were, with brandy sauce.

But over the way, about halfway down the table, the Ichwan Suliman ben Saoud, dead-cold-sober and abstemious, as befitted a fanatic, was talking, too. He was quite evidently talking against Abdul Ali, so that the Damascene kept looking at him with a troubled expression. He glanced frequently at the door, too, as if he expected some one who could put an end to Suliman ben Saoud's intrigue.

But it was a long time before the door opened and the second of his old-rose parasites came in. I had not noticed until then that the man was missing. He thrust a packet of some sort into Abdul Ali's hands. He whispered. The Damascene's face darkened instantly, and he swore like a pirate. Then, I suppose because he had to vent his wrath on somebody, he shouted to me in German all down the length of the table:

"Your cursed interpreter has nearly killed my secretary! He struck him in the mouth and knocked all his teeth out. What courteous servants you employ!"

"What was your secretary trying to do to him?" I retorted, but he saw fit not to answer that. He poured some more brandy instead for Ali Shah al Khassib.

So that was what Anazeh had been laughing at! The old humourist had either seen the fracas, or had come on the injured old-rose messenger of death nursing a damaged face. I began to share Grim's good opinion of ben Hamza. But though I watched Grim's face, and knew that he knew German, I could not detect a trace of interest. He kept on talking against Abdul Ali until after ten o'clock. By that time most of the notables were about as full as they could hold. Those who were not too drunk appeared ready for anything in or out of reason.

At that stage of the proceedings they ushered in the dancing girls. The servants cleared away most of the food, removed the table-cloths, and a ring was formed practically all around the room, the notables leaning their backs against the wall to ease overworked bellies. I set my cushion down next to a very drunken man just by the narrow door that opened on the stairway leading to the ramparts. He fell asleep with his head on my shoulder within five minutes, and as that, for some subtle reason, seemed to make me even more unnoticeable I let him snore away in peace.

Over in Abdul Ali's corner of the room there was a real council of war going on in whispers. Opposite to him, ten paces or so distant from me, Jimgrim Suliman ben Saoud was holding a rival show. It seemed about an even bet which was making greater headway. Those who were more or less drunk, and all the younger sheikhs, had eyes and ears for nothing but the dancing girls.

They were outrageous hussies. They wore more clothes than a Broadway chorus lady, and rather less paint, but if they were symbols of the Moslem paradise (as a learned Arab once assured me that they are meant to be) then, as I answered the Arab on that occasion, "me for hell." But none of those sheikhs had ever seen Broadway, so you could hardly blame them.

Abdul Ali of Damascus seemed to have his arrangements with the men in his corner cinched at last to his satisfaction. He walked a little unsteadily across the room, apparently to make his peace with Suliman ben Saoud. He held brazenly in one hand a leather wallet that bulged with paper money — doubtless the "documents" that he had sent for. He nodded to me as he passed with more familiarity than he had any right to, since he had so ostentatiously dismissed me to the dogs. I suppose he felt so sure of "convincing" Suliman ben Saoud, and was so bent on offsetting the reaction caused by Anazeh's behavior that he had been reviving that project about the school and therefore chose to appear on intimate terms with me. I met him more than halfway; any one who cared to might believe I loved him like a brother.

He stood in front of Suliman ben Saoud, rocking just a trifle from the effects of alcohol and smoke, and there was about five minutes' conversation of which, although I missed a lot of it, I caught the general drift. The men who had come under the Ichwan's influence kept joining in and raising objections. I gathered that they expected a proportionate percentage of the bribe for which Suliman ben Saoud was supposed to be maneuvering.

But even Abdul Ali, with a pouch of paper money in his hand, was not quite so barefaced as to bribe the Ichwan publicly. At the end of five minutes he suggested a private talk on the parapet. Suliman ben Saoud rose with apparent reluctance. Abdul Ali of Damascus took his arm. It was Suliman ben Saoud who opened the narrow door, and Abdul Ali who went through first. I did not wait for any invitation, but let my snoring neighbor fall on his side, hurried through after them, and closed the door behind me. Groping for the stick in the dark, I jammed it into the notches. It fitted perfectly. It held the door immovable and barred that stairway against all-comers. Then I followed them to the parapet.

The moon was about full and bathing the whole roof, and all the countryside, in liquid light. There was a certain amount of mist lower down, and you could only make out the Dead Sea through it here and there; but up where we were, and even in the moat eighty feet below us, it was almost like daylight without the glare and heat. I leaned over, but could see nobody in the moat, and there was no sign of Mahommed ben Hamza.

Abdul Ali led the way toward the corner where Grim had given his orders to ben Hamza that afternoon. Abdul Ali did not seem to realize that I was following. When he turned at last, with his back to the parapet and the moonlight full in his face, he demanded in German:

"Was machen Sie hier?"

I was about to answer him when there came a noise like subterranean thunder from the mouth of the stairway. They were trying to force that door below and follow us. The first words I used were in English, for Grim's benefit:

"I stuck a stick in the door. I should say it's good for ten or fifteen minutes unless they use explosives."

That gave the whole game away at once.

"So!" said Abdul Ali. He thrust the wallet into his bosom. With the other hand he pulled out a repeating pistol. "So!"

Grim said never a word. He closed with him. In a second we were all three struggling like madmen. The pistol was not cocked; I managed to get hold of Abdul Ali's wrist and wrench the weapon away before he could pull back the slide. Then we all three went down together on the stone roof, Abdul Ali yelling like a maniac, and Grim trying to squeeze the wind out of him. Even then, as we rolled and fought, I could still hear the thundering on the door. No doubt the noise they made prevented them from hearing Abdul Ali's yells for help.

The man's strength was prodigious, although he was puffy and short-winded. It began to look as if we would have to knock him on the head to get control of him. But even so, there was no rope — no sign of Mahommed ben Hamza and his men. You can think of a lot of things while you fight for your life eighty miles away from help. I wondered whether Grim would throw him over the parapet, and whether we two would have to take our chance of mountaineering down that ragged corner of the wall.

But suddenly about a hundred and eighty pounds of human brawn landed feet-first on my back. A voice said "Taib,[11] Jimgrim!" and two other men jumped after him from somewhere on the ruined wall above us. In another second Abdul Ali was held hand and foot, tied until he could not move, and then a wheat-sack was pulled down over his head and made fast between his legs.

"You're late!" said Grim. "Quick! Where's the rope? Are your men below?"

---

11   All right.

The thundering on the door had ceased. Either they were coming up the steps already, or had gone to reach the parapet some other way. It did not occur to me, or for that matter to any of us in the excitement of the minute, that they might be holding a consultation below, or might even have abandoned the idea of following, although I think now that must be the explanation, for what we did took more time than it takes to set it down.

Ben Hamza made one end of the rope fast around Abdul Ali's feet. He would not listen to argument. He said he knew his business, and certainly the knot was workmanlike. Then he called over the parapet (an Arab never whistles) and a voice answered from the southern side of the moat, where some fallen stones cast a shadow. Then the three of them lifted Abdul Ali over, and lowered him head-first.

It was a slow business, for otherwise he would have been stunned against the first projection. I thought that Grim looked almost as nervous as I felt, but Mahommed ben Hamza was having the time of his life, and could not keep his tongue still.

"Head upwards a man can yell," he explained to me, grinning from ear to ear. "Feet upwards, too afraid to yell!" Then the thundering on the door began again, louder than before it seemed to me. They were using a battering-ram. But they were too late. After what seemed like a long-drawn hour we saw shadowy arms below reach up and seize our prisoner. Then the loose rope came up again hand over hand.

"You next!" said Grim quietly. He pushed me forward, after carefully examining the loop Mahommed ben Hamza tied in the end of the rope.

CHAPTER TEN

"Money doesn't weigh much!"

Well — you don't stand on precedence or ceremony at times like that. Over I went in the bight of the rope. They let me fall about fifteen feet before they seemed to realize that I had let go of the parapet. Added to all that had gone before, that made about the climax of sensation. The pain of barking the skin of knees and elbows against projecting angles of stone was a relief.

I am no man of iron. I haven't iron nerves. Not one second of that descent was less than hell. I could hear the thunder of some kind of battering-ram on the door at the foot of the stair. I could imagine the rope chafing against the sharp edge of the parapet as they paid it out hand over hand. The only thing that made me keep my head at all was knowledge that Abdul Ali had had to do the trip feet-upward, with his head in a bag. When they let go too fast it was rather like the halfway stage of taking chloroform. When they slowed up, there was the agonizing dread of pursuit. And through it all there burned the torturing suggestion that the rope might break.

Mother Earth felt good that night, when strong hands reached up and lifted me out of the noose that failed of reaching the bottom by about a man's height. Come to think of it, it wasn't mother earth at that. It was the stinking carcass of a camel only half autopsied by the vultures, that my feet first rested on — brother, perhaps, to the beast I had put out of his agony that afternoon.

The others came down the rope hand-over-hand, Grim last. I suppose he stayed up there with his pistol, ready for contingencies. He had his nerve with him, for he had fastened the upper end of the rope to a piece of broken stone laid across a gap that the crusaders had made in the ramparts, centuries ago, for the Christian purpose of pouring boiling oil and water on their foes. It did not take more than a minute's violent shaking after he got down to bring the rope tumbling on our heads.

Then the next thing he did was to take a look at the prisoner.

Finding him not much the worse for wear, barring some bruises and a missing inch or two of skin, he ordered the bag pulled over his head again and gave the order for retreat. Mahommed ben Hamza went scouting ahead. The others picked up Abdul Ali as the construction gangs handle baulks of timber — horizontal — face-downward. When he wriggled they cuffed him into good behaviour.

You have to get down into an Arab moat before you can realize what the Hebrews meant by their word Gehenna. The smell of rotting carrion was only part of it. One stumbled into, and through, and over things that should not be. Heaps, that looked solid in the moonlight, yielded to the tread. Whatever liquid lay there was the product of corruption.

Yet we did not dare to climb out of the moat until we reached the shadows at the northern angle. Though the moonlight shone almost straight down on us it was a great deal brighter up above, and the walls cast some shadow. There was nothing for it but to pick our way in the comparative gloom of that vulture's paradise, praying we might find a stream to wade in presently.

Once, looking up behind me, I thought I saw men's heads peering over the parapet, but that may have been imagination. Grim vowed he did not see them, although I suspected him of saying that to avoid a panic. He shepherded us along, speaking in a perfectly normal voice whenever he had to, as if there were no such thing as hurry in the world. When we reached the farther corner of the moat it was he who climbed out first to con the situation. A look-out in a bastion on the ruined town wall promptly fired at him.

I expected him to fire back. I climbed up beside him to lend a hand with the pistol I had filched from Abdul Ali. But Grim shouted something about taking away for burial the corpse of a man who had died of small-pox. The man on the wall commanded us to Allah's mercy and warned us to beware lest we, too, catch that dreaded plague.

"Inshallah!" Grim answered. Then he summoned our men from the moat.

They passed up Abdul Ali, dragging him feet-first again with one man keeping a clenched fist ready to strike him in the mouth in case he should forget that corpses don't cry out. He looked like a corpse half cold, as they carried him jerkily along a track that roughly followed the line of the wall. I don't suppose that anything ever looked more like an Arab funeral procession than we did. The absence of noisy mourners, and the unusual hour of night, were plausibly accounted for by the dreaded disease that Grim had invented for the occasion. My golf-suit was the only false note, but I kept in shadow as much as I could, with the unseemly burden between me and the ramparts.

It was a long time before we had the town wall at our backs. A funeral, in the circumstances, might justifiably be rapid; but we could hardly run and keep up the pretense. But at last we passed over the shoulder of a hill into shadow on the farther side, and there was no more need of play-acting.

"Yalla bilagel!" [Run like the devil.] Grim ordered then, and we obeyed him like sprinters attempting to lower a record.

Twelve men running through the night can make a lot of noise, especially when they carry a heavy man between them. Our men were all from Hebron. Hebron prides itself on training the artfullest thieves in Asia. They boast of being able to steal the bed from under a sleeper without waking him. But even the stealthiest animals go crashing away from danger, and, now that the worst of the danger lay behind, more or less panic seized all of us.

Mahommed ben Hamza refused to follow the regular track, for fear of ambush or a chance encounter in the dark. Grim let him have his way. They dragged the wretched Abdul Ali like a sack of corn by a winding detour, and wherever the narrow path turned sharply to avoid great rocks they skidded him at the turn until he yelled for mercy. Grim pulled off the sack at last, untied his arms and legs, and let him walk; but whenever he lagged they frog-marched him again.

At last we reached a brook where we all waded to get rid of the filth and smell from that infernal moat, and Abdul Ali seized that opportunity to play his last cards. Considering Ben Hamza's reputation, the obvious type of his nine ruffians, the darkness and rough handling, it said a lot for Grim's authority that Abdul Ali still had that wallet-full of money in his possession. Sitting on a stone in the moonlight, he pulled it out. His nerve was a politician's, cynical, simple. Its simplicity almost took your breath away.

"How many men from Hebron?" he demanded.

"Ten. Well and good. I have here ten thousand piastres — one thousand for each of you, or divide it how you like. That is the price I will pay you to let me go. What can these other two do to you? Take the money and run. Leave me to settle with these others."

Ben Hamza, knee-deep in the brook, laughed aloud as he eyed the money. He made a gesture so good-humoured, so full of resignation and regret and broad philosophy that you would have liked the fellow even if he hadn't saved your life.

"Deal with those two first!" he grinned. "I would have taken your money long ago, but that I know Jimgrim! He would have made me give it up again."

"Jimgrim!" said Abdul Ali. "Jimgrim? Are you Major James Grim? A good thing for you I did not know that, when I had you in my power in the castle!"

Grim laughed. "Are we all set? Let's go."

We hurried all the faster now because our legs were wet. The night air on those Moab heights is chilly at any season. Perhaps, too, we were trying to leave behind us the moat-stench that the water had merely reduced, not washed away. A quarter of a mile before we reached the place appointed we knew that Anazeh had not failed to keep his tryst. Away up above us, beside the tomb, like an ancient bearded ghost, Anazeh stood motionless, silent, conning the track we should come by — a grand old savage keeping faith against his neighbours for the sake of friendship.

He did not challenge when he heard us. He took aim. He held his aim until Grim called to him. When our goat track joined the main road he was there awaiting us, standing like a sentinel in the shadow of a fanged rock. And there, if Abdul Ali of Damascus could have had his way, there would have been a fresh debate. He did not let ten seconds pass before he had offered Anazeh all the money he had with him to lend him a horse and let him go. Anazeh waved aside the offer.

"You shall have as much more money as you wish!" the Damascene insisted. "Let me get to my house, and a messenger shall take the money to you. Or come and get it."

All the answer Anazeh gave him was a curt laugh — one bark like a fox's.

"Where are all the horses?" Grim demanded. I could only see five or six.

"I wait for them."

"Man, we can't wait!"

"Jimgrim!" said the old sheikh, with a glint of something between malice and amusement in his eyes, "I knew you in the mejlis when you watched me read that letter! One word from me and —" He made a click between his teeth suggestive of swift death. "I let you play your game. But now I play my game, Allah willing. I have waited for you. Wait thou for me!"

"Why? What is it?"

Anazeh beckoned us and turned away. We followed him, Grim and I, across the road and up a steep track to the tomb on the overhanging rock, where he had stood when we first saw him.

He pointed. A cherry-red fire with golden sparks and crimson-bellied sulphur smoke was blazing in the midst of El-Kerak.

"The home of Abdul Ali of Damascus," said Anazeh with pride in his voice. It was the pride of a man who shows off the behaviour of his children. "My men did it!"

"How can they escape?" Grim asked him.

"Wallah! Will the gate guards stand idle? Will they not run to the fire — and to the looting? But they will find not much loot. My men already have it!"

"Loot," said Grim, "will delay them."

"Money doesn't weigh much," Anazeh answered. "Here my men come."

Somebody was coming. There came a burst of shooting and yelling from somewhere between us and El-Kerak, and a moment later the thunder of horses galloping full-pelt. Anazeh got down to the road with the agility of a youngster, ordered Abdul Ali of Damascus, the shivering Ahmed and me under cover. He placed his remaining handful of men at points of vantage where they could cover the retreat of the fifteen. And it was well he did.

There were at least two score in hot pursuit, and though you could hardly tell which was which in that dim light, Anazeh's party opened fire on the pursuers and let the fifteen through. I did not get sight of Grim while that excitement lasted, but he had two automatics. He took from me the one that I had taken from Abdul Ali, and with that one and his own he made a din like a machine-gun. He told me afterward that he had fired in the air.

"Noise is as good as knock-outs in the dark," he explained, while Anazeh's men boasted to one another of the straight shooting that it may be they really believed they had done. An Arab can believe anything — afterward. I don't believe one man was killed, though several were hit.

At any rate, whether the noise accomplished it or not, the pursuers drew off, and we went forward, carrying a cashbox now, of which Abdul Ali was politely requested to produce the key. That was the first intimation he had that his house had been looted. He threw his bunch of keys away into the shadows, in the first exhibition of real weakness he had shown that night. It was a silly gesture. It only angered his captors. It saved him nothing.

Four more of Anazeh's men had been wounded, all from behind, two of them rather badly, making six in all who were now unfit for further action. But we did not wait to bandage them. They affected to make light of their injuries, saying they would go over to the British and get attended to in hospital. Abdul Ali was put on Ahmed's miserable mount, with his legs lashed under the horse's belly. Ahmed, with Mahommed ben Hamza and his men were sent along ahead; being unarmed, unmounted, they were a liability now. But those Hebron thieves could talk like an army; they put up a prodigious bleat, all night long, about that cash-box. They maintained they had a clear right to share its contents, since unless they had first captured Abdul Ali, Anazeh's men could not have burned his house and seized his money. Anazeh's men, when they had time to be, were suitably amused.

It was not a peaceful retreat by any means. Time and again

before morning we were fired on from the rear. Our party deployed to right and left to answer — always boasting afterward of having killed at least a dozen men. I added up their figures on the fly-leaf of the pocket Bible, and the total came to two hundred and eighteen of the enemy shot dead and forever damned! I believe Anazeh actually did kill one of our pursuers.

By the time the moon disappeared we had come too close to Anazeh's country to make pursuit particularly safe. Who they were who pursued us, hauled off. We reached the launch, secure in its cove between the rocks, a few minutes after dawn. Anazeh ordered his six wounded men into it, with perfect assurance that the British doctors would take care of them and let them go unquestioned.

When Grim had finished talking with Anazeh I went up to thank the old fellow for my escort, and he acknowledged the courtesy with a bow that would have graced the court of Solomon.

"Give the old bird a present, if you've got one," Grim whispered.

So I gave him my watch and chain, and he accepted them with the same calm dignity.

"Now he's your friend for life!" said Grim. "Anazeh is a friend worth having. Let's go!"

The watch and chain was a cheap enough price to pay for that two days' entertainment and the acquaintance of such a splendid old king of thieves. Anazeh watched us away until we were out of earshot, he and Grim exchanging the interminable Arab farewell formula of blessing and reply that have been in use unchanged for a thousand years.

Then Abdul Ali produced his wallet again.

"Major Grim," he said, "please take this money. Keep it for yourself, and let me go. Surely I have been punished enough! Besides, you cannot — you dare not imprison me! I am a French subject. I have been seized outside the British sphere. I know you are a poor man — the pay of a British officer is a matter of common knowledge. Come now, you have done what you came to do. You have destroyed my influence at El-Kerak. Now benefit yourself. Avoid an international complication. Show mercy on me! Take this money. Say that I gave you the slip in the dark!"

Grim smiled. He looked extremely comical without any eyebrows. The wrinkles went all the way up to the roots of his hair.

"I'm incorruptible," he said. "The boss, I believe, isn't."

"You mean your High Commissioner? I have not enough money for him."

Grim laughed. "No," he said, "he comes expensive."

"What then?"

"Don't be an ass," said Grim. "You know what."

"Information?"

"Certainly."

"What information?"

"You were sent by the French," said Grim, "to raise the devil here in Palestine — no matter why. You were trying to bring off a raid on Judaea. Who are your friends in Jerusalem who were ready to spring surprises? What surprises? Who's your Jerusalem agent?"

"If I tell you?"

"I'm not the boss. But I'll see him about it. Come on — who's your agent?"

"Scharnhoff."

Grim whistled. That he did not believe, I was almost certain, but he whistled as if totally new trains of thought had suddenly revealed themselves amid a maze of memories.

"You shall speak to the boss," he said after a while.

I fell asleep then, wedged uncomfortably between two men's legs, wakened at intervals by the noisy pleading of Mahommed ben Hamza and his men for what they called their rights in the matter of Abdul Ali's wallet. They were still arguing the point when we ran on the beach near Jericho, where a patrol of incredulous Sikhs pounced on us and wanted to arrest Ahmed and Anazeh's wounded men. Grim had an awful time convincing them that he was a British officer. In the end we only settled it by tramping about four miles to a guard-house, where a captain in uniform gave us breakfast and telephoned for a commisariat lorry.

It was late in the afternoon when we reached Jerusalem and got the wounded into hospital. By the time Grim had changed into uniform and put courtplaster where his eyebrows should have been, and he, Abdul Ali and I had driven in an official Ford up the Mount of Olives to OETA, the sun was not far over the skyline.

Grim had telephoned, so the Administrator was waiting for us. Grim went straight in. It was twenty minutes before we two were summoned into his private room, where he sat behind the desk exactly as we had left him the other morning. He looked as if he had not moved meanwhile. Everything was exactly in its place — even the vase, covering the white spot on the varnish. There was the same arrangement of too many flowers, in a vase too small to hold them.

"Allow me to present Sheikh Abdul Ali of Damascus," said Grim.

The Administrator bowed rather elaborately, perhaps to hide the twinkle in his eyes. He didn't scowl. He didn't look tyrannical. So Abdul Ali opened on him, with all bow guns.

"I protest! I am a French subject. I have been submitted to violence, outrage, indignity! I have been seized on foreign soil, and brought here by force against all international law! I shall claim exemplary damages! I demand apology and satisfaction!"

Sir Louis raised his eyebrows and looked straight at Grim without even cracking a smile.

"Is this true, Major Grim?"

"Afraid it is, sir."

"Scandalous! Perfectly scandalous! And were you a witness to all this?" he asked, looking at me as if I might well be the cause of it all.

I admitted having seen the greater part of it.

"And you didn't protest? What's the world coming to? I see you've lost a little skin yourself. I hope you've not been breaking bounds and fighting?"

"He is a most impertinent man!" said Abdul Ali, trying to take his cue, and glowering at me. "He posed as a person interested in a school for El-Kerak, and afterward helped capture me by a trick!"

The Administrator frowned. It seemed I was going to be made the scape-goat. I did not care. I would not have taken a year of Sir Louis' pay for those two days and nights. When he spoke again I expected something drastic addressed to me, but I was wrong.

"An official apology is due to you, Sheikh Abdul Ali. Permit me to offer it, together with my profound regret for any slight personal inconvenience to which you may have been subjected in course of this — ah — entirely unauthorized piece of — ah — brigandage. I notice you have been bruised, too. You shall have the best medical attention at our disposal."

"That is not enough!" sneered Abdul Ali, throwing quite an attitude.

"I know it isn't. I was coming to that. An apology is also due to the French — our friends the French. I shall put it in writing, and ask you to convey it to Beirut to the French High Commissioner, with my compliments. I would send you by train, but you might be — ah — delayed at Damascus in that case. Perhaps Emir Feisal might detain you. There will be a boat going from Jaffa in two days' time. Two days will give you a chance to recover from the outrageous experience before we escort you to the coast. A first-class passage will be reserved for you by wire, and you will be put on board with every possible courtesy. You might ask the French High Commissioner to let me know if there is anything further he would like us to do about it. Now, I'll ring for a clerk to take you to the medical officer — under escort, so that you mayn't be subjected to further outrage or indignity. Good evening!"

"Anything more for me?" asked Grim, as soon as Abdul Ali had been led away.

"Not tonight, Grim. Come and see me in the morning." Grim saluted. The Administrator looked at me — smiled mischievously.

"Have a good time?" he asked. "Don't neglect those scratches. Good evening!"

No more. Not another word. He never did say another word to me about it, although I met him afterwards a score of times. You couldn't help but admire and like him.

Grim led the way up the tower stairs again, and we took a last look at El-Kerak. The moon was beginning to rise above the rim of the Moab Hills. The land beyond the Dead Sea was wrapped in utter silence. Over to the south-east you could make out one dot of yellow light, to prove that men lived and moved and had their being in that stillness. Otherwise, you couldn't believe it was real country. It looked like a vision of the home of dreams.

"Got anything to do tonight?" asked Grim. "Can you stay awake? I know where some Jews are going to play Beethoven in an upper room in the ancient city. Care to come?"

CHAPTER ELEVEN

"And the rest of the acts of Ahaziah —"

I have no idea what Grim did during the next few days. I spent the time studying Arabic, and saw nothing of him until he walked into my room at the hotel one afternoon, sat down and came straight to the point.

"Had enough?"

"No."

"Got the hang of it?"

"Yes, I think so," I answered. "Allah's peace, as they call it, depends on the French. They intend to get Damascus and all Syria. So they sent down Abdul Ali of Damascus to make trouble for the British in Palestine; the idea being to force the British to make common cause with them. That would mean total defeat for the Arabs; and Great Britain would save France scads of men and money. But you pulled that plug. I saw you do it. I heard Abdul Ali of Damascus tell you Scharnhoff's name. Did you go after Scharnhoff?"

"No, not yet," he answered. "You're no diplomat."

I knew that. I have never wished to be one, never having met a professional one who did not, so to speak, play poker with a cold deck and at least five aces. The more frankly they seem to be telling the truth, the more sure you may be they are lying.

"Neither are you," I answered. "You're a sportsman. Are you allowing Scharnhoff weight for age, and a fair start — or what?"

He chuckled. "You believed old Abdul-Ali of Damascus? He's a French secret political agent. So whatever he told us is certainly not true. Or, if it is true, or partially true, then it's the kind of truth that is deadlier deceptive than a good clean God-damned lie. Get this: such men as Abdul Ali would face torture rather than betray an associate — unless they're sure the associate is a traitor or about to become one. A government can't easily punish its own spies on foreign territory. But by betraying them, it can sometimes get the other government to do it. That Abdul Ali betrayed Scharnhoff to me, proves one of two things.

Abdul Ali was lying, and Scharnhoff harmless — or in some way Scharnhoff has fallen foul of his French paymasters and they want him punished. Very likely he has drawn French money, for their purposes, and has misused it for his own ends. Or perhaps they have promised him money, and wish to back down. Possibly he knows too much about their agents, and they want him silenced. They propose to have us silence him. I'm going to call on Scharnhoff."

"You suspect him of double treachery?"

"I suspect him of being a one-track-minded, damned old visionary."

I had met Hugo Scharnhoff. Long before the War he had been a professor of orientology at Vienna University. At the moment he was technically an "enemy alien." But he had lived so many years in Jerusalem, and was reputed so studious and harmless, that the British let him stay there after Allenby captured the city. A man of moderate private means, he owned a stone house in the German Colony with its back to the Valley of Hinnom.

"Care to come?" Grim asked me.

"Yes."

"Know your Bible?" He proceeded to quote from it: "And the rest of the acts of Ahaziah which he did are they not written in the book of the chronicles of the Kings of Israel?"'

"What of it?"

"That was set down in Aramaic, nowadays called Hebrew, something like three thousand years ago," said Grim. "It's Aramaic magic. Let's take a look at it."

We trudged together down the dusty Bethlehem Road, turned to the east just short of the Pool of the Sultan (where they now had a delousing station for British soldiers) and went nearly to the end of the colony of neat stone villas that the Germans built before the War, and called Rephaim. It was a prosperous colony until the Kaiser, putting two and two, made five of them and had to guess again.

The house we sought stood back from the narrow road, at a corner, surrounded by a low stone wall and a mass of rather dense shrubs that obscured the view from the windows. The front door was a thing of solid olive-wood. We had to hammer on it for several minutes. There was no bell.

A woman opened it at last — an Arab in native costume, gazelle-eyed, as they all are, and quite good looking, although hardly in her first youth. Her face struck me as haunted. She was either ashamed when her eyes met Grim's or else afraid of him. But she smiled pleasantly enough and without asking our business led the way at once to a room at the other end of a long hall that was crowded with all sorts of curios. They were mostly stone bric-a-brac — fragments of Moabite pottery and that kind of thing, with a pretty liberal covering of ordinary house dust. In fact, the house had the depressing "feel" of a rarely visited museum.

The room she showed us into was the library — three walls lined with books, mostly with German titles — a big cupboard in one corner, reaching from floor to ceiling — a big desk by the window — three armchairs and a stool. There were no pictures, and the only thing that smacked of ornament was the Persian rug on the floor.

We waited five minutes before Scharnhoff came in, looking as if we had disturbed his nap. He was an untidy stout man with green goggles and a grayish beard, probably not yet sixty years of age, and well preserved. He kept his pants up with a belt, and his shirt bulged untidily over the top. When he sat down you could see the ends of thick combinations stuffed into his socks. He gave you the impression of not fitting into western clothes at all and of being out of sympathy with most of what they represent.

He was cordial enough — after one swift glance around the room.

"Brought a new acquaintance for you," said Grim, introducing me. "I've told him how all the subalterns come to you for Palestinian lore —"

"Ach! The young Lotharios! Each man a Don Juan! All they come to me for is tales of Turkish harems, of which I know no more than any one. They are not interested in subjects of real importance. 'How many wives had Djemal Pasha? How many of them were European?' That is what they ask me. When I discuss ancient history it is only about King Solomon's harem that they care to know; or possibly about the modern dancing girls of El-Kerak, who are all spies. But there is no need to inform you as to that. Eh? I haven't seen you for a long time, Major Grim. What have you been doing?"

"Nothing much. I was at the Tomb of the Kings yesterday."

Scharnhoff smiled scornfully.

"Now you must have some whiskey to take the taste of that untruth out of your mouth! How can a man of your attainments call that obviously modern fraud by such a name? The place is not nearly two thousand years old! It is probably the tomb of a Syrian queen named Adiabene and her family. Josephus mentions it. This land is full — every square metre of it — of false antiquities with real names, and real antiquities that never have been discovered! But why should a man like you, Major Grim, lend yourself to perpetuating falsity?"

He walked over to the cupboard to get whiskey, and from where we sat we could both of us see what he was doing. The cupboard was in two parts, top and bottom, without any intervening strip of wood between the doors, which fitted tightly. When he opened the top part the lower door opened with it. He kicked it shut again at once, but I had seen inside — not that it was interesting at the moment.

He set whiskey and tumblers on the desk, poured liberally, and went on talking.

"Tomb of the Kings? Hah! Tomb of the Kings of Judah? Hah! If any one can find that, he will have something more important than Ludendorff's memoirs! Something merkwürdig, believe me!"

He stiffened suddenly, and looked at Grim through the green goggles as if he were judging an antiquity.

"Perhaps this is not the time to make you a little suggestion, eh?"

Grim's face wrinkled into smiles.

"This man knows enough to hang me anyhow! Fire away!"

"Ah! But I would not like him to hang me!"

"He's as close as a clam. What's your notion?"

"Nothing serious, but — between us three, then — you and I are both foreigners in this place, Major Grim, although I have made it my home for fifteen years. You have no more interest in this government and its ridiculous rules than I have. What do you say — shall we find the Tomb of the Kings together?"

Grim wrinkled into smiles again and glanced down at his uniform.

"Yes, exactly!" agreed Scharnhoff. "That is the whole point. They call me an enemy alien. I am to all intents and purposes a prisoner. You are a British officer — can do what you like — go where you like. You wear red tabs; you are on the staff; nobody will dare to question you. These English have stopped all exploration until they get their mandate. After that they will take good care that only English societies have the exploration privilege. But what if we — you and I, that is to say — between us extract the best plum from the pudding before those miscalled statesmen sign the mandate — eh? It can be done! It can be done!"

Grim chuckled:

"I suppose you already see a picture of you and me with an ancient tomb in our trunks — say a few tons of the more artistic parts — beating it for the frontier and hawking the stuff afterward to second-hand furniture dealers? Pour me another whiskey, prof, and then we'll go steal the Mosque of Omar!"

"Ach! You laugh at me — you jest — you mock — you sneer. But I know what I propose. Do you know what will be found in that Tomb of the Kings of Judah when we discover it?"

"Bones. Dry bones. A few gold ornaments perhaps. A stale smell certainly."

"The Book of the Chronicles of the Kings of Israel! Think of it! A parchment roll — perhaps two or three rolls — not too big to go into a valise — worth more than all the other ancient manuscripts in the world all put together! Himmel! What a find that would be! What a record! What a refutation of all the historians and the fools who set themselves up for authorities nowadays! What a price it would bring! What would your Metropolitan Museum in New York not pay for it! What would the Jews not pay for it! They would raise millions among them and pay any price we cared to ask! The Book of the Chronicles of the Kings of Israel — only think!"

"But why the Chronicles of the Kings of Israel in the tomb of the Kings of Judah?" Grim asked, more by way of keeping up the conversation, I think, than because he could not guess the answer. He is an omnivorous reader, and there is not much recorded of the Near East that he does not know.

"Don't you know your history? You know, of course, that after King Solomon died the Jews divided into two kingdoms. The latter-day Jews speak of themselves as Israelites, but they are nothing of the kind; they are Judah-ites. The tribe of Judah remained in Jerusalem, forming one small kingdom; their descendants are the Jews of today. Part of the tribe of Benjamin stayed with them. The other seceding ten tribes called themselves the kingdom of Israel."

"Everybody knows that," said Grim. "What of it?"

"Well, the Assyrians came down and conquered the kingdom of Israel — marched all the Israelites away into captivity — and they vanished out of history. From that day to this their Book of Chronicles, so often referred to in the Old Testament, has never been seen nor heard of."

"Of course not," said Grim. "The King of Assyria used it to wipe his razor on when he was through shaving every morning."

"Ach! You joke again; but I tell you I am not joking. Such people as those Hebrews are naturally secretive and so proud that they wrote down for posterity all the doings of their puny kings, would never have let their records fall into the hands of the Assyrians. They themselves were marched away in slave-gangs, but they left their Book behind them, safely hidden. Be sure of it! Ten years ago I found a manuscript in the place they now call Nablus, which in those days was Schechem. Schechem was the capital of the Kingdom of Israel, just as Jerusalem was the capital of the Kingdom of Judah, or the Jews. I sold that manuscript for a good price after I had photographed it. The idiots to whom I sold it — historians they call themselves! — value it only as a relic of antiquity. I made a digest of it — analyzed it — studied it — compared it with other authentic facts in my possession — and came to the definite conclusion that I hold the clue to the whereabouts of that lost Book of Chronicles."

"Let's see the photograph," Grim suggested.

"It has been impounded with other so-called 'enemy property' by your friends the British. I suppose they thought the German General Staff might get hold of it and conquer the Suez Canal! But what good would the sight of it do? You couldn't understand a word of it. It convinced me, after months of study, that when the Ten Tribes were carried away into captivity by the Assyrians they sent their records secretly to Jerusalem. Ever since the secession the Israelites and Jews had been jealous enemies. But they were relatives after all, boasting a common ancestor, proud of the same history, more or less observing the same religion. And Schechem was only about thirty miles from Jerusalem, which was considered an impregnable fortress until the Babylonians took it later on. So they sent their records to Jerusalem, and the Jews hid them. Where? Where do you suppose?"

"The likeliest place would be Solomon's Temple."

"You think so? Then you think superficially, my young friend. Let us return to that Tomb of the Kings again for a moment. That place that you visited is such an obvious fake that even the guide-books make light of it. The one all-important thing in Palestine that never yet has been discovered is the real Tomb of the Kings. Yet Jerusalem, where it certainly must be, has been searched and looted a hundred times from end to end. Therefore — you follow me? — the Jews must have concealed it very cunningly. Answer me, then: would the Jews, who were always a practical people and not corpse-worshippers like the Egyptians, have taken all that trouble to hide the tomb of their kings unless there were important treasure in it? Answer me!"

"So you expect to find treasure in addition to the lost Book of Chronicles?"

"Certainly I do! The treasure will make the whole proceeding safe. Let the British have it! The fools will be so blinded by the glamour of gold, that I shall easily extract the things of real value — the invaluable manuscripts! Then let the men who call themselves historians take a back seat!"

He rubbed his hands together in anticipation.

"Were you looking for the Tomb of the Kings, then, before the

War?" Grim asked him.

"Not exactly. Under the Turks it was difficult. The Turks were beautifully corrupt. By paying for it I could get permission to excavate on any property owned by Christians. But the minute I touched Moslem places the Turks became fanatical. The Arabs, now, are different — fanatics, too, but with a new sort of fanaticism — new to them, I mean — the kind that made the French revolutionists destroy everything their ancestors had set value on. There are plenty of Arabs so full of this disease of Bolshevism that they would make it easy for me to desecrate what others believe is holy ground. But these idiots of English are worse than the Turks! They have stopped all excavation. They are so afraid of Bolshevism that, if they could, they would imitate Joshua and make the sun stand still!"

"Well, what's the idea?" asked Grim, finishing his whiskey.

Scharnhoff shrugged his shoulders.

"You know my position. I am helpless — here on suffrance — obliged by idiotic regulations to sit in idleness. But if I could find a British officer with brains — surely there must be one somewhere! — one with some authority, who is considered above suspicion, I could show him, perhaps, how to get rich without committing any crime he need feel ashamed of."

I could not see Grim's eyes from where I sat, and he did not make any nervous movement that could have given him away. Yet I was conscious of a new alertness, and I think Scharnhoff detected it, too, for he changed his tactics on the instant.

"Hah! Hah! I was joking! Nobody who is fool enough to be a professional soldier would be clever enough to find the Tomb of the Kings and keep the secret for ten minutes! Hah! Hah! But I have a favour I would like to beg of you, Major Grim."

"I've no particular authority, you know."

"Ach! The Administrator listens to you; I am assured of that."

"He listens sometimes, yes, then usually does the other thing. Well, what's the request?"

"A simple one. There is a risk — not much, but just a little risk that some fool might stumble on that secret of the Tomb of the Kings and get away with the treasure. Now, did you ever set a thief to catch a thief? Hah! Hah! I would be a better watch-dog than any you could find. I know Jerusalem from end to end. I know all the likely places. Why don't you get permission for me to wander about Jerusalem undisturbed and keep my eye open for tomb-robbers? If I am not to have the privilege of discovering that Book of Chronicles, at least I would like to see that no common plunderer gets it. Surely I am known by now to be harmless! Surely they don't suspect me any longer of being an agent of the Kaiser, or any such nonsense as that! Why not make use of me? Get me a permit, please, Major Grim, to go where I please by day or night without interference. Tomb-robbers usually work at night, you know."

"All right," said Grim. "I'll try to do that."

"Ah! I always knew you were a man of good sense! Have more whiskey? A cigar then?"

"Can't promise anything, of course," said Grim, "but you shall have an answer within twenty-four hours."

Outside, as we turned our faces toward Jerusalem's gray wall, Grim opened up a little and gave me a suggestion of something in the wind.

"Did you see what he has in that cupboard?"

"Yes. Two Arab costumes. Two short crow-bars."

"Did you notice the grayish dust on the rug — three or four footprints at the corner near the cupboard?"

"Can't say I did."

"No. You wouldn't be looking for it. These men who pose as intellectuals never believe that any one else has brains. They fool themselves. There's one thing no man can afford to do, East of the sun or West of the moon. You can steal, slay, intrigue, burn — break all the Ten Commandments except one, and have a chance to get away with it. There's just one thing you can't do, and succeed. He's done it!"

"And the thing is?"

"Cheat a woman!"

"You mean his house keeper? She who answered the door?"

Grim nodded.

CHAPTER TWELVE

"You know you'll get scuppered if you're found out!"

Two days passed again without my seeing Grim, although I called on him repeatedly at the "Junior Staff Officers' Mess" below the Zionist Hospital. Suliman, the eight-year-old imp of Arab mischief, who did duty as page-boy met me on each occasion at the door and took grinning delight in disappointing me.

He was about three and a half feet high — coal-black, with a tarboosh worn at an angle on his kinky hair and a flashing white grin across his snub-nosed face that would have made an archangel count the change out of two piastres twice. Suliman and cool cheek were as obvious team-mates as the Gemini, and I was one of a good number, that included every single member of that unofficial mess, who could never quite see what Grim found so admirable in him. Grim never explained.

Taking the cue from his master, neither did Suliman ever explain anything to any one but Grim, who seemed to understand him perfectly.

"Jimgrim not here. No, not coming back. Much business. Good-bye!"

Somehow you couldn't suspect that kid of telling the truth. However, there was nothing for it but to go away, with a conviction in the small of your back that he was grinning mischievously after you.

Grim had found him one day starving and lousy in the archway of the Jaffa Gate, warming his fingers at a guttering candle-end preparatory to making a meal off the wax. He took him home and made Martha, the old Russian maid-of-all-work, clean him with kerosene and soft soap — gave him a big packing-case to sleep in along with Julius Caesar the near-bull-dog mascot — and thereafter broke him in and taught him things seldom included in a school curriculum.

In the result, Suliman adored Grim with all the concentrated zeal of hero-worship of which almost any small boy is capable;

but under the shadow of Grim's protection he feared not even "brass-hats" nor regarded civilians, although he was dreadfully afraid of devils. The devil-fear was a relic of his negroid ancestry. Some Arab Sheikh probably captured his great-grandmother on a slave-raid. Superstition lingers in dark veins longer than any other human failing.

I think I called five times before he confessed at last reluctantly that Grim was in. That was in the morning after breakfast, and I was shown into the room with the fireplace and the deep armchairs. Grim was reading but seemed to me more than usually reserved, as if the book had been no more than a screen to think behind, that left him in a manner unprotected when he laid it down. I talked at random, and he hardly seemed to be listening.

"Say," he said, suddenly interrupting me, "you came out of that El-Kerak affair pretty creditably. Suppose I let you see something else from the inside. Will you promise not to shout it all over Jerusalem?"

"Use your own judgment," I answered.

"You mustn't ask questions."

"All right."

"If any one in the Administration pounces on you in the course of it, you'll have to drop out and know nothing."

"Agreed."

"It may prove a bit more risky than the El-Kerak business."

"Couldn't be," I answered.

"You can't talk enough Arabic to get away with. But could you act deaf and dumb?"

"Sure — in three languages."

"You understand — I've no authority to let you in on this. I might catch hell if I were found out doing it. But I need help, of a certain sort. I want a man who isn't likely to be spotted by the gang I'm after. Get behind that screen — quick!"

It was a screen that hid a door leading to the pantry and the servants' quarters. There was a Windsor chair behind it, and it is much easier to keep absolutely still when you are fairly comfortable. I had hardly sat down when a man wearing spurs, who trod heavily, entered the room and I heard Grim get up to greet him.

"Are we alone?" a voice asked gruffly.

Instead of answering Grim came and looked behind the screen, opened the door leading to the pantry, closed it again, locked it, and without as much as a glance at me returned to face his visitor.

"Well, general, what is it?"

"This is strictly secret."

"I'll bet it isn't," said Grim. "If it's about missing explosives I know more than you do."

"My God! It's out? Two tons of TNT intended for the air force gone without a trace? The story's out?"

"I know it. Catesby sent me word by messenger last night from Ludd, after you put him under arrest."

"Damn the man! Well, that's what's happened. Catesby's fault. They'll blame me. The truck containing the stuff was run into a siding three days ago. Through young Catesby's negligence it was left there without a guard. Catesby will be broke for that as sure as my name is Jenkins. But, by the knell of hell's bells, Grim, more than Catesby will lose their jobs unless we find the stuff! Two tons. Half enough to blow up Palestine!"

"Too bad about Catesby," said Grim.

"Never mind Catesby. Damn him! Consider my predicament! How can I go to the Administrator with a lame-duck story about missing TNT and nothing done about it?"

"Nothing done? You've passed the buck, haven't you? Catesby is under arrest, you say."

"What do you mean?"

"I know Catesby," Grim retorted quietly. "He made that fine stand at Beersheba — when the Arabs rushed the camp, and you weren't looking. He took the blame for your carelessness, and never squealed. You took the credit for his presence of mind, and have treated him like a dog ever since. You expect me to try to save your bacon and forget Catesby's?"

"Nonsense, Grim! You're talking without your book. Here's what happened: the stuff arrived at Ludd in a truck attached to the end of a mixed train. The R.T.O.[12] sent me a memorandum and stalled the truck on a siding. I gave the memorandum to Catesby."

"He tells me in the note I received last night that you did nothing of the kind."

"Then he's a liar. He forgot all about it and did nothing. When the Air Force sent to get the stuff the truck was empty."

"And you want me to find it, I suppose?"

"Yes. The quicker the better!"

"And be a party to breaking Catesby? I like my job, but not that much!"

"You refuse then to hunt for the TNT?"

"I take my orders straight from the Administrator. He expects me in half an hour. You want me to smooth the way for you with Sir Louis. I'm much more interested in Catesby, who would face a firing party sooner than soak another fellow for his own fault. Catesby assures me in writing that the first he ever heard of that TNT was when you ordered him arrested after discovery of the loss. His word goes, as far as I'm concerned. If you want me to help you, find another goat than Catesby. That's my answer."

There followed quite a long pause. Perhaps Brigadier-General Jenkins was wondering what chance he would stand in a show-down. Whoever had heard the mess and canteen gossip knew that Jenkins' career had been one long string of miracles by which he had attained promotion without in any way deserving it, and a parallel series of even greater ones by which he had saved himself from ruin by contriving to blame some one else.

"You want me to white-wash Catesby?" he said at last. "If you pounce quickly on the TNT, no one need know it was lost."

"If you court-martial Catesby, the public shall know who lost it, and who didn't, even if it costs me my commission!"

"Blast you! Insubordination!"

"Is your car outside?" Grim answered. "Why don't you drive me up to the Administrator and charge me with it?"

12   Railway Traffic Officer.

"Don't be an idiot! I came to you to avoid a scandal. If this news gets out there'll be a panic. Things are touchy enough as it is."

"Yes."

"Well — if I drop the charge against Catesby —?"

"Then I shall not have to fight for him."

"I'll see what I can do."

"Be definite!"

"Damn and blast you! All right, I'll clear Catesby."

In that ominous minute, like the devil in an old-time drama, Suliman knocked at the door leading from the outer hall. Grim opened it, and I heard the boy's voice piping up in Arabic. The Administrator was in his car outside, waiting to know whether Major Grim was indoors.

"Where's your car?" I heard Grim ask.

"I sent the man to get a tire changed," Jenkins answered.

"Then Sir Louis needn't know you're here. Do you want to see him?"

"Of course not."

"You can get behind that screen if you like."

I thought Jenkins would explode when he found me sitting there. He was a big, florid-faced man with a black moustache waxed into points, and a neck the color of rare roast beef — a man not given to self-restraint in any shape or form. But he had to make a quick decision. Sir Louis' footsteps were approaching. He glared at me, made a sign to me to sit still, twisted his moustache savagely, and listened, breathing through his mouth to avoid the tell-tale whistle of his hairy nostrils. I heard Grim start toward the hall, but Sir Louis turned him back and came straight in.

"It occurred to me I'd save you the time of coming up to see me this morning, Grim, and look in on you instead before I start my rounds. Any new developments?"

"Not yet, sir. I'll need forty-eight hours. If we move too fast they may touch the stuff off before we get the whole gang in the net."

"You're sure you'd rather not have the police?"

"Quite. They mean well, but they're clumsy."

"Um-m-m! All the same, the thing's ticklish. There are rumours about all ready. The Grand Mufti[13] came to me before breakfast with a wild tale. I've promised him some Sikhs for special sentry duty. He'd hardly gone before some Zionists came with a story that the Arabs are planning to blow up their hospital; I gave them ten men and an officer."

"Is the city quiet?" Grim asked him.

"Fair to middling. The Jews refused to take their shutters down this morning. I had to issue an order about it. I hear now that they're doing business about as usual, but I've ordered the number of men on duty within the city walls to be doubled. At the first sign of disturbance I shall have the gates closed. Are you quite sure you're in touch?"

"Quite. sure, sir. I'm positive of what I told you last night. Will you be seeing Colonel Goodenough?"

"Yes, in ten minutes."

"Please ask him to hold his Sikhs at my disposal for the next two days. You might add, sir, that if he cares to see sport he could do worse than lend his own services."

"I'll do that. You can count on Goodenough. That's a soldier devoid of nonsense. Anything else?"

"That's all."

"Keep me informed. Remember, Grim, I'm responsible for all you do. I've endorsed you in blank, as it were. Don't overlook that point."

"I won't, sir."

Sir Louis walked out. Almost before his spurs ceased jingling in the tiled hall, Brigadier-General Jenkins strode out in a towering rage from behind the screen.

"'Pon my soul, a spy's trick!" he exploded. "Had an eavesdropper, did you? Listening from behind a screen while you tricked me into a promise on Catesby's account!"

"Sure," Grim answered, folding the screen back, and letting his face wrinkle in smiles all the way up to the roots of his hair.

13   The religious head of the Moslem community.

Very comical he looked, for his eyebrows were only partly sprouted again. "Had two of you to listen in on the Administrator!"

"Endorses you in blank, eh? How long would he let the endorsement stand if he knew I was behind that screen while he was talking to you?"

"Try him!" Grim suggested. "Shall I call him back? He doesn't want to break you — told me so, in fact, last night — but he could change his mind, I daresay. My tip to you is to get back to Ludd as fast as your car can take you, release Catesby, and say as little as possible to any one!"

"Damn you for a Yankee!" Jenkins answered. "You've got me cornered for the moment, and you make the most of it. But wait till my turn comes! As for you, sir," Jenkins turned and looked me up and down with all the arrogance that nice new crossed swords on his shoulder can give a certain sort of man, "don't let me catch you trying to interfere in any Administration business, that's all!"

I offered him a cigarette, grinning. There was no sense in picking a quarrel. No man likes to discover that a perfect stranger has overheard his intimate confessions. His annoyance was understandable. But he hadn't nice manners. He knocked the cigarette case out of my hand and kicked it across the room. So I got into one of the deep armchairs and laughed at him in self-defense, to preserve my own temper from boiling up over the top.

"To hell with both of you!" Jenkins thundered, and strode out like Mars on the war-path.

"Poor old Jinks!" said Grim, as soon as he had gone. "As Sir Louis said last night, he has a wife and family besides the unofficial ladies on his string. All they'll have to divide between them soon, at the rate he's going, will be his half pay. He has fought for promotion all his days, to keep abreast of expenses. What that string of cormorants will do with his four hundred pounds a year, when he oversteps at last and gets retired, beggars imagination! However, let's get busy."

Business consisted in dressing me up as an Arab with the aid of Suliman, and drilling me painstakingly for half an hour, both of them using every trick they knew to make me laugh or show surprise, and Grim nodding approval each time I contrived not to. More difficult than acting deaf and dumb was the trick of squatting with my legs crossed, but I had learned it after a fashion in India years ago, and only needed schooling.

"You'll get scuppered if you're caught," he warned me. "If Suliman wasn't so scared of devils I wouldn't risk it, but I must have somebody to keep an eye on him when the time comes; that'll be tomorrow, I think."

"Suppose you tell me the object of the game," I suggested. "I'm sick of only studying the rules."

"Well — your part will be to sit over those two tons of TNT and see that nobody explodes them ahead of time. There's a conspiracy on foot to blow up the Dome of the Rock."

"You mean the Mosque of Omar?"

"The place tourists call the Mosque of Omar. The site of Solomon's Temple — the Rock of Abraham — the threshing-floor of Araunah the Jebusite. Next after the shrine at Mecca it's the most sacred spot in the whole Mahommedan world."

"Good lord!" I said. "Are the Zionists so reckless?"

"No, the Arabs are. Remember what old Scharnhoff said the other day about the new fanaticism?"

"Is Scharnhoff mixed up in it?"

"He's being watched. If the Arabs pull it off, they'll accuse the Jews of doing it, and set to work to butcher every Jew in the Near East. That will oblige the British to protect the Jews. That in turn will set every Mohammedan in the world — 'specially Indians, but Egyptians, too — against the British. Jihad — green banner — holy war — all the East and Northern Africa alight while the French snaffle Syria. Sound good to you?"

"Sir Louis knows this?"

"He is paid to know things."

"And he lets you play cat and mouse with it?"

"Got to be careful. Suppose we draw the net too soon, what then? Most of the conspirators escape. The story leaks out. The Jews get the blame for the attempt, and sooner or later the massacre begins anyhow. What we've got to do is bag every last mother's son of them, and suppress the whole story — return the

TNT to store, and swear it was never missing."

"The Administrator has his nerve," I said.

"You'll need yours, too, before this game's played," Grim answered. "D'you see now why I picked on you for an accomplice?"

"I do not."

"You're the one man in Jerusalem whom nobody will suspect, or be on the look-out for. The men we're up against are the shrewdest rats in Palestine. They've got a list of British officers, my name included, of course. They'll know which men are assigned to special duty, and they'll keep every one of us shadowed."

"Won't that — I mean, how can you work if you're shadowed?"

"Me? I shall catch my spur in the carpet, fall downstairs and break a leg at ten-fifteen. At ten-thirty the doctor comes, and finds me too badly hurt to be moved. He sends word of it to Sir Louis by an orderly who can be trusted to talk to any one he meets on the way. I leave by the back way at ten forty-five. However, here's a chance for you to practise deaf-and-dumb drill. There's some one coming. Squat down in that corner. Look meek and miserable. That's the stuff. Answer the door, Suliman."

CHAPTER THIRTEEN

"You may now be unsafe and an outlaw and enjoy yourself!"

The man who entered was a short, middle-aged Jew of the type that writes political reviews for magazines — black morning coat, straw hat, gold pince-nez — a neatly trimmed dark beard beginning to turn gray from intense mental emotion — nearly bald — a manner of conceding the conventions rather than argue the point, without admitting any necessity for them — a thin-lipped smile that apologized for smiling in a world so serious and bitter. He wore a U.S.A. ten-dollar gold piece on his watch chain, by way of establishing his nationality.

"Well, Mr. Eisernstein? Trouble again? Sit down and let's hear the worst," said Grim.

Eisernstein remained standing and glanced at me over in the corner.

"I will wait until you are alone."

"Ignore him — deaf and dumb," Grim answered. "Half a minute, though — have you had breakfast?"

"Breakfast! This is no time for eating, Mister — I beg your pardon, Major Grim. I have not slept. I shall not break my fast until my duty is done. If it is true that the Emperor Nero fiddled while Rome burned, then I find him no worse than this Administrator!"

"Has he threatened to crucify you?" Grim asked. "Take a seat, do."

"He may crucify me, and I will thank him, if he will only in return for it pay some attention to the business for which he draws a salary! I drove to Headquarters to see him. He was not there. Nobody would tell me where he is. I drove down again from the Mount of Olives and luckily caught sight of his car in the distance. I contrived to intercept him. I told him there is a plot on foot to massacre every individual of my race in the Near East — a veritable pogrom. He was polite. He seems to think politeness is the Christian quality that covers the multitude of sins. He offered me a cigar!

"I offered him a telegram blank, with which to cable for reenforcements! He said that all rumours in Jerusalem become exaggerated very quickly, and offered me a guard of one soldier to follow me about! I insisted on immediate military precautions on a large scale, failing which I will cable the Foreign Office in London at my own expense. I offered to convince him with particulars about this contemplated pogrom but he said he had an urgent appointment and referred me to you, just as Nero might have referred a question regarding the amphitheatre to one of his subordinates!"

"Pogroms mean nothing in his young life," Grim answered smiling. "I'm here to do the dirty work. Suppose you spill the news."

"You must have heard the news! Yet you ignore it! The Moslems are saying that we Zionists have offered two million pounds, or some such ridiculous sum, for the site of Solomon's Temple. They are spreading the tale broadcast. Their purpose is to stir up fanaticism against us. The ignorant among them set such value on that rock and the mosque their cut-throat ancestors erected on it that Jews are now openly threatened as they pass through the streets. Yet there is not one word of truth in the story of our having made any such offer."

"There are plenty of troops," said Grim. "Any attempt at violence could be handled instantly."

"Then you will do nothing?"

"What do you suggest ought to be done?"

"Here is a list. Read it. Those are the names of fifty Arabs who are active in spreading anti-Zionist propaganda."

Grim read the list carefully.

"All talkers," he said. "Not a really dangerous man among them."

"Ah! There you are! I might have expected it!" Eisernstein threw up his hands in a gesture of contempt rather than despair. "Nobody cares what happens to Jews. Nobody cares for our sleepless agony of mind. Nobody cares how or what we suffer until afterward, when there will be polite expressions of regret, which the survivors will assess at a true valuation! It is the same wherever we turn. Last night — at half past one in the morning — a committee of us, every one American, called at the American consulate to tell our consul of our danger. The consul was unsympathetic in the last degree. Yet our coreligionists in the States are taxed to pay his salary. He said it was not his business. He referred us to the Administrator. The Administrator refers me to you. To whom do you refer me? To the devil, I suppose!"

"The best thing you can do," said Grim, "is to go ahead and deny that story about the offer to buy the Dome of the Rock. You Zionists have got the most efficient publicity bureau on earth. You can reach the public ear any time you want to. Deny the story, and keep on denying it."

"Ah! Who will believe us? To be a Zionist is to be a person about whom anybody will believe anything; and the more absurd the lie, the more readily it will be believed! Meanwhile, the Moslems are sharpening their swords against us from one end of this land to the other!"

I suppose that what Eisernstein really needed more than anything was sympathy, not good advice. Grim's deliberate coolness only irritated the passion of a man, whose whole genius and energy were bent on realizing the vision of a nation of Jews firmly established in their ancient home. A people that has been tortured in turn by all the governments can hardly be expected to produce un-nervous politicians. He was at the mercy of emotions, obsessed by one paramount idea. A little praise just then of his loyalty to an ideal, to which he had sacrificed time, means, health, energy, everything, would have soothed him and hurt nobody. But the acidity of his scorn had bitten beneath the surface of Grim's good humor.

"There'll be no pogrom," Grim said, getting up and lighting a cigarette. "There'll be nothing resembling one. But that won't be the fault of you Zionists. You accuse without rime or reason, but you yell for help the minute you're accused yourselves. I don't blame the Arabs for not liking you. Nobody expects Arabs to enjoy having their home invaded by an organization of foreigners. Yet if this Administration lifts a finger to make things easier for the Arabs you howl that it's unfair.

"If the Administrator refuses to arrest Arabs for talking a little wildly, you call him a Nero. I'm neither pro- nor anti-Zionist myself. You and the Arabs may play the game out between you for all of me. But I can promise you there'll be no pogrom. It is my business to know just what precautions have been taken."

"Words! Major Grim. Words!" sneered Eisernstein, getting up to go. "What do words amount to, when presently throats are to be cut? If your throat were in danger, I venture to say there would be something doing, instead of mere talk about precautions! I hope you will enjoy your little cigarette," he added bitterly. "Good morning!"

"Talk of fiddling while Rome burns!" Grim laughed as soon as the Zionist had left the room. "Has it ever occurred to you that Nero was possibly smothering his feelings? I wonder how long there'd be one Zionist left out here, if we simply stood aside and looked on. Go and change your clothes, Suliman. It's time I broke a leg."

Grim disappeared upstairs himself, and returned about ten minutes later in the uniform of a Shereefian officer — that is to say, of Emir Feisul's Syrian army. Nothing could be smarter, not anything better calculated to disguise a man. Disguise, as any actor or detective can tell you, is not so much a matter of make-up as suggestion. It is little mannerisms — unstudied habits that identify. The suggestion that you are some one else is the thing to strive for, not the concealment of who you really are.

Grim's skin had been sun-tanned in the Arab campaign under Lawrence against the Turks. The Shereefian helmet is a compromise between the East and West, having a strip of cloth hanging down behind it as far as the shoulders and covering the ears on either side, to take the place of the Arab head-dress. The khaki uniform had just enough of Oriental touch about it to distinguish it from that of a British officer. No man inexperienced in disguise would dream of choosing it; for the simple reason that it would not seem to him disguise enough. Yet Grim now looked so exactly like somebody else that it was hard to believe he was the same man who had been in the room ten minutes before. His mimicry of the Syrian military walk — blended of pride and desire not to seem proud — was perfect.

"I'm now staff-captain Ali Mirza of Feisul's army," he announced. "Ali Mirza a man notorious for his anti-British rancor, but supposed to be down here just now on a diplomatic mission. I've been seen about the streets like this for the last two days. But say: that doctor is a long time on the way."

He went to the telephone, but did not call the hospital; that would have been too direct and possibly too secret.

"Give me Headquarters — yes — who's that? — never mind who's speaking — say: I can't get the military hospital — something wrong with the wire — will you call Major Templeton and say that Major Grim has had an accident — yes, Grim — compound fracture of the thigh — very serious — ask him to go at once to Major Grim's quarters — thanks — that's all." He returned to the fireplace and stood watching me meditatively for several minutes.

"If you deceive Templeton, you'll do," he said at last. "Wait a minute."

He went to the desk and scribbled something in Arabic on a sheet of paper, sealed that in a blank envelope, and handed it to me.

"Hide it. You've two separate and quite distinct tasks, each more important and, in a way, dangerous than the other. The principal danger is to me, not you. If they spot you, my number's as good as hoisted from that minute. You mustn't kid yourself you're safe for one second until the last card has been played."

"Who are 'they'?"

"I'm coming to that. Your first job is to make it possible for me to get the confidence of one or two of these conspirators. You're a deaf-and-dumb man — stone deaf — with a message for staff-captain Ali Mirza, which you will only deliver to him in person. Suliman does the talking. You say nothing. You simply refuse to hand your message over to any one but me. They'll appreciate why a deaf and dumb man should be chosen for treasonable business. But perhaps you're scared — maybe you'd rather reconsider it? It's not too late."

I snorted.

"All right. These conspirators meet at Djemal's coffee shop on David Street. They talk to one another in French, because the proprietor and the other frequenters of the place only know Arabic. You know French and Arabic enough to understand a sentence here and there, so keep your ears wide open. I shan't show up until a Sikh named Narayan Singh tells me that a certain Noureddin Ali is in there. He's the bird I'm after. He's a dirty little murderer, and I'm going to be right pleasant to him.

"You may have to sit in the place all day waiting for me; but wait until after midnight if you must. Sooner or later Noureddin Ali is bound to show up. I shall be hard after him. If they offer you food, take it. Eat with your fingers. Eat like a pig. Lick the plate, if you like. The nearer mad you seem to be, the safer you are. After I get there, hang around until I give you money. Then beat it."

"Where to? I can't go to my room at the hotel in this disguise."

"I've thought of that. You know Cosmopolitan Oil Davey, of course? He lives at the hotel. I'll get word to him that he may expect a messenger from me after dark tonight. He'll leave word with the porter downstairs, who'll take you to Davey's room. You can tell Davey absolutely anything. He's white."

"Well, I think I can execute that maneuver. What's task number two?"

"To sit on the TNT! But one thing at a time is enough. Let's attend to this one first. Ah! Here comes Templeton!"

"Damn you, Grim!" said a calm voice in the doorway. A tall, lean man in major's uniform with the blue tabs of the medical staff strode in. He had the dried-out look of the Sudan, added to the self-reliance that comes of deciding life and death issues at a moment's notice.

"The hospital is crowded with patients, and here you immobilize me for half a morning. I can't pretend to set a compound fracture in ten minutes, you know! Why couldn't you break your neck and have me sign a death certificate?"

"Didn't occur to me," said Grim. "But never mind, doc. You need a rest. Here's tobacco, lots to read, and an armchair. Lock yourself in and be happy."

"Who's this?" asked Templeton, looking down at me.

"Deaf and dumb poor devil, earning a few piastres by

working for the Intelligence."

"Spy, eh? He looks fit for honest work if he had all his faculties. Is he dumb as well as deaf, or because he's deaf?"

"Dunno," said Grim. "He never speaks."

"Perhaps I can do something for him. Suppose you leave him here with me. I can give him a thorough examination instead of wasting my time here."

"He's got a job of work to do right now," said Grim.

"Does he know the sign language? Have you any way of telling him to come and see me at the hospital?"

"I give him written instructions in Arabic."

"That so? I'll look at his ears — tell you in a minute whether it's worth while to come to me."

He took my head between strong, authoritative hands and tilted it sidewise.

"Hello! What's this?"

The Arab head-dress I was wearing shifted and showed non-Arab symptoms.

"Open that bag of mine, will you, Grim, and pass me that big pair of forceps you'll find wrapped in oiled paper on top of everything. There's something I can attend to here at once."

It was an uncomfortable moment. Grim never cracked a smile. He dug out the instrument of torture and gave it to Templeton. But there were two points that occurred to me, in addition to the knowledge that nothing whatever was the matter with my ear. Doctors in good standing, who are usually gentlemen, don't operate without permission; and the forceps were much too big for any such purpose. So I sat still.

"Um-m-m! What he really needs is a red-hot needle run down close to the ear-drum. It wouldn't take five minutes, or hurt him — much. After that I think he'd be able to hear perfectly. Suppose we try."

"I can wait ten minutes yet," Grim answered.

"Very well. I've a platinum needle in the bag. I'll get out the spirit-lamp and we'll soon see. To be candid with you, I don't believe the man's any more deaf than you or I."

"If you run a hot needle through the lobe of his ear we'll find out whether he can really talk or not," said Grim in his pleasantest voice. "If he's shamming I don't mind. What we need in this service is a man who can endure without betraying himself."

"Well, we'll soon see."

I began to hate Grim pretty cordially. I hated him more when Suliman came in, dressed for the street in a rather dirty cotton smock, with a turban in place of his fez. He told the boy to hold the wooden handle of a paper-knife behind my ear to prevent the hot needle from going too far on its sizzling journey. It didn't seem to me the way to reciprocate volunteer secret service. Suliman's grin at the prospect of seeing a man tortured was enough to provoke murder. I brushed the boy aside, fly-fashion, got up, crossed the room, and sat down again in the corner.

"Good enough!" laughed Grim. "You'll do."

"Yes, I think he'll do," agreed Templeton.

But I took no notice. I had seen too many games lost and won with the last card. Templeton looked down at Suliman:

"Tell him the game's over. He may talk now."

"Mafish mukhkh!" [No brains!] the boy answered, grinning and tapping his own forehead. "Magnoon!" [Mad!]

"I think I can trust them both," said Grim, smiling in my direction. "All right, old man; time out! If you'd spoken once there'd have been nothing more between you and a life of safety and respectability!"

"Whereas," said Templeton, "you may now be unsafe and an outlaw and enjoy yourself! Are you sure they haven't marked him?" he asked Grim.

"Sure! Why should they suspect a tourist? But I've taken precautions. Word is on the way to the hotel to forward all his mail to Jaffa until further notice." He laughed at me again. "I hope you're not expecting important letters!"

Suliman had evidently been well schooled in advance, for at a nod from Grim he came over and took my hand, as if I were blind in addition to the other supposed infirmities. He led me out by a back-door, across a yard into an alley, which we followed as far as a main road and then turned toward the Jaffa Gate. Looking back once I saw Grim in his Shereefian uniform striding along behind us; but where the road forked he took the other turning.

There is contentment in walking disguised through crowded streets, even when you are in tow of eight-year-old iniquity that regards you as a lump of baggage to be pushed this and that way. Suliman plainly considered me a rank outsider, only admitted into the game on sufferance. Having said I was "magnoon" he lived up to the assertion, and warned people to make way for me if they did not want to be bitten and go mad, too; so as a general rule I received a pretty wide berth. But it was fun, in spite of Suliman. It was like seeing the world through a peep-hole. Men and women you knew went by without suspecting they were recognized, and in a puzzling sort of way the world, that had been your world yesterday, seemed now to belong wholly to other people, while you lived in a new sphere of your own.

We had to go slowly as we approached the Jaffa Gate, for the crowd was dense there, and a line of Sikhs was drawn across the gap where the street passes through the city wall. It was the gap the Turks once made by tearing down the wall to let the Kaiser through, when he made that famous meek and humble pilgrimage of his. The Sikhs were searching all comers for weapons, and we had to wait our turn.

Outside the gate, on the left-hand as you faced it, was the usual line of boot-blacks — the only cheap thing left in Jerusalem — a motley two dozen of ex-Turkish soldiers, recently fighting the British gamely in the last ditch, and now blacking their boots with equal gusto, for rather higher pay. Some of them still wore Turkish uniforms. Two or three were redheaded and blue-eyed, and almost certainly descended from Scotch crusaders. (The whole wide world bears witness that when the Scots went soldiering they were efficient in more ways than one.)

The rest of the crowd were mainly peasantry with basket-loads of stuff for market; but there was a liberal sprinkling among them of all the odds and ends of the Levant, with a Jew here and there, the inevitable Russian priest, and a dozen odd lots, of as many nationalities, whom it would have been difficult to classify.

And there was Police Constable Bedreddin Shah. You could not have missed noticing him, although I did not learn his name until afterwards. He came swaggering down the Jaffa Road with all the bullying arrogance of the newly enlisted Arab policeman. He shoved me aside, calling me a name that a drunken donkey-driver would hesitate to apply to a dog in the gutter. He was on his way to the lock-up that stands just inside the gate, and I wished him a year in it.

As he plunged into the crowd that checked and surged immediately in front of the line of Sikhs, a small man in Arab costume with the lower part of his face well covered by the kaffiyi,[14] rushed out from the corner behind the bootblacks and drove a long knife home to the hilt between the policeman's shoulder-blades. I wasn't shocked. I wasn't even sorry.

Bedreddin Shah shrieked and fell forward. Blood gushed from the wound. The crowd surged in curiously, and then fell back before the advancing Sikhs. A British officer who had heard the victim's cry came spurring his horse into the crowd from inside the gate. In his effort to get near the victim he only added to the confusion.

The murderer, who seemed in no particular hurry, dodged quietly in and out among the swarm of bewildered peasants, and in thirty seconds had utterly disappeared. A minute later I saw Grim offering his services as interpreter and stooping over the dying man to try to catch the one word he was struggling to repeat.

14   Head-dress that hangs down over the shoulders.

CHAPTER FOURTEEN

"Windy bellies without hearts in them."

Djemal's coffee shop is run by a Turkish gentleman whose real name is Yussuf. One name, and the shorter the better, had been plenty in the days when Djemal Pasha ran Jerusalem with iron ruthlessness, and consequent success of a certain sort. When Djemal was the Turkish Governor, every proprietor of every kind of shop had to stand in the doorway at attention whenever Djemal passed, and woe betide the laggard!

It would not have paid any one, in those days, to name any sort of shop after Djemal Pasha. Even the provider of the rope that throttled the offender would have made no profit, because the rope would simply have been looted from the nearest store. The hangman would have been the nearest soldier, whose pay was already two years in arrears. So Yussuf's own name done in Turkish characters used to stand over the door before the British came.

It was Djemal Pasha's considered judgment that Yussuf cooked the best coffee in Jerusalem. So whenever the despot was in the city he conferred on Yussuf the inestimable privilege of supplying him with coffee at odd moments, under threat of the bastinado if the stuff were not suitably sweet and hot. The only money that ever changed hands in that connection was when the tax-gatherer came down on Yussuf for an extra levy, because of the added trade that conceivably might be expected to accrue through the advertisement obtained by serving such an exalted customer. The tax-gatherer also threatened the bastinado; and as the man who likes that punishment, or who could soften the heart of a Turkish tax assessor, has yet to be discovered, Yussuf invariably paid.

But when Allenby conquered Palestine between bouts of trying to tame his Australians, and Djemal Pasha scooted hot-foot into exile with a two-hundred-woman harem packed in lorries at his rear, Yussuf remembered that old adage about better late than never. He put Djemal's name on the stone arch of the narrow door near the foot of David Street. He did it partly out of the disrespect that a small dog feels for a big one that is now on chain; but he was not overlooking the business value of it.

The first result was that he did quite a lot of trade with British officers, who came primarily because they were sick of eating sand and bully-beef, and drinking sand and tepid water in the desert. Later they flocked there by way of paying indirect homage to a governor who, whatever his obvious demerits, had at any rate never been answered back or thwarted with impunity. (There was a time, after the capture of Jerusalem, when if the British army could have voted on it, Djemal Pasha would have been brought back and given a free hand.)

But the officers began to discover that Yussuf was charging them four or five times the proper price. The seniors objected promptly, and deserted, to the inexpressible delight of the subalterns; but even the under-paid extravagant youths grew tired of extortion after a month or two, and Yussuf had to look elsewhere for customers.

Yussuf did some thinking behind that genial Turkish mask of his. Competition was keen. There are more coffee shops in Jerusalem than hairs on a hog's back, and the situation, down near the bottom of that narrow thoroughfare in the shadow of an ancient arch, did not lend itself to drawing crowds.

But there were others in Jerusalem besides the British officers who yearned for Djemal's rule again; and, unlike the irreverent men in khaki, they did not dare to voice their feelings in public. All the old political grafters, and all the would-be new ones savagely resented a regime under which bribery was not permitted; and, as always happens sooner or later, they began to show a tendency to meet in certain places, where they might talk violence without risk of incurring it.

So Yussuf permitted a rumour to gain ground that he, too, was a malcontent and that the British had deserted his coffee shop for that reason. He gave out that Djemal Pasha's name over the door stood for reaction and political intrigue. So his place began to be frequented by effendis in tarboosh and semi-European clothes, who could chew the cud of bitterness aloud between walls that the crusaders had built four feet thick. The only entrance was through the narrow front door, where Yussuf inspected every visitor before admitting him.

So Yussuf's "Cafe Djemal Pasha" was the place to go to for politics, of the red-hot, death-and-dynamite order that would make Lenin and Trotsky sound like small-town sports. But first you had to get by Yussuf at the door.

Suliman led me by the hand down David Street, through the smelly-yelly moil of flies and barter, past the meat and vegetable stalls, beneath the crusader arches from which Jewish women peered through trellised windows, across three transversing lanes of the ancient suk,[15] and halted at Yussuf's door.

He rapped on it three times. When Yussuf's wrinkled face appeared at last Suliman demanded to see Staff-Captain Ali Mirza. Yussuf's blood-shot eyes peered at me for a long time before he asked a question.

"Atrash! — akras! — majnoon!!" [Deaf! — dumb! — mad!!] said Suliman. Describing me as mad seemed to give him particular delight. He never overlooked a chance of doing it.

"Staff-Captain Ali Mirza is not here. What should a madman want with him?"

"He is not very mad — only stupid. He carries a message for the captain."

"But the captain is not here. He has not been here."

"He will come."

"How should a deaf-and-dumb man deliver a message?"

"It is in writing."

"Very well. He may leave the writing with me. If the captain comes I will deliver it."

"No. The message is from Esh-Sham (Damascus). He will give it only into the captain's own hand."

"What is your name?"

"Suliman."

"What is his?"

"God knows! He came with another man by train; and the

15   Bazaar

other man, who is much more mad than this one, gave me five piastres to bring this one to your kahwi!" [Coffee-pot]

Yussuf shut the door, and discussed the proposition with his customers. At the end of two or three minutes his head appeared again.

"You say Staff-Captain Ali Mirza is expected here?"

"So said the man at the station."

"What do you know of Staff-Captain Ali Mirza?"

"Nothing."

Once more the door closed and I could hear the murmur of voices inside — but only a confused murmur, for the door was thick. When it opened again two other heads were peering from behind Yussuf's.

"Has he money?" he asked.

"Kif? Ma indi khabar!" [How should I know?]

Yussuf opened the door wide and made a sign for me to enter. He seemed in two minds whether to let Suliman come in with me or not, but finally admitted him with a gruff admonition to keep still in one place and not talk.

The place was fairly full. It was a square room, with one window high in the wall on David Street. Around three sides, including that on which was the front door, ran a wooden seat furnished with thin cushions. Facing the front door was another one leading to a dark hole in the rear, where pots were washed and rice was boiled; beside that door, occupying most of the length of the fourth wall, was a thing like an altar of dressed stone, on which the coffee was prepared in dozens of little copper pots.

The benches being pretty well occupied, I was about to squat down on the floor, but they made room for me close to the front door, so I squatted on the corner of the bench and tucked my legs under me. Suliman dropped down on the floor in front of me with his head about level with my knees.

The other occupants of the room were all Syrian Arabs — not a Bedouin among them. All of them wore more or less European clothing, with the inevitable tarboosh, each set at a different angle. You can guess the mentality of the Syrian by the angle of that red Islamic symbol he wears on his head. The black tassel normally hangs behind, and the steady-going conservatives and all who take their religion seriously, wear the inverted flower-pot-shaped affair as nearly straight up as the cranium permits.

But once let a Syrian take up new politics, join the Young Turk Party, forswear religion, or grow cynical about accepted doctrine, and the angle of his tarboosh shows it, just as surely as the angle of the London Cockney's "bowler" betrays irreverence and the New York gangster's "lid" expresses self-contempt disguised as self-esteem.

The head-gears were set at every possible angle in that coffee-shop of Yussuf's, from the backward tilt of the breezy optimist to the far-forward thrust down over the eye of malignant cynicism, which usually went with folded arms, legs thrust out straight, and heels together on the floor.

Yussuf brought me coffee without waiting to be asked. I paid him a half piastre for it, which is half the proper price, and utterly ignored his expostulation. He touched me on the shoulder, displayed the coin in the palm of his hand and went through a prodigious pantomime. I did not even try to appear interested. He ordered Suliman to explain to me.

"Mafish mukhkh!" said the boy, touching his own forehead.

My real motive was to act as differently as possible from the white man, who always pays twice what he should. By establishing the suggestion of accustomed meanness, I hoped to offset any breaks I might make presently. Spies, and people of that kind, usually have plenty of money for their needs, so that by acting the part of a man unused to spending except in minute driblets I stood a better chance of not being detected.

But I was in luck. I have often noticed, so that it has become almost an article of creed with me, that luck invariably breaks that way. It almost never turns up blind. You sit down and wait for luck, and it all goes to the other fellow. But start to use your wits, even clumsily, and the luck comes along and squanders itself on you.

"He is certainly from Damascus," laughed one of the customers. "The price is a half piastre in Damascus at the meaner shops."

I did not know anything about Damascus then — had never

been there; but from that minute it never entered the mind of one of those men to doubt that Damascus was my home-city, so easily satisfied by trifling suggestions is the unscientific human. Yussuf went back to his charcoal stove grumbling to himself in Turkish.

But there was still one question in doubt. They seemed satisfied that I was really deaf and dumb, but in that land of countless mission schools and alien speech there is always a chance that even children know a word or two of French. They tested Suliman with simple questions, such as who was his mother and where was he born; but he did not need to act that part, he was utterly ignorant of French.

So they proceeded to ignore the two of us and turn their political acrimony loose in French, discussing the maddest, most unmoral schemes with the gusto of small boys playing pirates. There seemed to be almost as many rival political parties as men in the room. The only approach to unity was when they agreed to accuse and destroy. As for constructive agreement, they had none, and every one's suggestion for improvement was sneered at by all the rest. They were not even agreed about the Zionists, except hating them; they quarreled about what would be the best way to take advantage of them before wiping them out of existence.

But they all saw exquisite humour in the item of news that Eisernstein had taken so to heart.

"That was Noureddin Ali's idea! He is a genius! To accuse the Zionists of offering two million pounds for the Dome of the Rock — ah! who else could have thought of it! The story has spread all through Jerusalem, and is on its way to the villages. In two days it will be common gossip from Damascus to Beersheba. In a week it will be known from end to end of Egypt; then Arabia; then India! Ho! When the Indian Moslems get the news — the Indian troops in Palestine will send it by mail — then what a furor! Then what anger! That was finesse! That was true statesmanship! Never was a shrewder genius than Noureddin Ali!"

"Don't shout his name too loud," said somebody. "The Administration suspects him already."

"Bah! Who in this room is a friend of the Administration?

The Administrator is a broken shard; the British will summon him home for inefficiency. Besides, there is only one man in Jerusalem of whom Noureddin is in the least afraid — that Major Grim, the American. And whoever would give the price of a cup of coffee for a lease of the life of Major Grim in the circumstances would do better to toss the money to the first beggar he meets!"

"Hssh!"

"Hah! All the same, I would not choose to be Noureddin's enemy."

"There is another one who will share that opinion — or so I have heard. I was told that Bedreddin Shah, a recent recruit in the police, stumbled by accident on certain evidence and demanded a huge sum for silence. Hee-hee! How much will anybody give Bedreddin Shah for his prospect?"

"Hssh!"

"What did Bedreddin Shah discover?"

"Nobody knows."

"You mean nobody will tell."

"The same thing."

"How long could a secret be kept in Jerusalem, if you people were informed of what is going on? You are good for propaganda, that is all! You can talk — Allah! how you all talk! But as for doing anything, or keeping a secret until a thing is done, you are no better than magpies."

The last speaker was a rather fat man, over in the corner by the scullery door. He had a nose like Sultan Abdul Hamid's and large, elongated eyes that looked capable of seeing things on either side of him while he stared straight forward. Even in that dark corner you could see they had the alligator-hue that one associates with cruelty. He had the massive shoulders and forward-stooping position as he sat cross-legged on the seat that suggest deliberate purpose devoid of hurry.

They all resented what he said, but none seemed disposed to quarrel with him. One or two remonstrated mildly, but he ignored their remarks, busying himself with digging out a cigarette from a gold case set with jewels; after he had lighted it very thoughtfully and examined the end once or twice to make sure that it burned just right, he let it hang between his lips in a way that accentuated the angle of his bulbous nose. You wondered whether he owned a harem, and what the ladies thought of him.

"Will you sit and brag in here all day?" he asked after a few minutes. "Yussuf must be getting rich, you sip so much coffee. It is not particularly good for Yussuf to get rich; it will make him lazy, as most of you are."

The chattering had ceased, although there were several attempts to break that uncomfortable silence with inane remarks. His ravenish, unpleasant voice seemed to act on the company like a chill wind, depriving treason of its warm sociableness but leaving in the sting.

"I said you are good for propaganda," he resumed, tossing away ash with a reflective air. "But even that has no value within four walls. If Noureddin Ali should come and learn from me how much talking has been done in here, and how little done outside, I can imagine he will not be pleased. Are there no other kahawi?[16] Why is that story about the Zionists and their offer to buy the Dome of Rock not being spread diligently? You like the safety of this place with its four thick walls. But I tell you the jackal has to leave his hole to hunt."

They did not like taking orders, even when they were expressed more or less indirectly; no follower of the new political freedom does like it, for it rather upsets the new conceit. But he evidently knew his politicians, and they him. They got up one by one and made for the door, each offering a different excuse designed to cover up obedience under a cloak of snappy independence. Not one of them drew a retort from him, or as much as a farewell nod.

When the last one was gone, and the process took up all of half an hour, he sat and looked down his nose at me for several minutes without speaking. You could have guessed just as easily what an alligator was thinking about, and I tried to emulate him, pretending to go off into the brown study that the Turks call kaif, out of which it is considered bad manners to disturb your best

16   Coffee-shops

friend, let alone a stranger. But manners proved to be no barrier in his case.

He began talking to me in Arabic — directly at me, slowly and deliberately, but I did not understand very much of it and it was not difficult to pretend I did not hear. However, Suliman was in different case; the boy began to get very restless under the monolog, and I tugged at his back hair more than once to remind him of the part he had to play.

Discovering that the Arabic took no effect on me, the alligator person changed to French.

"They speak French in Damascus. I know you are not deaf. You are a spy. I know your name. I know what your business was before you came here. I know why you want to see the staff-captain. You have a letter for him; I know what is in it. No use trying to deceive me; I have ways of my own of discovering things. Do you know what happens to spies who refuse to answer my questions? They are attended to. Quite simple. They receive attention. Nobody hears of them again.

"There are drains in Jerusalem — big, dark, smelly, ancient, full of rats — very useful drains. You think the Staff-Captain Ali Mirza will protect you. At a word from me he will make the request that you receive immediate attention. You will disappear down a drain, where even Allah will forget that you ever existed. Staff-Captain Ali Mirza is my old friend. Better let me see that letter."

I felt like laughing at the drain threats although Suliman was still shivering from the effect of the earlier Arabic version. But the statement that he knew the real Ali Mirza might be true, in which case Grim's disguise was not going to last long. However, the fact that he had not yet seen through my disguise was some comfort. The wish being father of the thought, I decided he was bluffing first and last. But he had not finished yet. He tried me in English.

"The captain will give that letter to me in any case. It is intended for me. I have other business now, and wish to save time, so give it to me at once. Here, I will give you ten piastres for it."

He pulled out a purse and unfolded a ten-piastre note. I took no notice. He shook it for me to see, and I awoke like a pelican at the sight of fish.

"Yours for that letter," he said, shaking it again.

I nudged Suliman and nodded to him. He crossed the room, seized the ten-piastre note, and brought it back to me. I stowed it away under my shirt.

"Come, now give me the letter."

I took utterly no notice, so he turned his attention to Suliman again, and resumed in Arabic.

"Feel in his pocket and find the letter."

"I'm afraid," the boy answered.

"Of what? Of him? I will protect you. Take the letter from him."

Suliman chose to play the small boy, as he could very well indeed when nothing could be gained by being devilish and ultra-grown-up. He shook his head and grinned sheepishly.

"Has he any weapons?" was the next question.

"Ma indi khabar." [I don't know.]

Evidently assault and battery was to be the next item on the program. He had not the eyes or the general air of a man who will part with ten piastres for nothing. He called to Yussuf, who came hurrying out of the scullery place. They held a whispered conference, and Yussuf nodded; then he came over to the front door and locked it, removing the key.

"Tell him to hand over that letter!" he ordered Suliman.

"Mafish mukhkh!" said the boy, tapping his forehead once more.

Suliman's notion was the right one after all — at any rate the only one available. Old alligator rolled off his perch and started for me. Yussuf timed his own assault to correspond. They would have landed on me simultaneously, if Suliman had not reminded me that madness is a safe passport nearly anywhere in the East.

So I went stark, raving mad that minute. I once spent a night in the room of an epileptic who had delirium tremens, and learned a lot from him; some of it came to mind just when I needed it. If ever a man got ten piastres' worth of unexpected side-show it was that old Syrian with the alligator eyes. By the time I was quite out of breath there wasn't a cushion or a coffee-pot fit for business. Suliman was standing out of reach on the bench in a corner yelling with laughter, while the two men struggled to get through the scullery door, which was too narrow to admit them both at once. I earned that ten piastres. By the same token I did not let the kaffiyi fall off my head and betray my western origin.

Unable to think up any more original motions, and having breath for none, I sat on the floor and spat repeatedly, having seen a madman do that on the Hebron Road and get feared, if not respected for it. There seems to be a theory prevalent in that part of the world that the sputum of a madman is contagious.

But I overdid it. Most amateurs do overdo things.

They got so afraid that they decided to put me out into the street at all costs, where those enemies of society, the police, might demonstrate their ingenuity. Yussuf made a dash for the front door, and I suppose he would have called in help and ended my share in the adventure, if something had not happened.

The "something" was Noureddin Ali very much something in his own opinion.

"Why didn't you open the door sooner?" he demanded. "I have been knocking for two minutes."

He watched Yussuf lock the door again behind him, and then eyed the disheveled room with amused curiosity. He was a rat-faced little man dressed in a black silk jacket, worsted pants and brown boots, with the inevitable tarboosh set at an angle of sheer impudence — a man at least fifty years old by the look of him, but full of that peppery vigor that so often clings to little men in middle life. On the whole he looked more like a school-teacher, or a lawyer than a conspirator; but Yussuf addressed him with great deference as "Noureddin Ali Bey," and even old alligator-eyes became obsequious.

Both Yussuf and the other man began explaining the situation to him in rapid-fire Arabic. I, meanwhile, recovering from the fit as fast as I dared and trying to remember how to do it. Noureddin Ali was plainly for having me thrown out, until they mentioned the name of Staff-Captain Ali Mirza; at that he tried to cross-examine Suliman at great length, but could get nothing out of him. Suliman had evidently overheard Grim talking about Noureddin Ali, and was very much afraid of him.

"All right," Noureddin Ali said at last. "No more business today, Yussuf. Keep the door locked, but admit the captain. We must find out what this message is about."

Yussuf went to tidying up the place, while Noureddin Ali and the alligator person talked excitedly in low tones in the corner near the scullery door. I lay on the floor with one eye open, expecting Grim every minute; but it must have been four in the afternoon before he came, and all that while, with only short intervals for food and coffee, Noureddin Ali and the other man talked steadily, discussing over and over again the details of some plan.

Shortly after midday Suliman began to whimper for food. Yussuf produced a mess of rice and mutton, of which the two Syrians ate enormously before giving any to the boy; then they put what was left in the dish on the floor in front of me, pretty much in the way you feed a dog, and I hate to remember what I did to it. It is enough that I did not overlook Grim's advice to eat like a lunatic, and however suspicious of me Noureddin Ali might otherwise have been he was satisfied at the end of that performance.

Several people tried the door, and some of them made signals on it but Yussuf had a peep-hole where one of the heavy iron nails had been removed, and after a cautious squint through it at each arrival he proceeded to ignore them. One man thundered on the door for several minutes, but was allowed to go away without as much as a word of explanation.

That was the first incident that made me feel quite sure Nourreddin Ali was in fear of the police. All the time the thundering was going on he glanced furtively about him like a rat in a trap. I saw him feel for a weapon under his arm-pit. When the noise ceased and the impatient visitor went away he sighed with relief. The place was certainly a trap; there was no back way out of it.

When Grim came at last he knocked quietly, and waited in silence while Yussuf applied his eye to the nail-hole. When he entered, the only surprising thing about him seemed to me the thinness of his disguise. In the morning, when I had seen him change in ten minutes from West to East, it had seemed perfect; but, having looked for him so long with the Syrian disguise in mind, it seemed impossible now that any one could be deceived by it. He was at no pains to keep the kaffiyi thing close to his face, and I held my breath, expecting to see Noureddin Ali denounce him instantly.

But nothing of that sort happened. Grim sat down, thrust his legs out in front of him, leaned back and called for coffee. It was obvious at once that the alligator person had been lying when he boasted of knowing Staff-Captain Ali Mirza, for he made no effort to claim acquaintance or to denounce him as an impostor. But he nodded to Suliman, and Suliman came over and nudged me.

I let the boy go through a lot of pantomimic argument before admitting that I understood, but finally I crossed the room to Grim and offered him the envelope. He looked surprised, examined the outside curiously, spoke to me, shrugged his shoulders when I did not answer, tossed a question or two to Suliman, shrugged again and tore the letter open. Then his face changed, and he glanced to right and left of him as if afraid of being seen. He stuffed the letter into his tunic pocket and I went back to the corner by the front door.

Yussuf was pottering about, still rearranging all the pots and furniture that I had scattered, but his big ears projected sidewise and suggested that he might have another motive. However, it was a simple matter to evade his curiosity by talking French, and Noureddin All could contain himself no longer.

"Pardon me, sir? Staff-Captain Ali Mirza?"

Grim nodded suspiciously.

"I have heard of you. We have all heard of you. We are proud to see you in Jerusalem. We wish all success to your efforts on behalf of Mustapha Kemal, the great Turkish Nationalist leader. Our prayer is that he may light such a fire in Anatolia as shall spread in one vast conflagration throughout the East!"

"Who are you?" asked Grim suspiciously. (Evidently the real Ali Mirza had a reputation for gruff manners.)

"Noureddin Ali Bey. It may be you have heard of me. I am

not without friends in Damascus."

"Oh, are you Noureddin Ali?" Grim's attitude thawed appreciably. "We have been looking for more action and less talk from you. I made an excuse to visit Jerusalem and discover how much fire there is under this smoke of boasting."

"Fire! Ha-ha! That is the right word! There is a camouflage of talk, but under it — Aha! You shall see!"

"Or is that more talk?"

"We are not all talkers. Wait and see!"

"Oh, more waiting? Has Mustapha Kemal Pasha waited in Anatolia? Has he not set you all an example of deeds without words? Am I to wait here indefinitely in Jerusalem to take him news of deeds that will never happen?"

"Not indefinitely, my dear captain! And this time there will really be a deed that will please even such a rigorous lover of action as Mustapha Kemal!"

Grim shrugged his shoulders again.

"I leave for Damascus at dawn," he said cynically. "I don't care to be mocked there for bringing news of promises. We have had too many of those barren mares. I shall say that I have found everything here is sterile — the talk abortive — the men mere windy bellies without hearts in them!"

CHAPTER FIFTEEN

"I'll have nothing to do with it!"

Noureddin Ali was pained and upset. Grim had pricked his conceit — had sent thrust home where he kept his susceptibilities. He blinked, peered this and that way, exchanged glances with the alligator person, and then tucked his legs up under him.

"In me you see a doer!" he announced. He looked the part. His lean, pointed nose and beady little eyes were of the interfering, meddling type. You could not imagine him, like the yellow-eyed ruminant next to him, sitting and waiting ruthlessly for things to happen. Noureddin Ali looked more likely to go out and be ruthless.

"So they all say!" Grim retorted.

"Some one should forewarn them in Damascus what a deed will occur here presently. Above all, word should reach Mustapha Kemal, in Anatolia, as soon as possible, so that he may be ready to act."

"All day long," said Grim, "I have wandered about Jerusalem, listening to this and that rumour of something that may happen. But I have not found one man who can tell me a fact."

"That is because you did not meet me. I am — hee-hee! I am the father of facts. You say you leave for Damascus at dawn? You are positive? I could tell you facts that would put a sudden end to my career if they were spread about Jerusalem!"

"That is the usual boast of men who desire credit in the eyes of the Nationalist Party," Grim retorted.

"I see you are skeptical. That is a wise man's attitude, but I must be cautious, for my life is at stake. Now — how do you propose to leave Jerusalem? There is no train for Damascus at dawn tomorrow."

"I am on a diplomatic mission," answered Grim. "The Administration have placed a car at my disposal to take me as far as the border."

"Ah! And tonight? Where will you be tonight?"

"Why?"

"Because I propose to make a disclosure. And — ah — hee-hee! — you would like to live, I take it, and not be sent back to Damascus in a coffin? I have — ah — some assistants who — hee-hee! — would watch your movements. If you were to betray me afterwards to the Administration, there would remain at least — the satisfaction — of — you understand me? — the certainty that you would suffer for it!"

Grim laughed dryly.

"I shall be at the hotel," he answered. "In bed. Asleep. The car comes before dawn."

"That is sufficient. I shall know how to take essential precautions. Now — you think I am a man of words, not deeds? You were near the Jaffa Gate this morning, for I saw you there. You saw a man killed — a policeman, name Bedreddin. That was an unwise underling, who stumbled by accident on a clue to what I shall tell you presently. He had the impudence to try to blackmail me — me, of all people! You saw him killed. But did you see who killed him? I — I killed him, with this right hand! You do not believe? You think, perhaps, I lack the strength for such a blow? Look here, where the force of it broke my skin on the handle of the knife! Now, am I a man of words, not deeds?"

"You want me to report to Mustapha Kemal that all the accomplishment in Jerusalem amounts to one policeman killed?"

"No, no! You mistake my meaning. My point is that having proved to you I am a ruthless man of action, I am entitled to be believed when I tell you what next I intend to do."

"Well — I listen."

"There is going to be — hee-hee! — an explosion!"

"Where? When? Of what?"

"In Jerusalem, within a day or two, and of what? Why, of high explosive, what else?"

"Much good an explosion in this city will do Mustapha Kemal!" Grim grumbled. "You may kill a few beggars and break some windows. The British will double the guards afterward at all the city gates, and that will be the end of it; except that some of you, who perhaps may escape being thrown into jail, will apply to Mustapha Kemal for high commissions in his army on the strength of it! Great doings! Mustapha Kemal will have me bastinadoed."

"Hee-hee! You are going to be surprised. What would you say to an explosion, for instance, that destroyed the Dome of the Rock?"

"That might accomplish results."

"Hee-hee! You admit it! An explosion to be blamed on the Zionists, who must afterward be protected by the British from the mob! Would that not set India on fire?"

"It might help. But who is to do it?"

"You see the doer before you! I will do it."

"If I thought such a thing was really going to take place —"

"You would think that news worth carrying, eh? You would hurry to Damascus, wouldn't you? And let me assure you, my dear captain, speed is essential. There are reasons why the explosion has not yet occurred — reasons of detail and difficulties to be overcome. But now there is little further prospect of delay. Everything is nearly ready. The explosive is not yet in place, but is at hand. The authorities suspect nothing. There remains only a little excavation work, and then — hee-hee! — nothing to do but choose the hour when hundreds are in the mosque. Houp-la! Up she goes. Does not the idea appeal to you?"

"Sensational — very," Grim admitted.

"Ah! But the utmost must be made of the sensation. Men must be ready in Damascus to stir public feeling on the strength of it. Word must go to Mustapha Kemal to strike hard while the iron is hot. There must be reprisals everywhere. Blood must flow.

"The Europeans, French as well as British, must be goaded into making rash mistakes that will further inflame the populace. It must be shouted from the house-tops that the Jews have blown up a Moslem sacred place, and that the British are protecting them. There must be a true jihad[17] proclaimed against all non-Moslems almost simultaneously everywhere. Do you understand now how swiftly you must travel to Damascus?"

17   Holy war.

Grim nodded. "Yet these foreigners are cunning," he said doubtfully. "Are you sure your plan is not suspected?"

"Quite sure. There was one man — a cursed interfering jackanapes of an American, whom they all call Jimgrim, of whom I was afraid. He is clever. He goes snooping here and there, and knows how to disguise himself. But he fell downstairs this morning and broke his thigh in two places. If anything could make me religious, that would! If I were not a nationalist, I would say 'Glory to God, and blessed be His Prophet, who has smitten him whom we feared!'"

"That broken leg might be a trick to put you off your guard," Grim suggested pleasantly.

"No. I made secret enquiries. He is in great pain. He may lose the leg. The doctor who has charge of the case is a Major Templeton, an irritable person and, like most of the English, too big a fool to deceive anybody. No, luckily for Mister Jimgrim it is not a trick. Otherwise he would have shared the fate today of Bedreddin Shah the constable. The trap was all ready for him. With the inquisitive and really clever out of the way there is nothing to be feared. Now — pardon me, Captain Ali Mirza, but that letter you received just now; would you like to show it to me?"

"Why?" Grim demanded, frowning, and bridling all over.

"Hee-hee! For the sake of reciprocity. I have told you my secret. If it were not that I am more than usually circumspect, and accustomed to protect myself, one might say that my life is now in your hands, captain. Besides — hee-hee! — I might add that Jerusalem is my particular domain. I would have no difficulty in seeing that letter in any case. But there should be no need for — hee-hee! — shall we call them measures? — between friends."

"I see you are a man of resource," said Grim.

"Of great resource, with picked lieutenants. May I see the letter now?"

Grim produced it. Noureddin Ali took it between spidery fingers and examined it like a schoolmaster conning a boy's composition. But the expression of his face changed as he took in the contents, holding the paper so that alligator-eyes could read it, too.

"Who wrote this?" he asked.

"Can't you read the signature? Enver Eyub."

"Who is he?"

"One of Mustapha Kemal's staff."

"So. 'In pursuing your mission you will also take steps to ascertain whether or not Noureddin Ali Bey is a person worthy of confidence.' Aha! That is excellent! So Mustapha Kemal Pasha has heard of me?"

Grim nodded.

"And the rest of your mission?"

"Is confidential."

"And are you satisfied that I am to be trusted?"

"I think you mean business."

"Then you should tell me what is the nature of your secret mission to Jerusalem. Possibly I can give you needed information. If you have obtained information of value, you should confide in me. I can be most useful when I know most."

Grim frowned. He began to look uneasy. And the more he did that, the more delight Noureddin Ali seemed to take in questioning him, but he pleaded his own case, too.

"The trouble with the Nationalist movement," he insisted, "is lack of unity. There is no mutual confidence — consequently no combination. There are too many intellects working at cross purposes. You should tell me what is being done, so that I may fit in my plans accordingly. When the Dome of the Rock has been blown up there will be ample opportunity for putting into execution a combined plan. You must confide in me."

"Suppose I get rid of that messenger and the boy first," Grim suggested.

Grim felt in his pocket and produced a purse full of bank notes. But they were all big ones.

"Never mind, I have change," said Noureddin Ali. "How much will you give him?"

"No," said Grim. "The boy can take him to the hotel. Let him wait for me there. He has no further business here. He should return to Damascus. He had better travel with me in the car tomorrow morning. Take him to the hotel, and wait for me there, you," he added in Arabic to Suliman.

Yussuf came and opened the door. Suliman took my hand and led me out. The door slammed shut behind me, and a great Sikh, leaning on his rifle at a corner thirty feet away, came to life just sufficiently to follow me up-street with curious brown eyes.

"That is Narayan Singh," announced Suliman when we had passed him. "He is Jimgrim's friend."

There was another Sikh just in sight of him at the next corner, and another beyond him again, all looking rather bored but awfully capable. None except the first one took the slightest notice of us.

It was some consolation to know that "Jimgrim's friend" was on guard outside Yussuf's. I had no means of knowing what weapons Grim carried, if any, but was positive of one thing: if either Noureddin Ali or the man with alligator eyes should get an inkling of his real identity his life would not be worth ten minutes' purchase. Including Yussuf, who would likely do as he was told, there would be three to one between those silent walls, and it seemed to me that Narayan Singh might as well be three miles away as thirty feet. However, there was nothing I could do about it.

It was late afternoon already, and the crowd was swarming all one way, the women carrying the baskets and the men lording it near enough to keep an eye on them. If Suliman and I were followed, whoever had that job had his work cut out, for we were swallowed up in a noisy stream of home-going villagers, whose baskets and other burdens made an effectual screen behind us as well as in front.

The hotel stands close by the Jaffa Gate, and there the crowd was densest, for the outgoing swarm was met by another tide, of city-folk returning. In the mouth of the hotel arcade stood an officer whom I knew well enough by sight — Colonel Goodenough, commander of the Sikhs, a quiet, gray little man with a monocle, and that air of knowing his own mind that is the real key to control of Indian troops. Up a side-street there were a dozen troop-horses standing, and a British subaltern was making himself as inconspicuous as he could in the doorway of a store. It did not need much discernment to judge that those in authority were ready to deal swiftly with any kind of trouble.

But the only glimpse I had of any mob-spirit stirring was when three obvious Zionist Jews were rather roughly hustled by some Hebron men, who pride themselves on their willingness to brawl with any one. Two Sikhs interfered at once, and Goodenough, who was watching, never batted an eyelash.

I was tired, wanted a whiskey and soda and a bath more than anything else I could imagine at the moment. I was eager to get to my room in the hotel. Suliman, being not much more than a baby after all, wanted to go to sleep. We went past Goodenough, who eyed me sharply but took no further notice, and we entered the hotel door. But there we were met by Cerberus in the shape of an Arab porter, who cursed our religion and ordered us out again, threatening violence if we did not make haste.

Suliman argued with him in vain, and even whimpered. There was nothing for it but to return to the arcade, where I sat down on a step, from which a native policeman drove me away officiously. I had about made up my mind to go and speak to Goodenough in English, when Grim appeared. Not even Goodenough recognized him, his Syrian stride was so well acted. He saluted, and the salute was returned punctiliously but with that reserve toward a foreigner that the Englishman puts on unconsciously. When Grim spoke to him in Arabic Goodenough answered in the same language. I did not hear what was said at first, but as I drew closer I heard the sequel, for Grim changed suddenly to English.

"If you can't recognize me through that magnifying-glass of yours, colonel, I must be one leopard who can really change his spots. I'm Grim. Don't change your expression. Quick: look around and tell me if I'm followed."

"Hard to say. Such a crowd here. There's a Syrian over the way with a bulbous nose, who came along after you; he's leaning with his back to the wall now, watching us."

"He's the boy."

"I see Narayan Singh has left his post. Did you give him orders?"

"Yes. Told him to follow any one who followed me. I don't want that fellow interfered with. He may stay there, or more likely he'll call others to take his place; they'll watch all night, if they're allowed to; let them. Wish you'd give orders they're to be left alone. Then, please let Narayan Singh go off duty and get some sleep; I'm going to want him all day tomorrow."

"All right, Grim; anything else?"

"First opportunity, I wish you'd come to Davey's room upstairs. Now — long distance stuff again, sir — if any Syrian asks you about me, you might say I was making sure the car would come for me at dawn."

They exchanged salutes again as one suspicious alien to another. Grim looked suitably surprised at sight of me, and led me and Suliman back to the hotel, where Suliman wanted him to wreak dire vengeance on the porter; he grew sulky when he discovered that his influence with Grim was not sufficient for the purpose, but forgot it, small boy fashion, ten minutes later, when he fell asleep on the floor in a corner of Davey's room.

Davey did not look exactly pleased to see us, although he seemed to like Grim personally, and was the first that day to see through Grim's disguise at the first glance. Mrs. Davey, on the other hand, was radiant with smiles — thrilled at the prospect of learning secrets. She produced drinks and pushed the armchairs up. When she learned who I was, her husband could hardly keep her from putting on a costume too, to make a party of it.

Davey was reserved. He asked no questions. A gray-headed, gray-eyed, stocky, sturdy-looking man, who had made impossibilities come true on three continents, he waited for trouble to come to him instead of seeking it. There was silence for several minutes over the cigars and whiskey before Grim opened fire at last. He talked straight out in front of Mrs. Davey, for she had mothered Cosmopolitan Oil men in a hundred out-of-the-way places. She knew more sacred secrets than the Sphinx.

"Any news about your oil concessions, Davey?"

"No. Not a word. We've got every prospect in the country marked out. Nothing to do now but wait for the mandate, while the Zionists go behind our backs to the Foreign Office and scheme for the concessions. It's my belief the British mean to favor the Zionists and put us in the ditch. The fact that we were first on the ground, and lodged our applications with the Turks before the war seems to make no difference in their lives."

"Well, old man, I've arranged for you to change your policy," said Grim.

"What in thunder do you mean?"

Mrs. Davey giggled with delight, but her husband frowned ominously.

"I'm supposed to be Staff-Captain Ali Mirza of the Shereefian army."

"I've heard of him. He's a bad one, Jim. He is one of those Syrian Arabs who will accept any one's money, but who never stays bought. Why masquerade as a scoundrel?"

"I was in a place just now with a bunch of murderers, who'd have made short work of me if I couldn't give them a sound reason for being in Jerusalem just now."

"Why not have 'em all arrested?"

"For the same reason, Davey, that your Oil Company isn't piping ten thousand barrels a day from Jericho. The time is not yet. Things haven't reached that stage. I told them your Oil Company gave up hope long ago of getting a concession from the British, and has decided to finance Mustapha Kemal."

Davey flung his cigar out of the window, and laid both hands on his knees. His face was a picture of baffled indignation. But his wife laughed.

"They were tickled to death," Grim continued. "I'm supposed to be going to Damascus tomorrow morning with a hundred thousand dollars in U.S. gold, obtained from you in ten small bags. We've got to find some bags and pack them full of something heavy."

"I'll have nothing to do with it!" Davey exploded at last. "It's a damned outrage! Why — this tale will be all over the place. The Jews will get hold of it, and make complaints in London. Next you know, the U.S. State Department will be raising blue hell. Questions asked in Congress. Headlines in all the papers! What do you suppose our people will think of me?"

"Refer them to your wife, Davey. She's got you out of much worse messes."

"I'll drive the car straight up to OETA and lodge my protest against this in less than fifteen minutes!"

"No need; Davey, old man. Goodenough will be in here presently. Kick to him."

Mrs. Davey went into the next room and returned with a roll of coarse cotton cloth.

"I've no bags, Jim, but if this stuff will do I can sew some right now."

"Good enough, Emily, go to it."

"D'you want to lose me my job?" demanded Davey. But his wife took up the scissors and smiled back at him.

"You know better than that. We've trusted Jim before."

"Listen, Davey; this thing's serious," said Grim.

"I know it is! So'm I! Nothing doing!"

"You're on the inside of an official secret."

"Curse all official secrets! My business is oil!"

"There'll be no oil in this man's land for any one for fifty years if you won't play. There'll be a jihad instead. They're planning to blow up the Dome of the Rock."

"Jee-rusalem!"

"Straight goods, Davey. Two tons of TNT stolen, and our friend Scharnhoff, the Austrian, hunting for the Tomb of the Kings — digging for it day and night — conspirators waiting to run in the explosive as soon as the tunnel is complete."

"Why not arrest 'em at once?"

"We want to catch the principals red-handed, explosive and all. We don't know where the explosive is yet. Bag the lot, and kill the story. Otherwise, d'you see what it means, if the news leaks out? They'll blame the attempt on the Jews. And the minute the British protect the Jews there'll be all Moslem Asia on fire. Get me?"

"Get you? Yes, I get you. I'll get hell from the home office, though, for meddling in politics."

Goodenough came in then, rather a different man from the stern little martinet who had stood in the throat of the arcade. He was all smiles.

"Evening, Mrs. Davey," he said genially. "That one man went away, Grim, and three took his place. They shan't be disturbed. Narayan Singh has gone off duty. Now, Mrs. Davey, I've been told that Americans all went dry, on account of a new religion called the Volstead Act. D'you mean to say you'd tempt a thirsty soldier with a dry martini?"

CHAPTER SIXTEEN

"The enemy is nearly always useful if you leave him free to make mistakes."

The next item on the program was to awaken Suliman. He did not want to wake up. He had lost all interest in secret service for the time being. Even the sight of Mrs. Davey's New York candy did not stir enthusiasm; he declared it was stuff fit for bints,[18] not men.

"All right then," Grim announced at last. "School for you, and I'll get another side-partner."

That settled it. The boy, on whose lips the word dog was a foul epithet, was actually proud to share a packing-case bedroom with Julius Caesar the mess bull-dog. School, where there would be other iniquitous small boys to be led into trouble, had no particular terrors. But to lose his job and to see another boy, perhaps a Jew or a Christian, become Jimgrim's Jack-of-all-jobs was outside the pale of inflictions that pride could tolerate.

"I am awake!" he retorted, rubbing his eyes to prove it.

"Come here, then. D'you know where to find your mother?"

"At the place where I went yesterday."

"Take her some of Mrs. Davey's candy. Don't eat it on the way, mind. Get inside the place if you can. If she won't let you in try how much you can see through the door. Ask no questions. If she asks what you've been doing, tell her the truth: say that you cleaned my boots and washed Julius Caesar. Then come back here and tell me all you've seen."

"Sending him to spy on his own mother, Jim?" asked Mrs. Davey as Suliman left the room with candy in both fists. She paused from stitching at the cotton bags to look straight at Grim.

"His mother is old Scharnhoff's housekeeper," Grim answered. "Scharnhoff wouldn't stand for the boy, and drove

18   Women

him out. The mother liked Scharnhoff's flesh-pots better than the prospects of the streets, so she stayed on, swiping stuff from Scharnhoff's larder now and then to slip to the kid through the back door. But he was starving when I found him."

Mrs. Davey laid her sewing down.

"D'you mean to tell me that that old butter-wouldn't-melt-in-his-mouth professor is that child's father?"

"No. The father was a Turkish soldier — went away with the Turkish retreat. If he's alive he's probably with Mustapha Kemal in Anatolia. Old Scharnhoff used to keep a regular harem under the Turks. He got rid of them to save his face when our crowd took Jerusalem. He puts up with one now. But he has the thorough-going Turk's idea of married life."

"And to think I had him here to tea — twice — no, three times! I liked him, too! Found him interesting."

"He is," said Grim.

"Very!" agreed Goodenough.

"If it weren't for that harem habit of his," said Grim, "some acquaintances of his would have blown up the Dome of the Rock about this time tomorrow. As it is, they won't get away with it. Suliman came and told me one day that his mother was carrying food to Scharnhoff, taking it to a little house in a street that runs below the Haram-es-Sheriff. I looked into that. Then came news that two tons of TNT was missing, on top of a request from Scharnhoff for permission to go about at night unquestioned. After that it was only a question of putting two and two together —"

"Plus Narayan Singh," said Goodenough. "I still don't see, Grim, how you arrived at the conclusion that Scharnhoff is not guilty of the main intention. What's to prove that he isn't in the pay of Mustapha Kemal?"

"I'll explain. All Scharnhoff cares about is some manuscripts he thinks he'll find. He thinks he knows where they are. The Chronicles of the Kings of Israel. I expect he tried pretty hard to get the Turks to let him excavate for them. But the Turks knew better than to offend religious prejudices. And perhaps Scharnhoff couldn't afford to bribe heavily enough; his harem very likely kept him rather short of money. Then we come along, and stop all excavation — cancel all permits — refuse to grant new ones.

"Scharnhoff's problem is to dig without calling attention to what he's doing. As a technical enemy alien he can't acquire property, or even rent property without permission. But with the aid of Suliman's mother he made the acquaintance of our friend Noureddin Ali, who has a friend, who in turn has a brother, who owns a little house in that street below the Haram-es-Sheriff."

"Strange coincidence!" said Goodenough. "It'll need a better argument than that to save Scharnhoff's neck."

"Pardon me, sir. No coincidence at all. Remember, Scharnhoff has lived in Jerusalem for fifteen years. He seems to have satisfied himself that the Tomb of the Kings is directly under the Dome of the Rock. How is he to get to it? The Dome of the Rock stands in the middle of that great courtyard, with the buildings of the Haram-es-Sheriff surrounding it on every side, and hardly a stone in the foundations weighing less than ten tons.

"He reasons it out that there must be a tunnel somewhere, leading to the tomb, if it really is under the Dome of the Rock. I have found out that he went to work, while the Turks were still here, to find the mouth of the tunnel. Remember, he's an archae-ologist. There's very little he doesn't know about Jerusalem. He knows who the owner is of every bit of property surrounding the Haram-es-Sheriff; he's made it his business to find out. So when he finally decided that this little stone house stands over the mouth of the tunnel, all that remained to do was to get access to it. He couldn't do that himself, because of the regulations. He had to approach the Arab owner secretly and indirectly. That's where Suliman's mother came in handy.

"She contrived the introduction to Noureddin Ali. Innocent old Scharnhoff, who is an honest thief — he wouldn't steal money — sacrilege is Scharnhoff's passion — was an easy mark for Noureddin Ali. Noureddin Ali is a red-minded devil, so smart at seeing possibilities that he is blind to probabilities. He is paid by the French to make trouble, and he's the world's long-distance double-crosser. I don't believe the French have any hand in this job. Scharnhoff needed explosives. Noureddin Ali saw at once that if that tunnel can be found and opened up there could be an atrocity perpetrated that would produce anarchy all through the East."

"As bad as all that?" asked Mrs. Davey.

"That's no exaggeration," Goodenough answered. "I've lived twenty-five years in India, commanding Sikh and Moslem troops. The Sikhs are not interested in the Moslem religion in any way, but they'd make common cause with Moslems if that place were blown up and the blame could be attached to Jews. It's the second most sacred place in Asia. Even the Hindus would be stirred to their depths by it; they'd feel that their own sacred places were insecure, and that whoever destroyed them would be protected afterwards by us."

"Gosh! Who'd be an Englishman!" laughed Davey.

"I don't see that it's proved yet that the idea of an explosion wasn't Scharnhoff's in the first place," Goodenough objected.

"For one thing, he wouldn't want to destroy antiquities," said Grim. "They're his obsession. He worships ancient history and all its monuments. No, Noureddin Ali thought of the explosion. He knew that Scharnhoff needed money, so he gave him French money, knowing that would put old Scharnhoff completely in his power. Then he tipped off some one down at Ludd to watch for a chance to steal some TNT. He had better luck than he expected. He got two tons of it. He didn't have all the luck, though. His plan, I believe, was to time the fireworks simultaneously with a French-instigated raid from El-Kerak. But the raid didn't come off."

"Scharnhoff will hang!" said Goodenough.

"I think not, sir. He'll prove as meek as an old sheep when we land on him."

"There, will the bags do?" asked Mrs. Davey.

"What are they for?" Goodenough asked.

"We're supposed to have a slush fund in this room of a hundred thousand dollars," Davey answered dourly. "My Oil Company is supposed to be buying up Mustapha Kemal! I see my finish, if news of this ever reaches the States — or unless my version of it gets there first!"

Grim turned to me.

"We've got to find two people to take your place and mine in the car tomorrow morning. Perhaps you'd better go in any case; you'll enjoy the ride as far as Haifa — stay there a day or two, and come back when you feel like it. We'll find some officer to masquerade as me."

But there I rebelled — flat, downright mutiny.

"If I haven't made good so far," I said, "I'll consider myself fired, and hold my tongue. Otherwise, I see this thing through! Send some one else on the joy-ride."

"Good for you!" said Davey.

"Dammit, man!" said Goodenough, staring at me through his monocle. "The rest of us get paid for taking chances. The only tangible reward you can possibly get will be a knife in your back. Better be sensible and take the ride to Haifa."

"My bet is down," said I.

"Good," Grim nodded. "It goes. All the same, you get a joy-ride. Can't take too many chances. Tell you about that later. Meanwhile, will you detail an officer to come and spend the night in this hotel and masquerade as me at dawn, sir? He can wear this uniform that I've got on — somebody about my height."

"Turner will do that. What are you going to put in the bags?" asked Goodenough.

"Cartridges. They're heavy. You might tell Turner over the phone to bring them with him."

At that point Suliman returned, sooner than expected, with news that made Grim whistle. Suliman had not been inside the place where his mother was. She would not let him. But he had seen around her skirts as she stood in the partly opened door.

"There was a hole in the floor," said Suliman, "and a great stone laid beside it. Also much gray dust. And I think there was a light a long way down in the hole."

But that was not what made Grim whistle.

"What else? Did your mother say anything?"

"She was ill-tempered."

"That Scharnhoff had beaten her."

"I knew he'd make a bad break sooner or later. What did he beat her for?"

"Because she was afraid."

"That's a fine reason. Afraid of what?"

"He says she is to sell oranges. Four wooden benches have been brought, and tomorrow they are to be set outside the door in the street. Oranges and raisins have been bought, and she is to sit outside the door and sell them. She is afraid."

"Fruit bought already? Can't be. Was it inside there?"

"No. It is to come tomorrow. She says she does not know how to sell fruit, and is afraid of the police."

Grim and Goodenough exchanged glances.

"She says that if the police come everybody will be killed, and that I am to keep watch in the street in the morning and give warning of the police."

"That should teach you, young man, never to take a woman into your confidence — eh, Mrs. Davey?" said Goodenough.

"We're certainly the slow-witted sex," she answered, piling the finished bags one on top of the other on the table.

Grim took me after that to the hotel roof, whence you can see the whole of Jerusalem. It was just before moonrise. The ancient city lay in shadow, with the Dome of the Rock looming above it, mysterious and silent. Down below us in the street, where a gasoline light threw a greenish-white glare, three Arabs in native costume were squatting with their backs against the low wall facing the hotel.

"Noureddin Ali's men," said Grim, chuckling. "They'll help us to prove our alibi. The enemy is nearly always useful if you leave him free to make mistakes. You may have to spend the whole night in the mosque — you and Suliman. I'll take you there presently. Two of those men are pretty sure to follow us. One will probably follow me back here again. The other will stay to keep an eye on you. About an hour before dawn, in case nothing happens before that, you and Suliman come back here to the hotel. The car shall be here half an hour before daylight. You and Turner pile into it, and those three men watch you drive away. They'll hurry off to tell Noureddin Ali that Staff-Captain Ali Mirza and the deaf-and-dumb man have really started for Damascus, bags of gold and all.

"Turner must remember to drop a couple of bags and pick

them up again, to call attention to them. There'll be a change of clothes in the car for you. When you've gone a mile or so, get into the other clothes and walk back. If I don't meet you by the Jaffa Gate, Suliman will, or else Narayan Singh. Things are liable to happen pretty fast tomorrow morning. Let's go.

"I'm supposed to have found out somehow that you're awful religious and want to pray, so it's the Dome of the Rock for yours. Any Moslem who wants to may sleep there, you know. But any Christian caught kidding them he's a Moslem would be for it — short shrift. He'd be dead before the sheikh of the place could hand him over to the authorities. If the TNT were really in place underneath you, which I'm pretty sure it won't be for a few hours yet, that would be lots safer than the other chance you're taking. So peel your wits. Let Suliman sleep if he wants to, but you'll have to keep awake all night."

"But what am I to do in there? What's likely to happen?"

"Just listen. The tunnel isn't through to the end yet, I'm sure of it. If it were, they'd have taken in the TNT, for it must be ticklish work keeping it hidden elsewhere, with scores of Sikhs watching day and night. But they're very near the end of the tunnel, or they wouldn't be opening up that fruit stand. You'll hear them break through. When you're absolutely sure of that, come out of the mosque and say Atcha — just that one word — to the Sikh sentry you'll see standing under the archway through which we'll enter the courtyard presently. That sentry will be Narayan Singh, and he'll know what to do."

"What shall I do after that?"

"Suit yourself. Either return to the mosque and go to sleep, if you can trust yourself to wake in time, or come and sit on the hotel step until morning. Have you got it all clear? It's a piece of good luck having you to do all this. No real Moslem would ever be able to hold his tongue about it. They're superstitious about the Dome of the Rock. But ask questions now, if you're not clear; you mustn't be seen speaking in the street or in the mosque, remember. All plain sailing? Come along, then. If you're alive tomorrow you'll have had an adventure."

CHAPTER SEVENTEEN

"Poor old Scharnhoff's in the soup."

We ate a scratch dinner with the Daveys in their room and started forth. Grim as usual had his nerve with him. He led me and Suliman straight up to the three spies who were squatting against the wall, and asked whether there were any special regulations that would prevent my being left for the night in the famous mosque. On top of that he asked one of the men to show him the shortest way. So two of them elected to come with us, walking just ahead, and the third man stayed where he was, presumably in case Noureddin Ali should send to make enquiries.

You must walk through Jerusalem by night, with the moon just rising, if you want really to get the glamour of eastern tales and understand how true to life those stories are of old Haroun-al-Raschid. It is almost the only city left with its ancient walls all standing, with its ancient streets intact. At that time, in 1920, there was nothing whatever new to mar the setting. No new buildings. The city was only cleaner than it was under the Turks.

Parts of the narrow thoroughfares are roofed over with vaulted arches. The domed roofs rise in unplanned, beautiful disorder against a sky luminous with jewels. To right and left you can look through key-hole arches down shadowy, narrow ways to carved doors through which Knights Templar used to swagger with gold spurs, and that Saladin's men appropriated after them.

Yellow lamplight, shining from small windows set deep in the massive walls, casts an occasional band of pure gold across the storied gloom. Now and then a man steps out from a doorway, his identity concealed by flowing eastern finery, pauses for a moment in the light to look about him, and disappears into silent mystery.

Half-open doors at intervals give glimpses of white interiors, and of men from a hundred deserts sitting on mats to smoke great water-pipes and talk intrigue. There are smells that are stagnant with the rot of time; other smells pungent with spice, and mystery, and the alluring scent of bales of merchandise that, like the mew of gulls, can set the mind traveling to lands unseen.

Through other arched doors, even at night, there is a glimpse of blindfold camels going round and round in ancient gloom at the oil-press. There are no sounds of revelry. The Arab takes his pleasures stately fashion, and the Jew has learned from history that the safest way to enjoy life is to keep quiet about it. Now and then you can hear an Arab singing a desert song, not very musical but utterly descriptive of the life he leads. We caught the sound of a flute played wistfully in an upper room by some Jew returned from the West to take up anew the thread of ancient history.

Grim nudged me sharply in one shadowy place, where the street went down in twenty-foot-long steps between the high walls of windowless harems. Another narrow street crossed ours thirty feet ahead of us, and our two guides were hurrying, only glancing back at intervals to make sure we had not given them the slip. The cross-street was between us and them, and as Grim nudged me two men — a bulky, bearded big one and one of rather less than middle height, both in Arab dress — passed in front of us. There was no chance of being overheard, and Grim spoke in a low voice:

"Do you recognize them?" "I shook my head.

"Scharnhoff and Noureddin Ali!"

I don't see now how he recognized them. But I suppose a man who works long enough at Grim's business acquires a sixth sense. They were walking swiftly, arguing in low tones, much too busy with their own affairs to pay attention to us. Our two guides glanced back a moment later, but they had vanished by then into the gloom of the cross-street.

There was a dim lamp at one corner of that crossing. As we passed through its pale circle of light I noticed a man who looked like an Arab lurking in the shadow just beyond it. I thought he made a sign to Grim, but I did not see Grim return it.

Grim watched his chance, then spoke again:

"That man in the shadow is a Sikh — Narayan Singh's side-kick — keeping tabs on Scharnhoff. I'll bet old Scharnhoff has cold feet and went to find Noureddin Ali to try and talk him out of it. Might as well try to pretty-pussy a bob-cat away from a hen-yard! Poor old Scharnhoff's in the soup!"

Quite suddenly after that we reached a fairly wide street and the arched Byzantine gateway of the Haram-es-Sheriff, through which we could see tall cypress trees against the moonlit sky and the dome of the mosque beyond them. They do say the Taj Mahal at Agra is a lovelier sight, and more inspiring; but perhaps that is because the Taj is farther away from the folk who like to have opinions at second-hand. Age, history, situation, setting, sanctity — the Dome of the Rock has the advantage of all those, and the purple sky, crowded with coloured stars beyond it is more wonderful over Jerusalem, because of the clearness of the mountain air.

In that minute, and for the first time, I hated the men who could plot to blow up that place. Hitherto I had been merely interested.

Because it was long after the hour when non-Moslem visitors are allowed to go about the place with guides, we were submitted to rather careful scrutiny by men who came out of the shadows and said nothing, but peered into our faces. They did not speak to let us by, but signified admittance by turning uninterested backs and retiring to some dark corners to resume the vigil. I thought that the Sikh sentry, who stood with bayonet fixed outside the arch, looked at Grim with something more than curiosity, but no sign that I could detect passed between them.

The great white moonlit courtyard was empty. Not a soul stirred in it. Not a shadow moved. Because of the hour there were not even any guides lurking around the mosque. The only shape that came to life as we approached the main entrance of the mosque was the man who takes care of the slippers for a small fee.

Grim, since he was in military dress, allowed the attendant to tie on over his shoes the great straw slippers they keep there for that purpose. Suliman had nothing on his feet. I kicked off the red Damascus slippers I was wearing, and we entered the octagonal building by passing under a curtain at the rear of the deep, vaulted entrance.

Nobody took any notice of us at first. It was difficult to see, for one thing; the light of the lamps that hung on chains from the arches overhead was dimmed by coloured lenses and did little more than beautify the gloom. But in the dimness in the midst you could see the rock of Abraham, surrounded by a railing to preserve it from profane feet. Little by little the shadows took shape of men praying, or sleeping, or conversing in low tones.

The place was not crowded. There were perhaps a hundred men in there, some of whom doubtless intended to spend the night. All of them, though they gave us a cursory glance, seemed disposed to mind their own business. It looked for a minute as if we were going to remain in there unquestioned. But the two spies who had come with us saw a chance to confirm or else disprove our bona fides, and while one of them stayed and watched us the other went to fetch the Sheikh of the Mosque.

He came presently, waddling very actively for such a stout man — a big, burly, gray-bearded intellectual, with eyes that beamed intelligent good-humour through gold-rimmed glasses. He did not seem at all pleased to have been disturbed, until he drew near enough to scan our faces. Then his change of expression, as soon as he had looked once into Grim's eyes, gave me cold chills all down the back. I could have sworn he was going to denounce us.

Instead, he turned on the two spies. He tongue-lashed them in Arabic. I could not follow it word for word. I gathered that they had hinted some suspicion as to the genuineness of Grim's pretension to be Staff-Captain Ali Mirza. He was rebuking them for it. They slunk away. One went and sat near the door we had entered by. The other vanished completely.

"Jimgrim! What do you do here at this hour?" asked the sheikh as soon as we stood alone.

"Talk French," Grim answered. "We can't afford to be overheard."

"True, O Jimgrim! It is all your life and my position is worth for you to be detected in here in that disguise at such an hour! And who are these with you?"

"It is all your life and mosque are worth to turn us out!" Grim answered. "When was I ever your enemy?"

"Never yet, but — what does this mean?"

"You shall know in the morning — you alone. This man, who can neither hear nor speak, and the child with him, must stay in here tonight, and go when they choose, unquestioned."

"Jimgrim, this is not a place for setting traps for criminals. Set your watch outside, and none shall interfere with you."

"'Shall the heart within be cleansed by washing hands?'" Grim quoted, and the sheikh smiled.

"Do you mean there are criminals within the mosque? If so, this is sanctuary, Jimgrim. They shall not be disturbed. Set watchmen at the doors and catch them as they leave, if you will. This is holy ground."

"There'll be none of it left to boast about this time tomorrow, if you choose to insist!" Grim answered.

"Should there be riddles between you and me?" asked the sheikh.

"You shall know all in the morning."

The sheikh's face changed again, taking on a look of mingled rage and cunning.

"I know, then, what it is! The rumour is true that those cursed Zionists intend to desecrate the place. This fellow, who you say is deaf and dumb, is one of your spies — is he not? Perhaps he can smell a Zionist — eh? Well, there are others! Better tell me the truth, Jimgrim, and in fifteen minutes I will pack this place so full of true Moslems that no conspirator could worm his way in! Then if the Jews start anything let them beware!"

"By the beard of your Prophet," Grim answered impiously, "this has nothing to do with Zionists."

"Neither have I, then, anything to do with this trespass. You have my leave to depart at once, Jimgrim!"

"After the ruin —"

"There will be no ruin, Jimgrim! I will fill the place with men."

"Better empty it of men! The more there are in it, the bigger the death-roll! Shall I say afterwards that I begged leave to set a watch, and you refused?"

"You — you, Jimgrim — you talk to me of ruin and a death-roll? You are no every-day alarmist."

"Did you ever catch me in a lie?"

"No, Jimgrim. You are too clever by far for that! If you were to concoct a lie it would take ten angels to unravel it! But — you speak of ruin and a death-roll, eh?" He stroked his beard for about a minute.

"You have heard, perhaps, that Moslems are sharpening their swords for a reckoning with the Jews? There may be some truth in it. But there shall be no gathering in this place for any such purpose, for I will see to that. You need set no watch in here on that account."

"The time always comes," Grim answered, "when you must trust a man or mistrust him. You've known me eleven years. What are you going to do?"

"In the name of God, what shall I answer! Taib,[19] Jimgrim, I will trust you. What is it you wish?"

"To leave this deaf-and-dumb man and the boy, below the Rock, undisturbed."

"That cannot well be. Occasionally others go to pray in that place. Also, there is a Moslem who has made the pilgrimage from Trichinopoli. I myself have promised to show him the mosque tonight, because he leaves Jerusalem at dawn, and only I speak a language he can understand. There will be others with him, and I cannot refuse to take them down below the Rock."

"That is nothing," Grim answered. "They will think nothing of a deaf-and-dumb man praying or sleeping in a a corner."

"Is that all he wishes to do? He will remain still in one place? Then come."

"One other thing. That fellow who went and fetched you — he sits over there by the north door now — he will ask you questions about me presently. Tell him I'm leaving for Damascus in the morning. If he asks what we have been speaking about so long, tell him I brought you the compliments of Mustapha Kemal."

"I will tell him to go to jahannam!"

"Better be civil to him. His hour comes tomorrow."

19   All right.

The sheikh led the way along one side of the inner of three concentric parts into which the mosque is divided by rows of marble columns, until we came to a cavernous opening in the floor, where steps hewn in the naked rock led downward into a cave that underlies the spot on which tradition says Abraham made ready to sacrifice his son.

It was very dark below. Only one little oil lamp was burning, on a rock shaped like an altar in one corner. It cast leaping shadows that looked like ghosts on the smooth, uneven walls. The whole place was hardly more than twenty feet wide each way. There was no furniture, not even the usual mats — nothing but naked rock to lie or sit on, polished smooth as glass by centuries of naked feet.

I was going to sit in a corner, but Grim seized my arm and pointed to the centre of the floor, stamping with his foot to show the exact place I should take. It rang vaguely hollow under the impact, and Suliman, already frightened by the shadows, seized my hand in a paroxysm of terror.

"You've got to prove you're a man tonight and stick it out!" Grim said to him in English; and with that, rather than argue the point and risk a scene, he followed the sheikh up the steps and disappeared. Grim's methods with Suliman were a strange mixture of understanding sympathy and downright indifference to sentiment that got him severely criticized by the know-it-all party, who always, everywhere condemn. But he certainly got results.

A legion of biblical and Koranic devils owned Suliman. They were the child's religion. When he dared, he spat at the name of Christianity. Whenever Grim whipped him, which he had to do now and again, for theft or for filthy language, he used to curse Grim's religion, although Grim's religion was a well-kept secret, known to none but himself. But the kid was loyal to Grim with a courage and persistence past belief, and Grim knew how to worm the truth out of him and make him keep his word, which is more than some of the professional reformers know how to do with their protégés. I believe that Suliman would rather have earned Grim's curt praise than all the fabulous delights of even a Moslem paradise.

But the kid was in torment. His idea of manliness precluded any exhibition of fear in front of me, if he could possibly restrain himself. He would not have minded breaking down in front of Grim, for he knew that Grim knew him inside out. On the contrary, he looked down on me, as a mere amateur at the game, who had never starved at the Jaffa Gate, nor eaten candle-ends, or gambled for millièmes[20] with cab-drivers' sons while picking up odds and ends of gossip for a government that hardly knew of his existence. In front of me he proposed to act the man — guide — showman — mentor. He considered himself my boss.

But it was stern work. If there had been a little noise to make the shadows less ghostly; if Suliman had not been full of half digested superstition; or if he had not overheard enough to be aware that a prodigious, secret plot was in some way connected with that cavern, he could have kept his courage up by swaggering in front of me.

He nearly fell asleep, with his head in my lap, at the end of half an hour. But when there was a sound at last he almost screamed. I had to clap my hand over his mouth; whereat he promptly bit my finger, resentful because he knew then that I knew he was afraid.

It proved to be approaching footsteps — the sheikh of the mosque again, leading the man from Trichinopoli and a party of three friends. Their rear was brought up by Noureddin Ali's spy, anxious about me, but pretending to want to overhear the sheikh's account of things.

The sheikh reeled it all off in a cultured voice accustomed to using the exact amount of energy required, but even so his words boomed in the cavern like the forethought of thunder. You couldn't help wondering whether a man of his intelligence believed quite all he said, however much impressed the man from Trichinopoli might be.

"We are now beneath the very rock on which Abraham was willing to sacrifice his only son, Isaac. This rock is the centre of

20   The smallest coin of the country.

the world. Jacob anointed it. King Solomon built his temple over it. The Prophet of God, the Prince Mahommed, on whose head be blessings! said of this place that it is next in order of holiness after Mecca, and that one prayer said here is worth ten elsewhere. Here, in this place, is where King Solomon used to kneel in prayer, and where God appeared to him. This corner is where David prayed. Here prayed Mahommed.

"Look up. This hollow in the roof is over the spot where the Prophet Mahommed slept. When he arose there was not room for him to stand upright, so the Rock receded, and the hollow place remains to this day in proof of it. Beneath us is the Bir-el-Arwah, the well of souls, where those who have died come to pray twice weekly. Listen!"

He stamped three times with his foot on the spot about two feet in front of where I sat, and a faint, hollow boom answered the impact.

"You hear? The Rock speaks! It spoke in plain words when the Prophet prayed here, and was translated instantly to heaven on his horse El-Burak. Here, deep in the Rock, is the print of the hand of the angel, who restrained the Rock from following the Prophet on his way to Paradise. Here, in this niche, is where Abraham used to pray; here, Elijah. On the last day the Kaaba of Mecca must come to this place. For it is here, in this cave, that the blast of the trumpet will sound, announcing the day of judgment. Then God's throne will be planted on the Rock above us. Be humble in the presence of these marvels."

He turned on his pompous heel and led the way out again without as much as a sidewise glance at me. The spy was satisfied; he followed the party up the rock-hewn steps, and as a matter of fact went to sleep on a mat near the north door, for so I found him later on.

The silence shut down again. Suliman went fast asleep, snoring with the even cadence of a clock's tick, using my knees for a pillow with a perfect sense of ownership. He was there to keep care of me, not I of him. The sleep suggestion very soon took hold of me, too, for there was nothing whatever to do but sit and watch the shadows move, trying to liken them to something real as they changed shape in answer to the flickering of the tiny, naked flame. Thereafter, the vigil resolved itself into a battle with sleep, and an effort to keep my wits sufficiently alert for sudden use.

I had no watch. There was nothing to give the least notion of how much time had passed. I even counted the boy's snores for a while, and watched one lonely louse moving along the wall — so many snores to the minute — so many snores to an inch of crawling; but the louse changed what little mind he had and did not walk straight, and I gave up trying to calculate the distance he traveled in zigzags and curves, although it would have been an interesting problem for a navigator. Finally, Suliman's snoring grew so loud that that in itself kept me awake; it was like listening to a hair-trombone; each blast of it rasped your nerves.

You could not hear anything in the mosque above, although there were only eleven steps and the opening was close at hand; for the floor above was thickly carpeted, and if there were any sounds they were swallowed by that and the great, domed roof. When I guessed it might be midnight I listened for the voice of the muezzin; but if he did call the more-than-usually faithful to wake up and pray, he did it from a minaret outside, and no faint echo of his voice reached me. I was closed in a tomb in the womb of living rock, to all intents and purposes.

But it must have been somewhere about midnight when I heard a sound that set every vein in my body tingling. At first it was like the sort of sound that a rat makes gnawing; but there couldn't be rats eating their way through that solid stone. I thought I heard it a second time, but Suliman's snoring made it impossible to listen properly. I shook him violently, and he sat up.

"Keep still! Listen!"

Between sleeping and waking the boy forgot all about the iron self-control he practised for Grim's exacting sake.

"What is it? I am afraid!"

"Be still, confound you! Listen!"

"How close beneath us are the souls of the dead? Oh, I am afraid!"

"Silence! Breathe through your mouth. Make no noise at all!"

He took my hand and tried to sit absolutely still; but the

gnawing noise began again, more distinctly, followed by two or three dull thuds from somewhere beneath us.

"Oh, it is the souls of dead men! Oh —"

"Shut up, you little idiot! All right, I'll tell Jimgrim!"

Fear and that threat combined were altogether too much for him. One sprig of seedling manhood remained to him, and only one — the will to smother emotion that he could not control a second longer. He buried his head in my lap, stuffing his mouth with the end of the abiyi to choke the sobs back. I covered his head completely and, like the fabled ostrich, in that darkness he felt better.

Suddenly, as clear as the ring of glass against thick glass in the distance, something gave way and fell beneath us. Then again. Then there were several thuds, followed by a rumble that was unmistakable — falling masonry; it was the noise that bricks make when they dump them from a tip-cart, only smothered by the thickness of the cavern floor. I shook Suliman again.

"Come on. We're going. Now, let me have a good account of you to give to Jimgrim. Shut your teeth tight, and remember the part you've got to play."

He scrambled up the steps ahead of me, and I had to keep hold of the skirts of his smock to prevent him from running. But he took my hand at the top, and we managed to get out through the north door without exciting comment, and without waking the spy, although I would just as soon have wakened him, for Grim seemed to think it important that his alibi and mine should be well established; however, there were two others watching by the hotel. Ten minutes later I was glad I had not disturbed him.

I gave Suliman a two-piastre piece to pay the man who had charge of my slippers at the door, and the young rascal was so far recovered from his fright that he demanded change out of it, and stood there arguing until he got it. Then, hand-in-hand, we crossed the great moonlit open court to the gate by which Grim had brought us in.

Looking back, so bright was the moon that you could even see the blue of the tiles that cover the mosque wall, and the inter-woven scroll of writing from the Koran that runs around like a frieze below the dome. But it did not look real. It was like a dream-picture — perhaps the dream of the men who slept huddled under blankets in the porches by the gate. If so, they dreamed beautifully.

There was a Sikh, as Grim had said there would be, standing with fixed bayonet on the bottom step leading to the street. He stared hard at me, and brought his rifle to the challenge as I approached him — a six-foot, black-bearded stalwart he was, with a long row of campaign ribbons, and the true, truculent Sikh way of carrying his head. He looked strong enough to carry an ox away.

"Atcha!" said I, going close to him.

He did not answer a word, but shouldered his rifle and marched off. Before he had gone six paces he brought the rifle to the trail, and started running. Another Sikh — a younger man — stepped out of the shadow and took his place on the lower step. He was not quite so silent, and he knew at least one word of Arabic.

"Imshi!" he grunted; and that, in plain U.S. American, means "Beat it!"

I had no objection. It sounded rather like good advice. Remembering what Grim had said about the danger I was running, and looking at the deep black shadows of the streets, it occurred to me that that spy, who slept so soundly by the mosque door, might wake up and be annoyed with himself. When men of that type get annoyed they generally like to work it off on somebody.

Rather, than admit that he had let me get away from him, he might prefer to track me through the streets and use his knife on me in some dark corner. After that he could claim credit with Noureddin Ali by swearing he had reason to suspect me of something or other. The suggestion did not seem any more unreal to me than the moonlit panorama of the Haram-es-Sheriff, or the Sikh who had stepped out of nowhere-at-all to "Imshi" me away.

On the other hand, I had no fancy for the hotel steps. To sit and fall asleep there would be to place myself at the mercy of the other two spies, who might come and search me; and I was conscious of certain papers in an inner pocket, and of underclothes made in America, that might have given the game away.

Besides, I was no longer any too sure of Suliman. The boy was so sleepy that his wits were hardly in working order; if those two spies by the hotel were to question him he might betray the two of us by some clumsy answer. If there was to be trouble that night I preferred to have it at the hands of Sikhs, who are seldom very drastic unless you show violence. I might be arrested if I walked the streets, but that would be sheer profit as compared to half a yard of cold knife in the broad of my back.

"Take me to the house where you talked with your mother," I said to Suliman.

So we turned to the left and set off together in that direction, watched with something more than mild suspicion by the Sikh, and, if Suliman's sensations were anything like mine, feeling about as cheerless, homeless and aware of impending evil as the dogs that slunk away into the night. I took advantage of the first deep shadow I could find to walk in, less minded to explore than to avoid pursuit.

CHAPTER EIGHTEEN

"But we're ready for them."

Without in the least suspecting it I had gone straight into a blind trap, into which, it was true, I could not be followed by Noureddin Ali's spy, but out of which there was no escape without being recognized. The moment I stepped into the deep shadow I heard an unmistakable massed movement behind me. Sure that I could not be seen, I faced about. A platoon of Sikhs had appeared from somewhere, and were standing at ease already, across the end of the street I had entered, with the moonlight silvering their bayonets.

Well, most streets have two ends. So I walked forward, not taking much trouble about concealment, since it was not easy to walk silently. If the Sikh can't see his enemy he likes to fire first and challenge afterwards. I preferred to be seen. The sight of those uncompromising bayonets had changed my mind about the choice of evils. The knife of a hardly probable assassin seemed a wiser risk than the ready triggers of the Punjaub. Halfway down the street Suliman tugged at my cloak.

"That is the place where my mother is," he said, pointing to a narrow door on the left.

But I was taking no chances in that direction — not at that moment. The little stone house was all in darkness. There were no windows that I could see. No sound came from it. And farther down the street there was a lamp burning, whose light spelled safety from shots fired at the sound of foot-fall on suspicion. I wanted that light between me and the Sikh platoon, yet did not dare run for it, since that would surely have started trouble. It is my experience of Sikhs that when they start a thing they like to finish it. They are very good indeed at explanations after the event.

The Sikhs must have seen us pass through the belt of gasoline light, but they did not challenge, so I went forward more slowly, with rather less of that creepy feeling that makes a man's spine seem to belong to some one else. Toward its lower end the street curved considerably, and we went about a quarter of a mile before the glare of another light began to appear around the bend.

That was at a cross-street, up which I proposed to turn more or less in the direction of the hotel. But I did nothing of the sort. There was a cordon of Sikhs drawn across there, too, with no British officer in sight to enforce discretion.

Come to think of it, I have always regarded a bayonet wound in the stomach as the least desirable of life's unpleasantries.

So Suliman and I turned back. I decided to investigate that dark little stone house, after all; for it occurred to me that, if that was the centre of conspiracy, then Grim would certainly show up there sooner or later and straighten out the predicament. Have you ever noticed how hungry you get walking about aimlessly in the dark, especially when you are sleepy in the bargain? Suliman began to whimper for food, and although I called him a belly on legs by way of encouragement he had my secret sympathy. I was as hungry as he was; and I needed a drink, too, which he didn't. The little devil hadn't yet included whiskey in his list of vices.

The side of the street an which the little stone house stood was the darker, so we sat down with our backs against its wall, and the boy proceeded to fall asleep at once. The one thing I was sure I must not do was imitate him. So I began to look about me in the hope of finding something sufficiently interesting to keep me awake.

There was nothing in the street except the makings of a bad smell. There was plenty of that. I searched the opposite wall, on which the moon shone, but there was nothing there of even architectural interest. My eyes traveled higher, and rested at last on something extremely curious.

The wall was not very high at that point. It formed the blind rear of a house that faced into a court of some sort approached by an alley from another street. There were no windows. A small door some distance to my left belonged obviously to the next house. On top of the wall, almost exactly, but not quite, in the middle of it, was a figure that looked like a wooden carving — something like one of those fat, seated Chinamen they used to set over the tea counter of big grocer's shops.

But the one thing that you never see, and can be sure of not seeing in Jerusalem outside of a Christian church, is a carved human figure of any kind. The Moslems are fanatical on that point. Whatever exterior statues the crusaders for instance left, the Saracens and Turks destroyed. Besides, why was it not exactly in the middle?

It was much too big and thick-set to be a sleeping vulture. It was the wrong shape to be any sort of chimney. It was certainly not a bale of merchandise put up on the roof to dry. And the longer you looked at it the less it seemed to resemble anything recognizable. I had about reached the conclusion that it must be a bundle of sheepskins up-ended, ready to be spread out in the morning sun, and was going to cast about for something else to puzzle over, when it moved. The man who thinks he would not feel afraid when a thing like that moves in the dark unexpectedly has got to prove it before I believe him. The goose-flesh broke out all over me.

A moment later the thing tilted forward, and a man's head emerged from under a blanket. It chuckled damnably. If there had been a rock of the right size within reach I would have thrown it, for it is not agreeable to be chuckled at when you are hungry, sleepy, and in a trap. I know just how trapped animals feel.

But then it spoke in good plain English; and you could not mistake the voice.

"That's what comes of suiting yourself, doesn't it! Place plugged at both ends, and nowhere to go but there and back! Thanks for tipping off Narayan Singh — you see, we were all ready. Here's a pass that'll let you out — catch!"

He threw down a piece of white paper, folded.

"Show that to the Sikhs at either end. Now beat it, while the going's good. Leave Suliman there. I shall want him when he has had his sleep out. Say: hadn't you better change your mind about coming back too soon from that joy ride? Haven't you had enough of this? The next move's dangerous."

"Is it my choice?" I asked.

"We owe you some consideration."

"Then I'm in on the last act."

"All right. But don't blame me. Turner will give you orders. Get a move on."

I lowered Suliman's head gently from my knee on to a nice comfortable corner of the stone gutter, and went up-street to interview the Sikhs. It was rather like a New York Customs inspection, after your cabin steward has not been heavily enough tipped, and has tipped off the men in blue by way of distributing the discontent. I showed them the safe-pass Grim had scribbled. They accepted that as dubious preliminary evidence of my right to be alive, but no more. I was searched painstakingly and ignominiously for weapons. No questions asked. Nothing taken for granted. Even my small change was examined in the moonlight, coin by coin, to make sure, I suppose, that it wouldn't explode if struck on stone. They gave everything back to me, including my underwear.

A bearded non-commissioned officer entered a description of me in a pocket memorandum book. If his face, as he wrote it, was anything to judge by he described me as a leper without a license. Then I was cautioned gruffly in an unknown tongue and told to "imshi!" It isn't a bad plan to "imshi" rather quickly when a Sikh platoon suggests your doing it. I left them standing all alone, with nothing but the empty night to bristle at.

The rest of that night, until half an hour before dawn, was a half waking dream of discomfort and chilly draughts in the mouth of the hotel arcade, where I sat and watched the spies, and they watched me. The third man was presumably still sleeping in the mosque, but it was satisfactory to know that the other two were just as cold and unhappy as I felt.

About ten minutes before the car came the third man showed up sheepishly, looking surprised as well as relieved to find me sitting there. He put in several minutes explaining matters to his friends. I don't doubt he lied like a horse-trader and gave a detailed account of having followed me from place to place, for he used a great deal of pantomimic gesture. The other two were cynical with the air of men who must sit and listen to another blowing his own trumpet.

The car arrived with a fanfare of horn-blowing, the chauffeur evidently having had instructions to call lots of attention to himself. Turner came out at once, with the lower part of his face protected against the morning chill by a muffler. Being about the same height, and in that Syrian uniform, he looked remarkably like Grim, except that he did not imitate the stride nearly as well.

He stumbled over me, clutched my shoulder and made signs for the benefit of the spies. Then he whispered to me to help him carry out the "money" bags. So we each took three for the first trip, and each contrived to drop one. By the time all ten bags were in the car there can hardly have remained any doubt in the conspirators' minds that we were really taking funds to Mustapha Kemal, or at any rate to somebody up north.

But Davey was no halfway concession maker. Having lent himself unwillingly to the trick, he did his utmost to make it succeed, like a good sport. He stuck his head out of a bedroom window.

"Don't forget, now, to send me those rugs from Damascus!" he shouted.

It all went like clockwork. Glancing back as we drove by the Jaffa Gate I saw the three spies walk away, and there is very often more information in men's backs than in their faces. They walked like laborers returning home with a day's work behind them, finished; not at all like men in doubt, nor as if they suspected they were followed, although in fact they were. Three Sikhs emerged from the corner by the Gate and strolled along behind them. Detailed preparations for the round-up had begun. The unostentatious mechanism of it seemed more weird and terrible than the conspiracy itself.

There was a full company of Sikhs standing to arms in a side street leading off the Jaffa Road, but they took no notice of us. Their officer looked keenly at us once, and then very deliberately stared the other way, illustrating how some fighting men make pretty poor dissemblers; every one of his dark-skinned rank and file had observed all the details of our outfit without seeming to see us at all.

"We're using nothing but Sikhs on this job," said Turner. "British troops wouldn't appreciate the delicacy of the situation. Moslems couldn't be trusted not to talk. The Sikhs enjoy the surreptitious part of it, and don't care enough about the politics to get excited. Wish I might be in at the finish, though! Have you any notion what the real objective is?"

"No," said I, and tried not to feel, or look pleased with myself. But no mere amateur can conceal that, in the moment of discovery, he knows more about the inside of an official business than one of the Administration's lawful agents. That is nine-tenths of the secret of "bossed" politics — the sheer vanity of being on the inside, "in the know." I suppose I smirked. "Damn this ride to Haifa! What the hell have you done, I wonder, that you should have a front pew? Is the Intelligence short of officers?"

I had done nothing beyond making Grim's acquaintance and by good luck tickling his flair for odd friendship. I thought it better not to say that, so I went on lying.

"I don't suppose I know any more than you do."

"Rot! I posted the men who watched you into Djemal's place yesterday, and watched you out again. You acted pretty poorly, if you ask me. It's a marvel we didn't have to go in there and rescue you. I suppose you're another of Grim's favorites. He picks some funny ones. Half the men in jail seem to be friends of his."

I decided to change the subject.

"I was told to change clothes and walk back after a mile or so," I said. "Suppose we don't make it a Marathon. Why walk farther than we need to?"

"Uh!"

I think he was feeling sore enough to take me ten miles for the satisfaction of making me tramp them back to Jerusalem. But it turned out not to be his day for working off grievances. We were bowling along pretty fast, and had just reached open country where it would be a simple matter to change into other clothes without risk of being seen doing it, when we began to be overhauled by another, larger car that came along at a terrific pace. It was still too dark to make out who was in it until it drew almost abreast.

"The Administrator, by the Horn Spoon! What next, I wonder! Pull up!" said Turner. "Morning, sir."

The two cars came to a standstill. The Administrator leaned out.

"I think I can save you a walk," he said, smiling. "How about changing your clothes between the cars and driving back with me?"

I did not even know yet what new disguise I was to assume, but Turner opened a hand-bag and produced a suit of my own clothes and a soft hat.

"Burgled your bedroom," he explained.

All he had forgotten was suspenders. No doubt it would have given him immense joy to think of me walking back ten miles without them.

Sir Louis gave his orders while I changed clothes.

"You'd better keep going for some time, Turner. No need to go all the way to Haifa, but don't get back to Jerusalem before noon at the earliest, and be sure you don't talk to anybody on your way."

Turner drove on. I got in beside the Administrator.

"Grim tells me that you don't object to a certain amount of risk. You've been very useful, and he thinks you would like to see the end of the business. I wouldn't think of agreeing to it, only we shall have to call on you as a witness against Scharnhoff and Noureddin Ali. As you seem able to keep still about what you know, it seems wiser not to change witnesses at this stage. It is highly important that we should have one unofficial observer, who is neither Jew nor Moslem, and who has no private interest to serve. But I warn you, what is likely to happen this morning will be risky."

I looked at the scar on his cheek, and the campaign ribbons, and the attitude of absolute poise that can only be attained by years of familiarity with danger.

"Why do you soldiers always act like nursemaids toward civilians?" I asked him. "We're bone of your bone."

He laughed.

"Entrenched privilege! If we let you know too much you'd think too little of us!"

We stopped at a Jew's store outside the city for suspenders, and then made the circuit outside the walls in a whirlwind of dust, stopping only at each gate to get reports from the officers commanding companies drawn up in readiness to march in and police the city.

"It's all over the place that disaster of some sort is going to happen today," said Sir Louis. "It only needs a hatful of rumours to set Jerusalemites at one another's throats. But we're ready for them. The first to start trouble this morning will be the first to get it. Now — sorry you've no time for breakfast — here's the Jaffa Gate. Will you walk through the city to that street where Grim talked with you from a roof last night? You'll find him thereabouts. Sure you know the way? Good-bye. Good luck! No, you won't need a pass; there'll be nobody to interfere with you."

CHAPTER NINETEEN

"Dead or alive, sahib."

I did get breakfast nevertheless, but in a strange place. The city shutters were coming down only under protest, because, just as in Boston and other hubs of sanctity, shop-looting starts less than five minutes after the police let go control. There was an average, that morning, of about ten rumours to the ear. So the shop-keepers had to be ordered to open up. About the mildest rumour was that the British had decide to vacate and to leave the Zionists in charge of things. You couldn't fool an experienced Jew as to what would happen in that event. There was another rumour that Mustapha Kemal was on the march. Another that an Arab army was invading from the direction of El-Kerak. But there were British officers walking about with memorandum books, and a fifty-pound fine looked more serious than an out-break that had not occurred yet. So they were putting down their shutters.

I had nearly reached the Haram-es-Sheriff, and was passing a platoon of Sikhs who dozed beside their rifles near a street corner, when Grim's voice hailed me through the half open door behind them. He was back in his favourite disguise as a Bedouin, squatting on a mat near the entrance of a vaulted room, where he could see through the door without being seen.

"This is headquarters for the present," he explained. "Soon as we bag the game we'll run 'em in here quick as lightning. Most likely keep 'em here all day, so's not to have to parade 'em through the streets until after dark. A man's coming soon with coffee and stuff to eat."

"What's become of Suliman?"

"He's shooting craps with two other young villains close to where you left him last night. I'm hoping he'll get word with his mother."

Grim looked more nervous than I had ever seen him. There was a deep frown between his eyes. He talked as if he were doing it to keep himself from worrying.

"What's eating you?" I asked.

"Noureddin Ali. After all this trouble to bag the whole gang without any fuss there's a chance he's given us the slip. I watched all night to make sure he didn't come out of that door. He didn't. But I've no proof he's in there. Scharnhoff's in there, and five of the chief conspirators. Noureddin Ali may be. But a man brought me a story an hour ago about seeing him on the city wall. However, here's the food. So let's eat."

He sat and munched gloomily, until presently Goodenough joined us, looking, what with that monocle and one thing and another, as if he had just stepped out of a band-box.

"Well, Grim, the net's all ready. If that TNT is where you say it is, in that big barn behind the fruit-stalls near the Jaffa Gate, it's ours the minute they make a move."

"There isn't a doubt on that point," Grim answered. "Why else should Scharnhoff open a fruit-shop? The license for it was taken out by one of Noureddin Ali's agents, whose brother deals in fruit wholesale and owns that barn. Narayan Singh tracked some suspicious packages to that place four days ago. They'll start to carry it into the city hidden under loads of fruit just as soon as the morning crowd begins to pour in. We only need let them get the first consignment in, so as to have the chain of evidence complete. Are you sure your men will let the first lot go through?"

"Absolutely. Just came from giving them very careful instructions. The minute that first load disappears into the city they'll close in on the barn and arrest every one they find in there. But what are you gloomy about?"

"I'd hate to miss the big fish."

"You mean Noureddin Ali?"

"It looks to me as if he's been a shade too wise for us. One man swore he saw him on the wall this morning, but he was gone when I sent to make sure. We've got all the rest. There are five in Djemal's Cafe, waiting for the big news; they'll be handcuffed one at a time by the police when they get tired of waiting and come out.

"But I'd rather bag Noureddin Ali than all the others put together. He's got brains, that little beast has. He'd know how to use this story against us with almost as much effect as if he'd pulled the outrage off."

He had hardly finished speaking when Narayan Singh's great bulk darkened the doorway. He closed the door behind him, as if afraid the other Sikhs might learn bad news.

"It is true, sahib. He was on the wall. He is there again."

"Have you seen him?"

"Surely. He makes signals to the men who are loading the donkeys now in the door of the barn. It would be a difficult shot. His head hardly shows between the battlements. But I think I could hit him from the road below. Shall I try?"

"No, you'd only scare him into hiding if you miss. Oh hell! There are three ways up on to the wall at that point. There's no time to block them all — not if he's signalling now. He'll see your men close in on the barn, sir, and beat it for the skyline. Oh, damn and blast the luck!"

"At least we can try to cut him off," said Goodenough. "I'll take some men myself and have a crack at it."

"No use, sir. You'd never catch sight of him. I wish you'd let Narayan Singh take three men, make for the wall by the shortest way, and hunt him if it takes a week."

"Why not? All right. D'you hear that, Narayan Singh?"

"Atcha, sahib."

"You understand?" said Grim. "Keep him moving. Keep after him."

"Do the sahibs wish him alive or dead?"

"Either way," said Goodenough.

"If he's gone from the wall when you get there," Grim added, "bring us the news. You'll know where to find us."

"Atcha."

The Sikh brought his rifle to the shoulder, faced about, marched out, chose three men from the platoon in the street, and vanished.

"Too bad, too bad!" said Goodenough, but Grim did not answer. He was swearing a blue streak under his breath. The next to arrive on the scene was Suliman, grinning with delight because he had won all the money of the other urchins, but brimming with news in the bargain. He considered a mere colonel of cavalry beneath notice, and addressed himself to Grim without ceremony.

"My mother brought out oranges in baskets and set them on benches on both sides of the door. Then she went in, and I heard her scream. There was a fight inside."

"D'you care to bet, sir?" asked Grim.

"On what?"

"I'll bet you a hundred piastres Scharnhoff has tried to make his get-away, and they've either killed him or tied him hand and foot. Another hundred on top of that, that Scharnhoff offers to turn state witness, provided he's alive when we show up."

"All right. I'll bet you he hangs."

"Are you coming with us, sir?"

"Wouldn't miss it for a king's ransom."

"The back way out, then."

Grim beckoned the Sikhs into the room, left one man in there in charge of Suliman, who swore blasphemously at being left behind, and led the way down a passage that opened into an alley connecting with a maze of others like rat runs, mostly arched over and all smelly with the unwashed gloom of ages. At the end of the last alley we entered was a flight of stone steps, up which we climbed to the roof of the house on which I had seen Grim the night before.

There was a low coping on the side next the street, and some one had laid a lot of bundles of odds and ends against it; lying down, we could look out between those without any risk of being seen from below, but Goodenough made the Sikhs keep well in the background and only we three peered over the edge. About two hundred yards in front of us the Dome of the Rock glistened in the morning sun above the intervening roofs. The street was almost deserted, although the guards at either end had been removed for fear of scaring away the conspirators. We watched for about twenty minutes before any one passed but occasional beggars, some of whom stopped to wonder why oranges should stand on sale outside a door with nobody in charge of them. Three separate individuals glanced right and left and then helped themselves pretty liberally from the baskets.

But at last there came five donkeys very heavily loaded with oranges and raisins, in charge of six men, which was a more than liberal allowance. When they stopped at the little stone house in front of us there was another thing noticeable; instead of hitting the donkeys hard on the nose with a thick club, which is the usual way of calling a halt in Palestine, they went to the heads and stopped them reasonably gently. So, although all six men were dressed to resemble peasants, they were certainly nothing of the kind.

Nor were they such wide-awake conspirators as they believed themselves, for they were not in the least suspicious of six other men, also dressed as peasants, who followed them up-street, and sat down in full view with their backs against a wall. Yet I could see quite plainly the scabbard of a bayonet projecting through a hole in the ragged cloak of the nearest of those casual wayfarers.

They had to knock several minutes before the door opened gingerly; then they off-loaded the donkeys, and it took two men to carry each basketful, with a third lending a hand in case of accident. Only one man went back with the donkeys, and two of the casual loafers against the wall got up to saunter after him; the other five honest merchants went inside, and we heard the bolt shoot into its iron slot behind them.

"How about it, Grim?" asked Goodenough then.

"Ready, sir. Will you give the order?"

We filed in a hurry down the steps into the alley, ran in a zig-zag down three passages, and reached another alley with narrow door at its end that faced the street. Grim had made every preparation. There was a heavy baulk of timber lying near the door, with rope-handles knotted into holes bored through it at intervals. The Sikhs picked that up and followed us into the street.

The mechanism of the Administration's net was a thing to wonder at. As we emerged through the door the "peasants" who were loafing with their backs against the wall got up and formed a cordon across the street. Simultaneously, although I neither saw nor heard any signal, a dozen Sikhs under a British officer came down the street from the other direction at the double and formed up in line on our lefthand. A moment later, our men were battering the door down with their baulk of timber, working all together as if they had practised the stunt thoroughly.

It was a stout door, three inches thick, of ancient olivewood and reinforced with forged iron bands. The hinges, too, had been made by hand in the days when, if a man's house was not his fortress, he might just as well own nothing; they were cemented deep into the wall, and fastened to the door itself with half inch iron rivets. The door had to be smashed to pieces, and the noise we made would have warned the devils in the middle of the world.

"We shouldn't have let them get in with any TNT at all," said Goodenough. "They'll touch it off before we can prevent them."

"Uh-uh! They're not that kind," Grim answered. "They'll fight for their skins. Have your gun ready, sir. They've laid their plans for a time-fuse and a quick getaway. They'll figure the going may be good still if they can once get past us. Look out for a rush!"

But when the door went down at last in a mess of splinters there was no rush — nothing but silence — a dark, square, stone room containing two cots and a table, and fruit scattered all over the floor amid gray dust and fragments of cement. Grim laughed curtly.

"Look, sir!"

The fruit-baskets were on the floor by one of the cots, and the TNT containers were still in them. They had tipped out the fruit, and then run at the sound of the battering ram.

Goodenough stepped into the room, and we followed him. Beyond the table, half hidden by a great stone slab, was a dark hole in the floor. Evidently the last man through had tried to cover up the hole, but had found the stone too heavy. The Sikhs dragged it clear and disclosed the mouth of a tunnel, rather less than a man's height, sloping sharply downward.

"What we need now is mustard gas. Smoke 'em out," said Goodenough.

"Might kill 'em," Grim objected.

"That'd be too bad, wouldn't it!"

"We could starve 'em out, for that matter," said Grim. "But they've probably got water down there, and perhaps food. Every hour of delay adds to the risk of rioting. We've got to get this hole sealed up permanently, and deny that it was ever opened."

"We could do that at once! But I won't be a party to sealing 'em up alive."

"Besides, sir, they've certainly got firearms, and they might just possible have one can of TNT down there."

"All right," said Goodenough. "I'll lead the way down."

"I've a plan," said Grim.

He took one of the fruit-baskets and began breaking it up.

"Who has a white shirt?" he asked.

I was the haberdasher. The others, Sikhs included, were all clothed in khaki from coat to skin. Grim's Bedouin array was dark-brown. I peeled the shirt off, and Grim rigged it on a frame of basket-work, with a clumsy pitch-forked arrangement of withes at the bottom. The idea was not obvious until he twisted the withes about his waist; then, when he bent down, the shirt stood up erect above him.

"If you don't mind, sir, we'll have two or three Sikhs go first. Have them take their boots off and crawl quietly as flat down as they can keep. I'll follow 'em with this contraption. They'll be able to see the white shirt dimly against the tunnel, and if they do any shooting they'll aim at that. Then if the rest of you keep low behind me we've a good chance to rush them before they can do any damage."

I never met a commanding officer more free from personal conceit than Goodenough, and as I came to know more of him later on that characteristic stood out increasingly. He was not so much a man of ideas as one who could recognize them. That done, he made use of his authority to back up his subordinates, claiming no credit for himself but always seeing to it that they got theirs.

The result was that he was simultaneously despised and loved — despised by the self-advertising school, of which there are plenty in every army, and loved — with something like fanaticism by his junior officers and men.

"I agree to that," he said simply, screwing in his monocle. Then he turned and instructed the Sikhs in their own language.

"You follow last," he said to me. "Now — all ready?"

He had a pistol in one hand and a flashlight in the other, but had to stow them both away again in order to crawl in the tunnel. Grim had no weapon in sight. The two Sikhs who were to lead had stripped themselves of everything that might make a noise, but the others kept both boots and rifles, with bayonets fixed, for it did not much matter what racket they made. In fact, the more noise we, who followed, made, the better, since that would draw attention from the Sikhs in front. All we had to do was to keep our bodies below Grim's kite affair, out of the probable line of fire.

Nevertheless, that dark hole was untempting. A dank smell came out of it, like the breath of those old Egyptian tombs in which the bones of horses, buried with their masters, lie all about on shelves. You couldn't see into it more than a yard or two, for the only light came through the doorway of the windowless room, and the tunnel led into the womb of rock where, perhaps, no light had been since Solomon's day.

But the leading Sikhs went in without hesitation and got down on their bellies. They might have been swallowed whole for all that I heard or saw of them from that minute. You could guess why the Turks and Germans had not really craved to meet those fellows out in No-man's-land.

Grim went in on all-fours like a weird animal, with my shirt dancing on its frame above his back. Goodenough went next, peering through that window-pane monocle like a deep-sea fish. All the rest of the Sikhs went after him in Indian file, dragging their rifle-butts along the tunnel floor and making noise enough to remind you of the New York subway.

I went in at the tail end, trying at intervals to peer around a khaki-covered Punjaub rump, alternately getting my head and fingers bruised by heels I could not see and a rifle-butt that only moved in jerks when you didn't expect it to. My nose was bleeding at the end of ten yards.

But you couldn't keep your distance. Whenever the men in front checked at some obstruction or paused to listen, all those behind closed up; and by the time those behind had run their noses against iron-shod heels the men in front were on their way again. You couldn't see a thing until you rammed your head into it, and then the sense of touch gave you a sort of sight suggestion, as when you see things in a dream. As for sound, the tunnel acted like a whispering gallery, mixing all the noises up together, so that you could not guess whether a man had spoken, or a stone had fallen, or a pistol had gone off, or all three.

Once or twice, when the line closed up on itself caterpillar-fashion, I was able to make out my white shirt dancing dimly; and once, where some trick of the tunnel sorted out the sounds, I caught a scrap of conversation.

"D'you suppose they'll be able to see the shirt?"

"God knows. I can hardly make it out from here."

"When it looks like the right time to you, sir, turn the flashlight on it."

"All right. God damn! Keep on going — you nearly knocked out my eye-glass!"

Even over my shoulder, looking backward, I could see practically nothing, for what little light came in through the opening was swallowed by the first few yards. There was a suspicion of paleness in the gloom behind, and the occasional suggestion of an outline of rough wall; no more.

Nor was the tunnel straight by any means. It turned and twisted constantly; and at every bend the men who originally closed it had built up a wall of heavy masonry that Scharnhoff had had to force his way through. In those places the broken stones were now lying in the fairway, as you knew by the suffering when you came in contact with them; some of the split-off edges were as sharp as glass.

It was good fun, all the same, while it lasted. If we had been crawling down a sewer, or a modern passage of any kind, the sense of danger and discomfort would, no doubt, have overwhelmed all other considerations. But, even supposing Scharnhoff had been on a vain hunt, and the veritable Tomb of the Kings of Judah did not lie somewhere in the dark ahead of us, we were nevertheless under the foundations of Solomon's temple, groping our way into mysteries that had not been disclosed, perhaps, since the days when the Queen of Sheba came and paid her homage to the most wise king. You could feel afraid, but you couldn't wish you weren't there.

I have no idea how long it took to crawl the length of that black passage. It seemed like hours. I heard heavy footsteps behind me after a while. Some one following in a hurry, who could see no better than we could, kept stumbling over the falling masonry; and once, when he fell headlong, I heard him swear titanically in a foreign tongue. I called back to whoever it was to crawl unless he wanted to be shot, but probably the words were all mixed up in the tunnel echoes, for he came on as before.

Then all at once Goodenough flashed on the light for a fraction of a second and the shirt showed like a phantom out of blackness. The instant answer to that was a regular volley of shots from in front. The flash of several pistols lit up the tunnel, and bullets rattled off the walls and roof. The shirt fell, shot loose from its moorings, and the leading Sikhs gave a shout as they started to rush forward.

We all surged after them, but there was a sudden check, followed by a babel worse than when a dozen pi-dogs fight over a rubbish-heap. You couldn't make head or tail of it, except that something desperate was happening in front, until suddenly a man with a knife in his hand, too wild with fear to use it, came leaping and scrambling over the backs of Sikhs, like a forward bucking the line. The Sikh in front of me knelt upright and collared him round the knees. The two went down together, I on top of both of them with blood running down my arm, for the man had started to use his knife at last, slashing out at random, and I rather think that slight cut he gave me saved the Sikh's life. But you can make any kind of calculation afterwards, about what took place in absolute darkness, without the least fear of being proven wrong. And since the Sikh and I agreed on that point no other opinion matters.

I think that between the two of us we had that man about nonplused, although we couldn't see. I had his knife, and the Sikh was kneeling on his stomach, when a hundred and eighty pounds of bone and muscle catapulted at us from the rear and sprawled on us headlong, saved by only a miracle from skewering some one with a bayonet as he fell.

He laughed while he fought, this newcomer, and even asked questions in the Sikh tongue. He had my arm in a grip like a vise and wrenched at it until I cursed him. Then he found a leg in the dark and nearly broke that, only to discover it was the other Sikh's. Still laughing, as if blindfolded fighting was his meat and drink, he reached again, and this time his fingers closed on enemy flesh. Judging by the yells, they hurt, too.

There must have been at least another minute of cat-and-dog-fight struggling — hands being stepped on and throats clutched — before Goodenough rolled himself free from an antagonist in front and, groping for the flashlight, found it and flashed it on. The first thing I recognized by its light was the face of Narayan Singh, with wonderful white teeth grinning through his black beard within six inches of my nose.

"Damn you!" I laughed. "You weigh a ton. Get off — you nearly killed me!"

"Nearly, in war-time, means a whole new life to lose, sahib. Be pleased to make the most of it!" he answered.

Within two minutes after that we had eight prisoners disarmed and subdued, some of them rather the worse for battery. The amazing thing was that we hadn't a serious casualty among the lot of us. We could have totaled a square yard of skin, no doubt, and a bushel of bruises (if that is the way you measure them) but mine was the only knife-wound. I felt beastly proud.

By the light of the electric torch we dragged and prodded the prisoners back whence they had come, and presently Grim or somebody found a lantern and lit it. We found ourselves in a square cavern — a perfect cube it looked like — about thirty feet wide each way.

In the midst was a plain stone coffer with its lid removed and set on end against it. In the coffer lay a tall man's skeleton, with the chin still bound in linen browned with age. There were other fragments of linen here and there, but the skeleton's bones had been disturbed and had fallen more or less apart.

Over in one corner were two large bundles done up in modern gunny-bags, and Grim went over to examine them.

"Hello!" he said. "Here's Scharnhoff and his lady friend!"

He ripped the lashings of both bundles and disclosed the Austrian and the woman, gagged and tied, both almost unconscious from inability to breathe, but not much hurt otherwise.

The Sikhs herded the prisoners, old alligator-eyes among them, into another corner. Grim tore my shirt into strips to bandage my arm with. Goodenough talked with Narayan Singh, while we waited for Scharnhoff to recover full consciousness.

"Those murderers!" he gasped at last. "Schweinehunde!"

"Better spill the beans, old boy," Grim said, smiling down at him. "You'll hang at the same time they do, if you can't tell a straight story."

"Ach! I do not care! There were no manuscripts — nothing! I don't know whose skeleton that is — some old king David, perhaps; for that is not David's real tomb that the guides show. Hang those murderers and I am satisfied!"

"Your story may help hang them. Come on, out with it!"

"Have you caught Noureddin Ali?"

"Never mind!"

"But I do mind! And you should mind!"

Scharnhoff sat up excitedly. He was dressed in the Arab garments I had seen in his cupboard that day when Grim and I called on him, with a scholar's turban that made him look very distinguished in spite of his disarray.

"That Noureddin Ali is a devil! Together we would look for the Tomb of the Kings. Together we would smuggle out the manuscripts — translate them together — publish the result together. He lent me money. He promised to bring explosives. Oh, he was full of enthusiasm! It was not until last night, when I had broken that last obstruction down and discovered nothing but this coffin, that I learned his real plan. The devil intended all along to fill this tomb with high explosive and to destroy the mosque above, with everybody in it! Curse him!"

"Never mind cursing him," said Grim, "tell us the story."

"He sent oranges here, all marked with the labels of a Zionist colony. When I told him that the explosive would arrive too late, he said I should use it to smash these walls and find another tomb. He himself disappeared, and when I questioned his men they told me the explosive would be brought in hidden under fruit in baskets. I waited then in the hope of killing him myself —"

"Hah-hah!" laughed Grim.

"That is true! But they bound me, and later on bound the woman, and laid us here to be blown up together with the mosque."

Grim turned to Goodenough, who had been listening.

"Do I win the bet, sir?"

"Ten piastres!" said Goodenough. "Yes. Narayan Singh says Noureddin Ali was gone by the time they reached the wall."

"Sure, or he'd have brought Noureddin Ali. I've been thinking, sir. We've one chance left to bag that buzzard. Will you give me carte blanche?"

"Yes. Go ahead."

Grim crossed the place to the corner where old alligator-eyes stood herded with the other prisoners.

"Are you guilty?" he demanded.

"No. Guilty of nothing. I came out of curiosity to see what was happening here."

"Thought so. Can you hold your tongue? Then go! Get out of here!"

Alligator-eyes didn't wait for a second urging, nor stay to question his good luck, but went off in a shambling hurry.

"You are mad!" exclaimed Scharnhoff. "That man is the next-worst!"

"Grim, are you sure that's wise?" asked Goodenough.

"We can get him any time we want him, sir," Grim answered. "He lacks Noureddin Ali's gift of slipperiness."

He turned to Narayan Singh.

"Follow that man, but don't let him know he's followed. He'll show you where Noureddin Ali is. Get him this time!"

"Dead or alive, sahib?"

"Either."

CHAPTER TWENTY

"All men are equal in the dark."

The first thing Goodenough did after Grim had sent Narayan Singh off on his deadly mission was to summon the sheikh of the Dome of the Rock. He himself went to fetch him rather than risk having the sheikh bring a crowd of witnesses, who would be sure to talk afterwards. The all-important thing was to conceal the fact that sacrilege had been committed. But it was also necessary to establish the fact that Zionists had had no hand in it.

"You see," Grim explained, sitting on the edge of the stone coffin, "we could hold Jerusalem. But if word of this business were to spread far and wide, you couldn't hold two or three hundred million fanatics; and believe me, they'd cut loose!"

"The sheikh must realize that," said I. "What do you bet me he won't try to black-mail the Administration on the strength of it?"

"I'll bet you my job! Watch the old bird. Listen in. He's downy. He knows a chance when he sees it, and he might try to cheat you at dominoes. But in a big crisis he's a number one man."

While we waited we tried to get an opinion out of Scharnhoff about the coffin and the skeleton inside it. But the old fellow was heart-broken. I think he told the truth when he said he couldn't explain it.

"What is there to say of it, except that it is very ancient? There is no decoration. The coffin is beautifully shaped out of one solid piece of stone, but that is all. The skeleton is that of an old man, who seems to have been wounded once or twice in battle. The linen is good, but there is no jewelry; no ornaments. And it is buried here in a very sacred place, so probably, it is one of the Jewish kings, or else one of the prophets. It might be King David — who knows? And what do I care? It is what a man sets down on parchment, and not his bones that interest me!"

The sheikh arrived at last, following Goodenough down the dark passage with the supreme nonchalance of the priest too long familiar with sacred places to be thrilled or frightened by them. He stood in the entrance gazing about him, blinking speculatively through the folds of fat surrounding his bright eyes. Goodenough took the lantern and held it close to the prisoners' faces one by one.

"You see?" he said. "All Syrians. All Moslems. Not a Jew among them. I'll take you and show you the others presently."

"What will you do with them?"

"That's for a court to decide. Hang them, most likely. They were plotting murder."

"They will talk at the trial."

"Behind closed doors!" said Goodenough.

"Ahum!" said the sheikh, stroking his beard. It would not have been compatible with either his religion or his racial consciousness not to try to make the utmost of the situation. "This would be a bad thing for all the Christian governments if the tale leaked out. Religious places have been desecrated. There would be inflammation of Moslem prejudices everywhere."

"It would be worse for you!" Grim retorted. The sheikh stared hard at him, stroking his beard again,

"How so, Jimgrim? Have I had a hand in this?"

"This is your famous Bir-el-Arwah, where, as you tell your faithful, the souls of the dead come to pray twice a week. This is the gulf beneath the Rock of Abraham that you tell them reaches to the middle of the world. Look at it! Shall we publish flashlight photographs?"

The sheikh's eyes twinkled as he recognized the force of that argument. He turned it over in his mind for a full minute before he answered.

"You cannot be expected to understand spiritual things," he said at last. "However," looking up, "this is not under the Rock. This is another place."

Goodenough pulled a compass from his pocket, but Grim shook his head.

"Go on," said Grim. "What of it?"

"It is better to close up this place and say nothing."

"Except this." Goodenough retorted: "you will say at the first and every succeeding opportunity that you know it is not true that Zionists tried to blow up the Dome of the Rock."

"How do I know they did not try?"

"Perhaps we'd better ask the Administrator to come and inspect this place officially and put the exact facts on the record," Goodenough retorted.

"You understand, don't you?" said Grim.

"Everything we've done until now has been strictly unofficial. There's a difference."

"And this effendi?" he asked, staring at me. "What of him?"

"He is commended to your special benevolence," Grim answered. "The way to keep a man like him discreet is to make a friend of him. Treat him as you do me, then we three shall be friends."

The sheikh nodded, and that proved to be the beginning of a rather intimate acquaintance with him that stood me in good stead more than once afterwards. The influence that a man in his position can exert, if he cares to, is almost beyond the belief of those who pin their faith to money and mere officialdom.

The prisoners were marched out. All except Scharnhoff and the woman were confined temporarily in the room in which Grim and I had breakfasted. The woman was taken to the jail until an American missionary could be found to take charge of her. They always hand the awkward cases over to Americans, partly because they have a gift for that sort of thing, but also because, in case of need, you can blame Americans without much risk of a reaction.

Goodenough left a guard of Sikhs outside the street entrance, to keep out all intruders until the sheikh could collect a few trustworthy masons to seal up the passage again. Grim, Scharnhoff and I walked quite leisurely to Grim's quarters, where Grim left the two of us together in the room downstairs while he changed into uniform.

"What will they do with me?" asked Scharnhoff. He was not far from collapse. He lay back in the armchair with his mouth open. I got him some of Grim's whiskey.

"Nothing ungenerous," I said. "If you were going to be hanged Grim would have told you."

"Do you — do you think he will let me go?"

"Not until he's through with you," said I, "if I'm any judge of him."

"What use can I be to him? My life is not worth a minute's purchase if Noureddin Ali finds me — he or that other whom they let go. Oh, what idiots to let Noureddin Ali give them the slip, and then to turn the second-worst one loose as well! Those English are all mad. That man Grim has been corrupted by them!"

Grim hardly looked corrupted, rather iron-hard and energetic when he returned presently in his major's uniform. You could tell the color of his eyes now; they were blue-gray, and there was a light in them that should warn the wary not to oppose him unless a real fight was wanted. His manner was brisk, brusk, striding over trifles. He nodded to me.

"You sick of this?" he asked me.

"How many times? I want to see it through."

"All right. Your own risk."

He turned on Scharnhoff, standing straight in front of him, with both arms behind his back.

"Look here. Have you any decency in that body of yours? Do you want to prove it? Or would you rather hang like a common scoundrel? Which is it to be?"

"I — I — I — I — do not understand you. What do you mean?"

"Are you game to risk your neck decently or would you rather have the hangman put you out of pain?"

"I — I was not a conspirator, Major Grim. If I had known what they intended I would never have lent myself to such a purpose. I needed money for my excavations — it has been very difficult to draw on my bank in Vienna. Noureddin Ali represented himself to me as an enthusiastic antiquarian; and when I spoke of my need he offered money, as I told you already. I never suspected until last night that he and Abdul Ali of Damascus are French secret agents. But last night he boasted to me about Abdul Ali. He laughed at me. Then he —"

"Yes, yes," Grim interrupted. "Will you play the man now, if I give you the chance?"

"If you will accord me opportunity, at least I will do my

best."

"Understand; you'll not be allowed to live here afterward. You'll be repatriated to Austria, or wherever you come from. All you're offered is a chance to clean your slate morally before you go."

"I shall be grateful."

"Will you obey?"

"Absolutely — to the limit of my power, that is to say. I am not an athlete — not a man of active habits."

"Very well. Listen." Grim turned to me again.

"Take Scharnhoff to his house. You know the way. When afternoon comes, set a table in the garden and let him sit at it. He may as well read. If nothing happens before dark, take him out a lamp and some food. He mustn't move away. He'd better change into his proper clothes first. Your job will be to keep an eye on him until I come. You'd better keep out of sight as much as possible, especially after dark. Better watch him through the window. And, by the way, take this pistol. If Scharnhoff disobeys you, shoot him."

He turned again on Scharnhoff.

"I hope you're not fooling yourself. I should say the chance is two or three to one that you'll come out of this alive. If you're killed, you may flatter yourself that's a mighty sight cleaner than hanging. If you come out with a whole skin, you shall leave the country without even going to jail. Time to go now."

I slipped the heavy pistol into my pocket and led the way without saying a word. Scharnhoff followed me, rather drearily, and we walked side by side toward the German Colony, he looking exactly like one of those respectable and devout educated Arabs of the old style, who teach from commentaries on the Koran. We excited no comment whatever.

"What will he do? What is his purpose?" Scharnhoff asked me after a while. "If a man is in danger of death, he likes to know the reason — the purpose of it."

I had a better than faint glimmering of Grim's purpose, but saw no necessity to air my views on the subject.

"I'm amused," said I, "at the strictly unofficial status of all this. You see, I'm no more connected with this administration than you are. I'm as alien as you. You might say, I'm a stranger in Jerusalem. Yet, here I am, with a perfectly official pistol, loaded with official cartridges, under unofficial orders to shoot you at the first sign of disobedience. And — strictly unofficially, between you and me — I shan't hesitate to do it!"

He contrived a smile out of the depths of his despondency.

"I wonder — should you shoot me — what they would do to you afterwards."

"Something unofficial," I suggested. "But we'll leave that up to them. The point is —"

"Oh, don't worry! You shall have no trouble from me." It took a long time to reach his house, for the poor old chap was suffering from lack of sleep, and physical weariness, as well as disappointment, and I had to let him sit down by the wayside once or twice. Being in hard condition, and not much more than half his age, I had almost forgotten that I had not slept the night before. Keen curiosity as to what might happen between now and midnight was keeping me going.

He could hardly drag himself into the house. But a bath, and some food that I found in the larder restored him considerably. He helped me carry out the table. He chose a book of Schiller's poems to take with him, but did not read it; he sat with his elbows on the table and his back toward the front door, resting his chin gloomily on both fists. He remained in that attitude all afternoon, and for all I know slept part of the time.

Between him and the window of the room I sat in were some shrubs that obscured the view considerably. I could see Scharnhoff through them easily enough, but I don't think he could see me, and certainly no one could have seen me from the road. I felt fairly sure that no one saw me until it began to grow dark and I carried out the lamp. Even then, it was Scharnhoff who struck the match and lit it, so that I was in shadow all the time — probably unrecognizable.

It had been fairly easy to keep awake until then, but as the room grew darker and darker, and nothing happened, the yearning to fall asleep became actual agony. It was a rather large, square room, crowded up with a jumble of antiquities. The only real furniture was the window-seat on which I knelt, and an oblong table; but even the table was laid on its side to make room for a battered Roman bust standing on the floor between its legs.

I had left the door of the room wide open, in order to be able to hear anything that might happen in the house; but the only sound came from a couple of rats that gnawed and rustled interminably among the rubbish in the corner.

It must have been nearly eight o'clock, and I believe I had actually dozed off at last, kneeling in the window, when all at once it seemed to me that the rats were making a different, and greater noise than I ever heard rats make. It was pitch-black dark. I couldn't see my hand in front of me. My first thought was to glance through the window at Scharnhoff, but something — intuition, I suppose — made me draw aside from the window instead.

Then, beyond any shadow of a doubt, I heard a man move, and the hair rose all up the back of my head. I remembered the pistol, clutched it, and found voice enough for two words: "Who's there?"

"Hee-hee!" came the answer from behind the table. "So Major Jimgrim lied about a broken leg, and thought to trap Noureddin Ali, did he! Don't move, Major Jimgrim! Don't move! We will have a little talk before we bid each other good-bye! I cannot last long in any case, for the cursed Sikhs are after me. I would rather that you should kill me than those Sikhs should, but I would like to kill you also. If you move before I give you leave you are a dead man, Major Jimgrim! Hee-hee! You cannot see me! Better keep still!"

If it was flattering to be mistaken for Grim in the dark, it was hardly pleasant in the circumstances. For a moment I was angry. It flashed across my mind that Grim had planned this. But on second thought I refused to believe he would deceive me about Scharnhoff and use me as a decoy without my permission. I decided to keep still and see what happened.

"Do you think you deserve to live, Major Jimgrim?" Noureddin Ali's voice went on. I heard him shift his position. He was probably trying to see my outline against the dark wall in order to take aim. "You, a foreigner, interfering in the politics of this land? But for you there would have been an explosion today that would have liberated all the Moslem world. But for that lie about a broken leg you would have died a little after ten o'clock this morning — hee-hee — instead of now! Don't move, Major Jim-grim! You and I will have a duel presently. There is lots of time. The Sikhs lost track of me."

I did move. I stooped down close to the floor, so that he might fire over my head if, as I suspected, he was merely gaining time in order to take sure aim. I tried to see which end of the table he was talking from, but he was hidden completely.

"Do you think you should go free, to perpetrate more cowardly interference, after spoiling that well-laid plan? Hee-hee! You poor fool! Busy-bodies such as you invariably overreach themselves. Having tricked me two or three times, you thought, didn't you? that you could draw me here to kill Scharnhoff, that poor old sheep. You were careful, weren't you? to let Omar Mahmoud go, in order that he might tell me how Scharnhoff had turned witness against us. And the Sikhs followed Omar Mahmoud, until Omar Mahmoud found me. And then they hunted me. Hee-hee! Don't move! Was that the plan? Simultaneously then, being yourself only a fool after all, you flatter me and underestimate my intelligence. Hee-hee!

"You were right in thinking I would not submit to capture and death without first wreaking vengeance. But vengeance on such a sheep as Scharnhoff? With Major Jimgrim still alive? What possessed you? Were you mad? I satisfied myself an hour ago that Scharnhoff was the bait, which the redoubtable Major Jimgrim would be watching. Perhaps I shall deal with Scharnhoff afterwards — hee-hee! — who knows? Now — now shall we fight that duel? Are you ready?"

I supposed that meant that he could not see me and had given up hope of it. He would like to have me move first, so as to judge my exact whereabouts by sound. I reached out very cautiously, and rapped the muzzle of my pistol on the floor twice.

He fired instantly, three shots in succession. The bullets went wild to my left and brought down showers of plaster from the wall. I feared he might have seen me by the pistol-flash. I did not fire back. There was no need. Something moved swiftly like a black ghost through the open door. There was a thud — and the ring of a steel swivel — and a scream.

"Has the sahib a match?" said a gruff voice that I thought I recognized.

I was trembling — excitement, of course — only children and women and foreigners ever feel afraid! It took me half a minute to find the match box, and the other half to strike a light.

Narayan Singh was standing by the end of the table. He was wiping blood off his bayonet with a piece of newspaper. He looked cool enough to have carried the paper in his pocket for that purpose. I got up, feeling ashamed to be seen crouching on the floor. But Narayan Singh smiled approval.

"You did well, sahib. All men are equal in the dark. Until he fired first there was nothing wise to do but hide."

"How long have you been here?" I asked.

"Five minutes. I only waited for a sure thrust. But hah? the sahib feels like a dead man come to life again, eh? Well I know that feeling!"

The match burned my fingers. I struck another. As I did that Grim stood in the doorway, smiling.

"Is he dead?" he asked.

"Surely, sahib. Shall I go now and get that other one — that Omar Mahmoud?"

"No need," said Grim. "They rounded him up five minutes after he had found Noureddin."

"Then have I done all that was required of me?"

"No, Narayan Singh. You haven't shaken hands with me yet."

"Thank you, Jimgrim."

The match went out. I struck a third one. Grim turned to me.

"Hungry?"

"Sleepy."

"Oh, to hell with sleep! Let's bring old Scharnhoff into the other room, dig out some eats and drinks, and get a story from him. All right, Narayan Singh; there'll be a guard here in ten minutes to take charge of that body. After that, dismiss. I'll report you to Colonel Goodenough for being a damned good soldier."

"My colonel sahib knew that years ago," the great Sikh answered quietly.

THE END

www.ingramcontent.com/pod-product-compliance
Lightning Source LLC
Chambersburg PA
CBHW030518020726
47494CB00004B/1148